MW01503043

Frank J. Musumici is an avid reader of mysteries and thrillers. He's been married for over twenty-eight years and has two children. He grew up in Hoboken, New Jersey, and currently resides in Hudson County. Frank's work history has always revolved around social services, including managing a crisis center for women in Harlem and running an illegal needle exchange program in a state that had outlawed it (New Jersey). He is currently writing a second novel.

Dedicated to my wife, Michele, and children, Jalisa and Frank Jr.

Frank J. Musumici

MARKED

AUSTIN MACAULEY PUBLISHERS™

LONDON • CAMBRIDGE • NEW YORK • SHARJAH

Ordering Information:
Quantity sales: special discounts are available on quantity purchases by corporations, associations, and others. For details, contact the publisher at the address below.

Publisher's Cataloging-in-Publication data
Musumici, Frank J.
Marked

ISBN 9781643788692 (Paperback)
ISBN 9781643788685 (Hardback)
ISBN 9781645365440 (ePub e-book)

Library of Congress Control Number: 2020908940

www.austinmacauley.com/us

First Published (2020)
Austin Macauley Publishers LLC
40 Wall Street, 28th Floor
New York, NY 10005
USA

mail-usa@austinmacauley.com
+1 (646) 5125767

Special thanks to:

Sarah of Eve White Literary Agency
Lorena Goldsmith of Daniel Goldsmith Associates
Austin Macauley Publishers

Chapter 1

"Get out of the way!" shouted Dean as he ran west on 54th street towards the Hudson River, "Move!" he shouted something else to try and get the attention of the pedestrians blindly walking between him and the armed scumbag he was chasing. Only in New York, do you have people look at you with disdain even as you are trying to warn them of impending danger. "Get down!" it was fucking insane. Now Dean was getting the, this person must be mental, look for his efforts. He knew if someone back on the Arizona reservation yelled for him to get out of their way, his ass would have dove into a cactus faster than an arrow hitting a buck, no questions asked.

"He has a gun!" ah, he should have remembered "gun" was a universal danger word. Once it was out of his mouth, some pedestrians realized that the running screaming maniac wasn't crazy or bullshitting. They parted like the Red Sea, instantly providing Dean with an opportunity to see Freddy running up ahead with his gun. Dean quickly guessed that he was about half a block from catching up with the prick. What made it even easier for him to close so rapidly was Dean had already shot Freddy twice, once in the leg. He was about twenty yards away and gaining fast when he saw Freddy suddenly stop just pass a Starbucks. He saw him raise his gun hand and swing it around so that it was level with Dean's chest.

"Gun, everyone down!" shouted Dean as the first bullet whizzed by his ear. He dove down to the ground just as another bullet sailed over his back. As he fell to the ground, he got his gun from his shoulder holster and was about to shoot back when he saw a young woman step out from the Starbucks.

"No!" yelled Dean. It was too late. Freddy had pulled the trigger at the same time the young woman stepped out from Starbucks. She had turned and stood in front of Freddy as he fired and took two bullets to the chest. The blows catapulted her backward onto the sidewalk. Freddy without hesitation turned away from the scene and ran further down 54th street.

Dean rushed to the side of the young woman. She had tears in her eyes as she looked up at Dean from the sidewalk. He knelt down like a football player taking a knee, put his gun into his jacket, and lifted her head and chest so that it lay across his thigh. When she spoke, all she could muster was the question, "why" before coughing up blood. Dean looked at her, told her the truth, which may offend most people but his mother, taught him that honesty was always the best policy. So, he told the young woman that it was her stupidity that caused her to be in her current dire situation.

When he said this, a look of confusion crept into her facial expression. The thing about being honest with someone is that it takes him or her by total surprise. Think about it, if a person asks you, "why," the most common answer given is a lie, usually, "I don't know." In reality, that person already knew the answer but to admit that would mean they acknowledged the truth that their actions showed either a lack of judgment or Dean's personal favorite their stupidity.

In this case, the girl was just plain stupid. Dean explained to the dying girl that while she was in Starbucks, spending five dollars for a coffee (stupid), she probably heard a commotion outside. And instead of using common sense and staying put, she wanted to be nosy and find out what the commotion was all about (again stupid), and in doing that she stood directly in the line of fire (severe stupidity) without a clue that she stood between him and an asshole trying to kill him.

Although his mother was right about honesty being the best policy, she forgot to mention that it also hurt like a motherfucker. Samantha (Dean later found out her name), just twenty-one and a senior in college, sobbed uncontrollably when she realized that she was going to be the cause of her own death.

At that moment, New York City First-Grade Detective Michael Duncan ran up alongside Dean, looked down and shouted, "Jesus Christ, Dean, did you shoot her by mistake?"

Dean looked up with a smirk, "The fuck you think, Duncan? When was the last time I shot an innocent bystander?"

Duncan nodded his head, "Sorry, you're right, but let EMS take care of her. There's nothing you could do for her now."

Dean yelled, "You fucking forgot that my sister was alone when she was abducted and in captivity last year. I wasn't there for her, the least I could do for this girl is comfort her until the end."

Duncan put his hands up, "OK, I get you, just point me the direction of that asshole."

"It was that scumbag, Freddy, I told you about earlier. He's heading down 54th street. You'll catch up with him, just look for the blood trail. I hit him twice, once in the shoulder and the other one in the fucking thigh."

Duncan acknowledged Dean with a nod and ran off looking for the shooter.

Dean again turned his attention to Samantha and with genuine concern spoke calmly, "Look at me and don't try and talk, everything will be alright. You have to save your strength. EMS will be here in a couple of minutes. I promise you that I won't leave your side until they've arrived."

The girl may have been stupid and her death fell on her, but she was still a human being in need of someone to comfort her in her final moments of life. She looked up at Dean with a look of clarity and managed a bloody smile that not only sent a shiver down his spine but also brought tears to his eyes. In that moment, Dean knew she could see and feel the spirit world as it enveloped her. His eyes moistened further and tears flowed not of sadness but pure joy because Samantha now understood that she was not alone and would be walking Earth's plains alongside her ancestors.

Detective Duncan followed the blood trail from Starbucks to the entrance of the alley in front of him. He smiled to himself, Dean was right. The bullet had to have nicked an artery because the amount of blood that led into the alley looked like pools of red water, not droplets. He supposed he had to make a quick decision, wait for backup and let the shooter bleed out or enter the alley with the intention of saving the gunman's life. Shit, he laughed with no one in particular and thought who was he kidding that motherfucker was better dead than alive.

Duncan entered the alley and saw the gunman leaning against a dumpster holding his right arm down alongside his leg with a gun in his hand. "Hey, Freddy, drop the fucking gun or get kissed by Ms. Smith and her brother, Mr. Wesson."

The gunman picked his head up and looked at Duncan with pleading eyes, "Please, Officer, I need help fast, I'm bleeding to death."

"Help, how about that young girl you just shot. Don't you think, she needs it more than you?" shouted Duncan.

"Please, that wasn't my fault. It was that fucking Geronimo chasing me. He pulled a gun and starting shooting. It was self-defense I swear, please, I can't feel my right side," cried Freddy.

Duncan gave the gunman an icy stare that made the gunman stop crying. Freddy immediately realized that this cop was not there to help, "Oh shit, you're going to kill me, God no, please, please, I'll do anything you…"

"Fucking pussy, you had no problem shooting a girl but come face to face with the gun barrel and shit yourself," laughed Duncan as he returned his gun to his holster after putting a well-placed bullet through Freddy's mouth mid-sentence.

Dean finished giving his statement to the officers on the scene when he noticed the coroner place Samantha into a body bag destined for the morgue.

Although he did not know her, it did not prevent him from mourning her. She was a daughter, granddaughter, sister, and probably had a boyfriend or girlfriend all of which would have their lives blacked with a cloud of emptiness and a lifetime of grief. It was then that he noticed Duncan walking towards him smiling.

"What the hell do you have to smile about," shouted Dean.

"Well, for one, that prick, Freddy won't be shooting any more innocent bystanders. Oh, and I wasn't hurt, you ungrateful bastard," retorted Duncan.

Dean smiled, "Sorry, Duncan, thanks for going after him. What happened?"

"Nothing really, I followed the blood trail into an alley. Before entering, I identified myself. The scumbag yelled out that he needed help because he was bleeding to death. I wanted to get to him in time to stem the bleeding so I rushed into the alley, which was dumb on my part. The moment he saw me he raised his gun. I yelled for him to drop it but he continued giving me no choice but to shoot him. End of story," explained Duncan.

Dean shook his head back in forth as if he was saying no, "Shit, the way you explained it sounds you've written the incident report already but I'm not complaining though. Thanks again."

Duncan smiled, "You are welcome and that's exactly how I'm writing it up for the Captain. Listen, let me also apologize for my reaction earlier, I should have known that the young girl getting shot must have triggered memories of your sister's ordeal."

Dean chuckled nervously, "Ordeal, better description than using her 'kidnapping and captivity' but no need to apologize. My sister was lucky, someone found her and brought her back to my family, unfortunately for Samantha, I wish I could have done the same for her."

Dean wanted to say more but noticed two tall men in black suits and cheap-ass sunglasses approaching him. He figured they were the feds, probably FBI, since one could not enter a crime scene if not in law enforcement. Moreover, local cops like to dress differently from their partners, unlike the feds who dressed similar either in an off the rack black or navy suit. Both men stopped in front of Dean and Duncan. Dean's first instinct was that they were there to talk about the shooting. He looked at both men and asked, "Why the heavy hitters, this fiasco is a local police crime scene. Did someone from the city call it in?"

"Shit no, no one from the city called theses fucking guys. We can take care of our own messes," interjected Duncan then added, "You shouldn't even be here, you don't have fucking jurisdiction here."

"Take it easy, cowboy. We're not here for you," the taller of the two agents stated. He then pointed at Dean, "It's you we came to get and bring back downtown."

Dean now had his antenna's up and paid close attention to them. "You guys got I.D.?" he asked. They both simultaneously flipped open their billfolds holding their FBI credentials for him to see. Dean laughed to himself, feds all right; they do love the opportunity to show off their "creds."

"You guys practice that move because it was smoother than a baby's ass," Laughed Dean.

"They said you were a smartass," replied the second agent. He told Dean his name was Lance Smith and his partner was Derrick Breshneck.

"Hey, Lance, how about giving me a clue as to why I need to be taken downtown?" Dean asked.

Agent Lance shrugged his shoulders, "Don't know or care, was told to head up here, pick you up and bring downtown after you gave your statement to the police."

"Shit, Dean, you don't have to go anywhere with these clowns. Let me call up the Captain. I'm sure we can get her to say you're still needed here," Duncan stated.

"Is there a reason you're being a prick. Could it be that you didn't pass the psych evaluation to get into the bureau? Is this your way of getting even," replied Agent Lance as he started walking towards Duncan.

Dean stepped between them, "Easy guys, I have no problem going downtown. Duncan, if you need anything, just give me a call. I'm curious as to what awaits me downtown. Once I'm done, I'll check back with you."

Duncan nodded, "Alright but if you feel like something's not right shut the fuck up and call me."

Dean laughed, "OK, Dad."

Duncan stuck his middle finger up at Dean as he passed by him.

Chapter 2

"Come on, Katharine, stop being a baby," chimed Hailey, "it's a tattoo of a white lily. No one's gonna notice. It will be on the back of your neck the size of your thumbnail. Plus, your hair will cover it."

Katharine, fifteen years old, head moving back and forth, looking unsure and scared "but you know my family looks down on girls with tattoos. Mom says it sends the wrong message to men. She says it tells them that the girl is not only easy but wild."

Hailey smiled, "Really, listen to what you just said, it doesn't even make sense."

Katharine continued, "My dad even said, he wouldn't hire anyone with tattoos especially girls."

Hailey snorted, "I bet he doesn't mind fucking tattooed girls."

Hailey could see that she may have gone too far. Katharine's face turned a bright crimson and she began to ball her hands at the side of her body as if to release some sort of pressure building in her. "Come on Katharine stop giving me that fucking look. We both know your father is no angel. Remember he came onto me a couple of times during his infrequent trips to the school, and I'm tatted."

Katharine's eyes watered, "I'm not easily fooled by your stupid mind games like those other girls you control, Hailey."

Hailey feigned as if she was hurt, "That's not true, Katharine."

"I know you saying shit about my dad to get me upset enough at him that I go with you to Hunter's shop as a way to get back at him. But I'm not that type of girl, and the answer is still no. Go look for some other idiot." Katharine stormed off to her dorm room leaving Hailey standing there shaking her head in frustration.

Just then, Hailey's phone rang. She saw the number and was immediately agitated but reluctantly picked up the call.

"Did you convince your friend to come over?" asked the caller.

Hailey whispered, "You have to let me work the girls my way. I'm still working on Katharine but if that doesn't work, there are others."

14

The caller unconvinced decided that Hailey needed reminding of what was required of her. "Listen, your fucking job is the easiest of them all, recruit girls. How hard is that? You better fucking remember the only reason I don't put you on the floor is we need your recruiting skills," the caller hissed.

Hailey could feel her blood rising causing her face to color, so she looked away from the girls walking up and down the hallway of the school. Her reply was through clenched teeth, "don't fucking worry, Hunter, I'll bring someone down tonight."

He softened his voice an octave, "Sorry about that, Hay, but we can't get Abraham angry with us for not delivering the goods on time."

Hailey containing her contempt lowered her voice, "I already told you that I would have someone for you tonight. When I commit to something, asshole, I always come through, it would serve you right to remember that."

Hunter heard Hailey's temperature rising from the low grumble in her voice and knew now was not the time to get her angry. They needed a girl for tonight so he softened his stance, "You know what, you're right. I should already know when you give your word it is golden. See you tonight can't wait to see the fresh meat you have on the hook for me."

Hailey hung up the phone, took a deep breath and relaxed the best way she could by thinking about her little sister and their favorite time of the day as she walked over to the school's Santa Anna Dormitory.

"Now, Mila, go brush your teeth, wash your face and jump into bed," smiled Hailey at her six-year sister, Mila.

Mila chuckled, "I already did, now tell me what you're reading me tonight?"

Hailey looked up at the ceiling with her pointer finger on her cheek, "Hmm, how about we go with Goldilocks and the three bears."

Mila's eyes lit up, "That's my favorite story. I just love hearing about the baby bear."

Hailey's face glowed as she not only saw her little sister's joy but felt it as well, "Now jump in." She padded the bed with one hand and held up the bedsheets with the other.

Hailey snapped back to reality when she reached the Santa Anna Dormitory. She entered with the intent of finding another freshman, Megan. She saw her coming down the stairway on her way to class. "Hey, Meg, you still looking to do something bad and exciting?" laughed Hailey while giving Megan a wink. Hailey remembered meeting Megan this past summer during the school's new student orientation. Hailey, now a junior, was the school's student liaison since she was freshman. Her job was to meet all incoming girls registered at Berkheart Academy located in upper Manhattan, New York. Her primary role was meet freshman, establish a rapport and provide any guidance to the girls ensuring an easy transition into the boarding school experience. Megan like most girls in the school, Hailey being one of the exceptions, came from wealthy white aristocratic families.

Megan was also the type of spoiled rich kid that riled Hailey. She had what Hailey like to call the "rich do-gooder" syndrome. A kid whose family earned their wealth on the backs of those less fortunate and would want to atone for those past family transgressions by volunteering for health and social projects. That part of the syndrome was fine with Hailey. It was the second part of the disease, the rankled her. They always wanted to get back at mommy and daddy for being the top 1% of the population with a catch, of course, it needed to be without their parents knowing because they didn't want to be written out of any inheritance. Hailey knew this was a normal thing with these girls. They usually did what most teenagers considered rebellious, smoking, drinking and getting high. That would be the extent of "danger" for those girls wanting to be different from their parents. However, those were a dime a dozen, what Hailey recruited were those girls that were not only rebellious but also adventurous and risk-takers. These girls were not only confident in their physical appearance but dressed as if they demanded attention. Men and women would fawn over them and teenage boys would stop dead in their tracks to leer at them. Their world consisted of playing games with those enamored with them. Their most popular game was "Geezer Teaser." The object of this game was to see who could persuade older men to do things for them. Things like buy gifts or give cash without having to do "anything" for it. Normally, it would be too easy for these girls to get it done so they made it interesting by targeting each other's fathers as their marks. These were the prizes, Hailey actively recruited and successfully turned into club girls.

The first time Megan made her impassioned speech about wanting to help those less fortunate; Hailey balked and struck her from her mental recruitment list. That changed when Megan had told Hailey, she caught one of her male professors leering at her. Hailey remembered telling her that wasn't something unique matter of fact she told Megan not only did male professors leer at her so did the female professors.

Megan nodded her head, "Yes that may be true but this pervert purposely dropped my exam on the floor in front of me then proceeded to walk behind me to watch me bend over and pick it up."

"And what you didn't do it because he might have seen your private parts," mocked Hailey.

16

"Actually, no, I gave him what he wanted. I slowly bent from the waist, making sure he got a good, long look at my ass and do you want to know why?" asked Megan.

"No, enlighten me, Megan," smiled Hailey.

"You never know when I might need a passing grade or anything else," laughed Megan.

"What would your parents think of your little perverted game?" asked Hailey.

Megan gave her a mischievous grin, "Come on, they won't find out unless you or I told them. Besides it gave me a feeling of power and control, it's so easy. No harm no foul."

At that point, Hailey changed her mind and made a run to recruit her into the club. She knew it was a risk with these girls. You never knew if one would turn and go to the police or the school but you had to try.

"You know you are not the only one that likes that type of control and power," Hailey countered and saw that those two words piqued Megan's interest.

"Really, now, do you like to do the same thing, Hailey?" asked a much more interested Megan.

"Let's just say that I belong to a group of schoolgirls that likes to see how far we could make older men go especially one's daddy," replied Hailey.

"Oh, that sounds like fun but you've not given me enough to go on. I need specifics, you know I gave you one, return the favor," pouted Megan.

"How about I do something better, I'll show you something instead, something no one knows about unless you part of the club," asked Hailey as she again saw Megan's intrigue rise through the widening of her eyes.

Hailey pulled back her long blond hair with her two hands and turned her body so that the back of her neck was visible to Megan. Megan could see at the base of Hailey's neck was a small tattoo of a White Lily. It looked as though a painter and not a tattooist created it.

"Holy shit that's beautiful so lifelike. Why would you hide such art?" asked Megan.

Hailey explained, "I'm not hiding it just choosing who gets to see it. That's the beauty Megan; I'm in control as to what I do and who I do it with. I show it to the people I deem worthy, like you."

Megan smiled at being in on a secret, "Thank you, does every girl in the club have one?"

Hailey nodded her head, "Yes."

"Are they all upperclassman like you?" asked Megan.

Hailey smiled inwardly, these fucking rich girls are so predictable, "Nope, we also have freshman and sophomores inducted."

"Who, besides you has one?" inquired Megan.

Hailey laughed, "Sorry, Megan, I can't tell you because only members are privy to that secret."

Megan looked frustrated, "Well, if that's true, why show me?"

Was I this damn naive thought Hailey? She guessed maybe in her early years, when her mother was still around, "If a member of the club thinks a freshman is worthy of recruitment, then they are allowed to recruit them. I think you're worthy so this is my way of recruiting you. Which I'm doing now."

"Come on, you only showed me a tattoo and made cryptic comments. Now, just come out and tell me what it's all about and it better not get me kicked out of school," replied a skeptical Megan.

Hailey smiled, "Our club is like a sorority. One has to get initiated before becoming a member."

Hailey raised the palm of her hand and chuckled, "Let me finish before you ask a question. The initiation is attending a weekly high-end exclusive party held at the famous Dakota Apartments. This party is by invitation only and is attended by rich prominent men from every industry."

"Sounds good so far but what's the catch?" Megan cut Hailey off.

Hailey threw up her hands in mock frustration, "I was about to tell you before you cut me off."

Hailey put her finger to her mouth to signify silence, "It's simple, just prove to us that you can get a minimum of three old men to buy you a drink and either offer to buy you something or bring you on a trip somewhere outside the of the United States."

"That's impossible, Hailey, first, I'm a minor and no bartender would risk his job like that. Second, if for some reason we did come across a dumb bartender, how can you verify that the man made an actual offer? You'll take my word?" asked a skeptical Megan.

"Shit no, that's why all members attend these parties. The drink order is the easy one to confirm because the bartender is with us. He'll simply give the recruiter thumbs up to show the first task was met," replied Hailey.

"OK like I said, it's not the drink that's hard to prove it's whether I was offered a gift or travel?" replied Megan.

Hailey shook her head, "This may shock you, Megan but you are not my first recruit. When a man offers to buy you something or take you somewhere, you are to tell him that you do not travel alone. If he's serious he will ask why. At that point, you tell him for safety reasons you don't travel without your best friend. You then point at me. I'll give him a seductive smile and walk over. He'll offer to take me with you. That will confirm that an offer was made. At that point, I'll politely decline for the both of us."

Megan laughed, "Damn that is brilliant but wait what if he just wants to buy me something?"

"Same thing, he has to buy for your friend as well," replied Hailey.

That was two weeks ago and every time Hailey spotted Megan in the corridor, she could see the teenager eagerly looking at everyone's neck hoping to see someone other than Hailey with the white lily.

Hailey sadly remembered the asshole, Hunter, saying that there was a sucker born every minute waiting to be set up.

"So what's it going to be, you in or were you just talking shit?" Hailey asked. Hailey could see uncertainty in Megan's eyes but like most teenagers, she didn't want to seem as though she was concerned or even scared.

"Fuck it, tell me where and when and remember, Hailey, once I'm in, you'll have to spill the beans on all members of the white lily club, right," replied Megan.

Hailey giggled and cupped her hands around Megan's cheeks. Although Hailey's outward appearance conveyed happiness to Megan, her true feelings were that of dread and regret. She knew she just condemned yet another innocent girl to a life of misery, hopelessness and quite possibility death. However, the alternative would mean her certain death, so she soldiered on as she has done over the last three years, "Cross my heart and hope to die."

Chapter 3

Hunter sat down after speaking with Hailey but didn't have a chance to relax as his phone vibrated. He looked at the screen and cringed, "What's up, Abraham."

"You have any prospects for tonight?" asked Abraham.

"Do you have to ask the same fucking question every week? You already know the answer. Just come down to the shop tonight. I'll have your boss's new lamb to add to his flock," replied Hunter.

"Why do you always get upset, if you know it's the same question, you should have no trouble answering it," laughed Abraham as he hung up the phone.

Hunter placed the phone on the counter and shook his head. He thought to himself, man did he fuck up his life. His father was right about him growing up to be a Class A fuckup and that irked him to no end. But sometimes he wished the piece of shit was still around to maybe help him out this fucking mess he made.

"Ha," he shouted to no one in particular and remembered what a piece of shit, coward, and drunkard his old man was. His way of coping with the world was to beat the shit out of his wife and kid.

Hunter got up and walked to the front of his shop. He stopped next to a young Puerto Rican man reading this month's Tattoo Magazine.

"Jesus, you available tonight, I have another girl coming in," asked Hunter.

Jesus smiled then laughed, "let me guess, another rich white girl wanting a white lily on the back of their neck."

"Wow and here I thought I had to explain things twice for you beaners," laughed Hunter.

"Fuck you, and for your information, I'm Puerto Rican," retorted Jesus.

"All you wetbacks are the same if you ask me. Just get your equipment ready they'll be here in an hour," replied Hunter.

"You know, I'm an artist whose work should not only be appreciated but shown. That fucking tattoo would have been a great addition to my collection of exclusive pieces but your girls killed it for me. Now, I'm known for that cookie-cutter design. To make matters more insulting, those girls have the nerve to hide my artistic expression under their hair."

Hunter shook his head, "Get the fuck out of here, I don't pay you to be an artist. Your job is to fucking ink who I tell you to do. Outside of here, I don't give a fuck what you do."

"Yo, chill the fuck out, Hunter. I was just yanking your chain," Jesus stated with his hands raised.

Hunter laughed, "Just stop complaining about it. You still get paid and I might add extra for staying late and keeping your spic mouth shut."

"Kiss my Puerto Rican ass, Redneck," countered Jesus, "By the way, it gets boring doing the same shit, sixteen fucking white lilies. You white people have no friggin imagination."

Chapter 4

"You think it's a good idea to use a hired gun, especially a man in your position?" asked Special Agent in Charge (SAC), Cecil Johnson.

"What choice do I have? Elizabeth doesn't want us to work it and even if she consented, having us or the locals involved could potentially affect whether or not we find Sofia," stressed a somber Christian Gates, Assistant Director of the New York FBI Office.

Cecil countered, "That may happen or by using our manpower and that of the NYPD we could flush out either the perps that may have taken your niece or get information on what may have happened to her. On both counts it's a win, win."

"I'm still leaning with Antonio's idea," replied Chris.

"How about this then, if internal affairs finds out you hired someone, not in law enforcement, you'll be called to the carpet, and for the life of me, I don't know why you're not the least bit worried about this guy?" pleaded Cecil.

Chris laughed, "Come on, Cecil, we're talking about Antonio here. You really think he'll fuck me like that."

Cecil's shoulders sagged a little, "Your right, like you I would trust my children's lives with him but you have to admit that it's shady. I mean all we know is that this person has a legitimate license to carry anywhere in the country and been involved in several cases where he has discharged his weapon. As a matter of fact, just this morning; he shot a man he went to just talk too."

Chris gave a genuine and sincere chuckle, "That's why I wanted you to be my second-in-command when I accepted this position. I knew you were going to have my back no matter the situation."

He could see Cecil ease up a bit so he decided to make him smile with a shared memory. "You remember back at the academy when Stanley Kowinski wanted you to sneak out of the dorms with him and hit the local strip club. Since we were roommates at the time you wanted me to cover for you just in case the sergeant happened to come by for the bed check."

Cecil laughed, "Really, you are going to rehash those memories now."

"Yep, because if I remember correctly, I told you not to go because if caught, you could be kicked out of the academy. You thanked me and told me that you had it under control. Sure enough, you were fucking right. You made it back in time for the midnight bed check. You even brought back some wild ass stories about threesomes, which by the way I didn't believe for a minute but you were able to do that because you knew that I had you covered."

Cecil shook his head, "Message received. Go ahead and use your hired hand. You already know however it plays; I'll be there for you."

"I know, brother, and thanks, again," replied Chris.

Chris watched his friend and colleague, leave his office. In a way, his friend was correct he really didn't know the whole story around this guy, Dean, but then again he was highly recommended by his oldest friend who he considered a blood brother and was his niece Sofia's godfather but more interestingly, his confidential informant for many years, Antonio Patrasini. He took out his personal cell phone and dialed Antonio's number.

"Hey, Antonio, you have some time this morning to talk to me about your man before he's brought downtown?" asked Chris.

"Ah, shit, Chris, don't tell me you changed your fucking mind. We have to find her as quick as possible," pleaded Antonio.

Chris lowered his voice, "I know and every minute that I don't hear that sweet voice or see those beautiful eyes, I die a little just like you."

"Uncle Chris, next week my school is going to have a career day, can you please, please come and tell all my friends about your job?" asked his ten-year-old niece, Sofia.

"Well, baby, you think your class would like to hear from an agent with the FBI?" smiled Chris. He could see his little sister's features in her angelic face and heartwarming smile. That smile could make you want to jump at the chance to do anything for her. He thought to himself, who is kidding he and Antonio would jump at the whim of this beautiful child.

She added with her patented pout, "Of course, those smelly boys will be jealous that their dads can't carry a gun like you. Plus, Erica's bringing her daddy, who's a fireman, so the boys will be talking about her dad if you don't come."

Ah, he thought she only needed him to one-up her friend Erica. He shook his head back and forth and with his finger, wagging back and forth, relaying disappointment, "Now, Sofia, you know we don't like to show off or brag."

There she goes with that killer smile he laughed inwardly, "Uncle, I know but it's not about showing off. It's that I want the kids in class to know that policemen and agents are good people."

Shit, she looked like my little sister but had the street presence and hustle of her father, God rest his soul. He already knew he was going to do it so he relented and put the date into his schedule.

"Hey, Chris, you still on the phone?" shouted Antonio.

"Yeah, just remembering how Sofia got me to the do the career day at her grammar school," replied Chris.

Antonio's mood brightened as he remembered that day as well, "Hah, you fucking sap, I remember that like it was yesterday. Damn, I cannot believe that was four years ago. I told her she should ask you to do it cause the kids would think it was cool that you carried a gun to work."

Antonio laughed so loud and much he started to choke.

"I hope you choke to death, prick. So you going to meet with me or what?" asked Chris.

"Yeah, yeah, calm your horses, just tell me where and what time?" replied Antonio.

"Now, at the coffee shop downtown," answered Chris.

Chapter 5

Chicago, Illinois 1982

"Where the fuck we going, Sal?" asked Carmine.

"No asshole your question should be, are you downstairs?" laughed Sal.

"You just fucking called me not ten minutes ago and told me to be downstairs," whined Carmine.

"Damn, you complain like some pansy," laughed Sal, "there's a card game that just started on the corner of West Taylor and South Miller. My contact called me about a high rollers poker game happening in his apartment. The opening ante is ten grands apiece. He said there were forty Gs on the table right now," explained Salvatore Patrasini to his friend Carmine Leggerio. Sal stopped the car outside Carmine's apartment building, "Come the fuck down, I'm in front."

Carmine grabbed his gun that was on the kitchen table and ran out of the apartment slamming his front door in the process. He could see Sal's car parked in front of the stoop. He ran down the stairs and hopped into the car. Carmine sat across Sal nodded his head, "What's the plan?"

"Hello, to you too, prick," laughed Sal.

"Yeah, yeah, you wanna rush so I bypassed the pleasantries," countered Carmine.

Sal looked at Carmine raised his left eyebrow, "Give you ten bucks if you could spell pleasantries and another ten if you tell me the definition."

"F.U.C.K. Y.O.U and it means kiss my ass," smiled Carmine, "Now what's the plan?"

"We hit them hard and fast, pop out and head to that spot off Ocean Avenue, Pompeii's. We pull into the alley and split the pot between us. It'll be the easiest twenty grand either of us ever made," shouted Salvatore.

"OK, genius, how the fuck you getting into a closed card game?" countered Carmine.

"I told you, I have a contact. He's the one lending his apartment to the guys running the game. He's gonna leave the key under the mat for me," replied Salvatore.

"Now the million-dollar question, why is he giving you this information if he's getting a kickback for letting the game be played in his apartment?" wondered Carmine aloud.

Shaking his head in disbelief and laughing at the same time, "You're fucking kidding right. Don't you run numbers off 18th street and have that no-show job at the convention center and yet your still here ready to do a stickup job. Why is that Carmine, let me tell you why, GREED! He's like you not satisfied with what you have, always looking for more money to get into your hands." Laughed Salvatore

"How much more?" questioned Carmine.

"Don't worry, you greedy fuck, he's getting a grand from me just for leaving the key. Now shut the fuck up and put your mask on we're coming up to the building," replied Salvatore as he steered the car down West Taylor.

He could hear his friend now grumbling about the President Reagan mask he had to wear, "Still don't know why the fuck we have to put this asshole's face on. You couldn't find a simple clowns mask."

Although Carmine was one fucking tough nut, he could whine like his twelve-year-old son, Antonio, no strike that worse than his son does. Salvatore made the turn into the ally and killed the engine. Turned to his friend and slapped him on the back, "Now enough bitching let's get this over with, Angie is making lasagna tonight."

"Nice, I'm friggin starving. You know I love her lasagna," replied Carmine.

"You got to be friggin shitting me, I have to pay my contact and feed you. I should be the one whining," smiled Salvatore as he put on his mask.

As he walked with Carmine toward the back-alley entrance to the apartment building, Salvatore was thinking about his share of the money. What he didn't tell Carmine was the real reason he decided to jump on this job. Last week, both he and his wife Angie decided that they were going to send their son, Antonio, to Saint Aloysius High School on Brentwood Avenue. That move meant, they would have to pay close to eighteen thousand dollars for his high school education. He laughed inwardly with the fact that people called him and his crew crooks.

"You ready to get paid, Mr. President," Salvatore came back to the present.

"Fuck you, asshole, let's just get this over with so I could eat," came Carmine's response.

Inside the apartment, four card players from Vegas were playing their hands. Sal's contact and owner of the apartment stood apart from where the game was being played. He was directly in line with the front door and closer to the hallway that leads to his bedroom. What the owner of the apartment did not know prior to calling Sal was that an armed man would be used for security. Unfortunately, there was no way of letting Sal know without tipping the gunman. He believed his current position would make him safe should anything go down. If the armed man got the jump on Sal and killed him, his betrayal would die with him. If Sal got him first, his secret would still be safe. However, to better his odds of surviving, should it all go to shit he could run and hide in the bedroom.

Sal stood to the side of the apartment door. He bent down retrieving the key left for him, slipped it into the lock, and slowly turned it until he felt the door pull from the door jam. He looked at Carmine, who stood to his right with a 9 mm in the ready position. Sal brought his hand up with five fingers splayed and began to tick each one off. When he dropped his last finger, he kicked open the door. Both he and Carmine burst into the room with guns in the air yelling, "Don't fucking move, hands on the table…"

However, Sal couldn't finish his sentence as he felt a quick gust of wind pass his right ear. He froze for a second knowing it was a bullet but wasn't expecting someone to have a gun. A second gust of wind hit the top of his mask with enough force to pull it up to his eyes. He was able to quickly pull the mask back over his face only to see a gunman poised to shoot at him again. If not for Carmine's quick trigger finger, Salvatore would have been dead. Carmine's bullet tore the right side of the gunman's face splattering the wall behind him with a pink mist and gore.

"Jesus Christ, who the fuck was that?" shouted Sal to no one in particular.

"You're fucking dead and don't even know it," shouted one of the card players who got see most of Sal's face.

Sal moved swiftly to the man grabbing a fist full of his hair. He picked his head up and with as much force as he could and slammed it back down on the table knocking poker chips all over the place.

"If you don't want to end up like him," Sal pointed at the dead man, "I suggest you keep your fucking mouth shut."

Carmine walked over to the dead man looked him over and started to shake his head back and forth as to say no. He pointed his arm towards Sal, "Get your ass over here quick."

Salvatore approached Carmine while still having his gun trained on the card players and his contact.

In a whisper, Carmine leaned next to Salvatore, "We fucked up real fucking bad, Sal. This asshole is an earner for one of Delaconte's capos."

Carmine could see wrinkles forming around Salvatore's eyes as well as his mouth forming a grimace, "Fuck me." He thought for a minute, "Look,

Carmine, these guys don't know who we are and they can't see our faces. Let's just get the money and get the hell out."

"OK, that sounds like a solid move but remember your contact gave you the info. He can't identify me, but you, he could. Once Delaconte picks him up it'll be a just a matter of time before he breaks and gives you up. We both know Delaconte won't stop there. A message will need to be sent out that fucking with the Delaconte Family means death to all those involved including their families like Angie and Antonio," reasoned Carmine.

"What the fuck are you saying, Carmine," a resigned Salvatore replied knowing what had to be done.

"Come on, Sal, we're not fucking Boy Scouts here. We both went into this life with eyes wide open. It has to be either him or your family. He knew the consequences if the shit hit the fan," counseled Carmine.

Sal thought to himself. Angie also knew the consequences when she married into the family but Carmine was right, family always comes first. Salvatore still looked pale but recovered quickly, "Alright, take the players and lock them in the bathroom. I'll take care of my contact."

Carmine walked towards the card players waving his gun and shouting, "Listen up assholes, get the fuck up and listen carefully. If any of you decide that you're tough enough to want to play hero then I'll have no choice but to paint the other wall with your fucking brains. Now fucking move to the bathroom!"

Salvatore pointed his gun at his contact, "You get your ass into the bedroom and don't say a fucking word."

The contact was confused by Sal's attitude change because it didn't match his facial feature. Sal yelled the order but winked at him through the mask and neither his partner nor the card players noticed since they were behind Sal as he ordered him to the bedroom. He figured Sal was doing it for his benefit, so he played along and went to the bedroom relieved that he was going to come out of this mess alive and a thousand dollars richer. As he opened his bedroom door and walked towards the window, he heard Sal walk up behind him.

The contact started turning from the window to face Sal, "Listen, thanks for not saying anything to me. I need them to think…" BAM the contact didn't even have a chance to realize what happened as his body fell backward onto his bed.

"Sorry, it was you or my family and that was an easy choice," said Sal to the dead man sprawled on the bed as he lowered his gun.

"What the fuck was that?" shouted one of the card players.

"What the fuck you think it was asshole!" shouted Carmine.

The four players looked as though they were going to be sick. The card player who got to see Salvatore's face started to whimper and beg, "Please don't kill us. We were here just to play cards. You got the money. We didn't see your faces. I swear to fucking God we won't say shit." The other card players shook their heads in agreement.

Carmine responded, "You heard what just happened in there, if someone comes looking for us, you are all dead as well as your families."

Sal came out from the bedroom alone. He pointed to Carmine, "Get them in the bathroom. Did you warn them about what happens if they say anything?"

Carmine nodded, "I believe we all have an understanding." And with that, he herded the men into the bathroom and told not to come out for at least fifteen minutes.

They exited the apartment quickly and ran down the stairs and out back to the car. Sal started the engine and eased out into the street, driving the speed limit. He didn't want to attract any attention from the police. A ticket now would place them in the area and he knew from experience the Delaconte Family had their share of cops on the payroll.

"Change of plans. We skip Pompeii's and meet later tonight over at Comiskey Park to talk this out. I need to head home and check on Angie and Antonio," a somber Sal stated.

"OK, sounds like a plan and hey Sal, don't worry they didn't see us, plus you took care of the only loose end. It's all going to work out," replied Carmine, although skeptical, he knew better than to express doubt to Sal for he did not want to suffer the same fate as Sal's contact.

Chapter 6

Antonio was by the Hoboken train station when Chris called. He immediately walked over and down the steps to the PATH underground trains. PATH has only two trains out of Hoboken, New Jersey into Manhattan; one went to 33rd street and the other to the World Trade Center (WTC). He boarded the WTC train and rode the three stops in eleven minutes. He walked out of the new WTC station towards Church Street in Manhattan. He stopped at a corner coffee shop on Church and Chambers and waited for his friend and brother to appear. He didn't have to wait long, five minutes later, Chris arrived. They both stood and greeted each other with kisses on the cheek along with a hug. In the Italian culture, it was customary for men who knew each well to greet one another warmly with a kiss on the cheek followed by a hug.

They both sat across from each other with Chris jumping into the conversation first, "Alright, make me feel more at ease about this guy you recommended and remember you didn't exactly mention what he did for a living either."

Chris held up his hand quickly as he could see Antonio start to move his mouth, "And I just got off the phone with one of my agents. It appears that your choice to find Sofia shot a guy up in Harlem this morning."

Antonio quickly cut in, "Knowing Dean, the guy probably had it coming."

Chris again put up his hand to stop him from continuing, "Antonio, if this guy is a nut, we can't be a part of the kind of shit storm that would accompany him."

Antonio starting laughing then coughing, "Listen, Chris, who gives a fuck what he did to the scumbag. The guy must have done something horrible and in our book, anything done to him was fair game."

Antonio's somberly added, "Listen, Sofia is my goddaughter and Elizabeth is practically my sister. I can't sleep at night wondering if I'll ever see her again. It sickens me to think that some fucking piece of shit could have snatched her and I couldn't do shit about it."

Chris adjusted his seat and looked as his childhood best friend but more importantly his brother with such heartache that it almost overwhelmed him,

"Sorry, it's been the same for me and I'm FBI and it hasn't helped one bit. It's making me feel so impotent and useless."

Antonio smiling warmly and with understanding, "You see that's why we need to try something different. I get it; a man in your position would be a little leery about someone you didn't know. But, Chris, you have to have trust in me."

Chris returned the smile, "You're right and I do trust you."

Antonio laughed, "Alright then let me give you some context on our man. He's what I like to call a 'doer.'"

"What the fuck is a doer? Is that even a word," Chris skeptically added.

"Of course, you could look it up; it means someone who gets things done. Should I continue or do you want to keep interrupting me?" replied Antonio.

Chris could see his pain but it was mixed with what looked like hope in his eyes. It was so infectious that he could not help but feel the same way, "Jesus, I was just saying, I've never heard of such a thing, go on."

Antonio sat up straighter as though a weight was lifted from his back, "Great, you remember when we dealt with that Tommy 'Shakes' Delfino thing."

Chris shook his head, "Yep, you provided me enough information to help me nail the shit bags that did the hit on him. Why, did you keep some information from me?"

Antonio shrugged lifting his two arms up and smiled, "Got to keep it like that my boy, it's the only way our agreement will work. Not everyone is happy that I, a Capo in a Jersey mafia family, has an FBI agent as a brother. The reason I agree to be your informant was those fucking southern mob families were stepping over the line when they started buying meth in bulk from those skinheads. The deal was that I would give you them so that you could stop them from spreading their hate and drugs as long as you left us here in Jersey alone."

Chris moved his hand back and forth to say move on, "I know the deal, remember I agreed to it but what does that have to do with Dean?"

"I'll tell you but you have to take it easy and let me finish. You do want to know about Dean, right?"

"Yes, you already know that," replied Chris.

"OK, do you remember a couple of years ago, I told you about Shakes and his loan sharking and gambling houses?" asked Antonio.

Once he saw Chris nod his head, he went on, "Well, last year, he had some Wall Street bigwig on the hook for over 100 Gs playing the ponies. The asshole wouldn't pay his debt and kept dodging Shakes on payday. Finally, Shakes got

31

tired of the guy ducking him when it came to pay…" Antonio was explaining when Chris jumped in.

"I know in the underworld all one has is your reputation, if someone steps on it like not paying a debt, you'll be known as being soft. This means you're either going to get robbed or killed for your territory, right," replied Chris.

"Where the fuck did you come up with 'Underworld' from some fucking PBS documentary on the Cosa Nostra." Antonio laughed so hard he almost fell off the chair.

Chris stuck his middle finger up at Antonio, "Kiss my ass."

Antonio put up his hands in mock surrender, "You are right, Shakes had to maintain his reputation if he was to continue collecting on his debts but to do that he had to send a message to this deadbeat, so Shakes decided to pay the scumbag a personal visit to his Wall Street office."

Chris starts to smile, "Man, Shakes did have some brass balls."

"No question. He gets to this guy's office and asks his receptionist to call him to her desk. She must have seen or felt that Shakes was not a person to mess with so she calls her boss and tells him that someone by the name of Tommy Delfino was outside. A minute passes when the door to the guy's office opens. The guy looks at Shakes recognized him and went back into his office locking the door," explained Antonio.

"Did the guy have him thrown out?" asked Chris.

"I'll get to that. He called security and once they get to the guy's office, the prick comes out and meets the guard by Shakes. He then has the balls to order the guard to physically escort Shakes out of the building." Antonio erupts with laughter and continues, "The guard takes one look at Shakes and they both start to laugh. The guy is pissed and embarrassed that his order is not followed up on. He also can't figure what the hell was so funny."

Chis nodded his head, "That makes two of us."

"Not after I tell you why. What the asshole didn't know was when he started to miss out on payments to Shakes, our friend made sure his cousin, Vito 'Big V' Salvatore was hired by the asshole's building's security company. He did that just in case he had to make a personal visit to the mark's office."

That got Chris laughing, "Damn, that son of a bitch, Shakes, always thinking two steps ahead. Especially when it came to money, but I'm still waiting for the Dean tie-in."

Antonio replies, "Don't worry it's coming, so Big V walks up to his cousin Shakes, kisses and hugs him. The mark looks at both of our boys turns white and starts to tremble. Shakes ordered the scumbag back into his office with him and Big V trailing."

Chris jumped in, "He didn't yell for help?"

32

"Why would he, security was already there," laughed Antonio, "now they all enter the office and closed the door. The guy was going to plead his case when Shakes punches him in the face breaking his nose. The guy starts crying and begging for his life offering to pay half the loan that day and rest by the end of the week."

"Fucking guy still didn't get it, huh," snorted Chris.

"That was the fucking problem. He thought his business status would intimidate Shakes but he learned that day that he was just another sucker. Shakes told him he had to pay for making him lose face on the street. Realizing he was about to get the shit kicked out of him he started spitting some shit about having credit with an escort service that specialized in young teenage girls."

Chris's face turned crimson, "After this, give me the piece of shit's name; I'll make sure he does some time with some hard men in prison."

"Easy, cowboy, you know I can't do that. Shakes and his crew started running him since that day."

"I don't understand why you don't give him up?" asked Chris.

"Come on, Chris, really. He's now part of Shake's street racket. He now has to give Shakes a percentage of his client's fees in cash so that he could continue breathing."

Chris nods his head in acknowledgment, "It's always about the hustle, isn't it?"

"You already know that so don't act surprised. Anyway, the asshole tells Shakes that he has a credit for one night and offered it to Shakes as a bonus to the money owed."

Chris stared dumbfounded, "Damn, I know Shakes is no saint but he did have four daughters who he dotted like no other father. I know he didn't take that offer."

"That's right, he was disgusted the moment he heard it. Now he knew this guy wasn't going to go there anymore, he would see to that. However, he also thought he could help at least one girl get out of that situation."

"Just one girl, why didn't he just close the operation?" asked Chris.

"We both know the world is not made up of unicorns and princesses, you just talked about our need to have a hustle to make money. Sure, Shakes was disgusted but he probably knew some other crew was running this hustle. Remember it's not his job to be the cop but he could his small part by both removing this predator from those girls and maybe save one."

"Sorry, sometimes I get carried away thinking everyone will do the right thing," responded Chris.

"That's what I love about you, always hopeful but again, he did want to some good. So he accepts the offer, gives the prick an address for him to send the girl." Antonio stopped and took a sip of his coffee. Chris motioned with his hand to get the point.

Laughing Antonio continued, "After the girl arrived at Shakes, he talks with her and finds out her situation. That's when he calls me and asks a favor but doesn't tell me anything on the phone. He asked me to come meet him and gave me an address."

Chris shaking his head in disbelief, "You're fucking out of your mind. Even I know, an invite like that usually meant you were going get whacked."

"You're so fucking dramatic. That's because you saw Goodfellas too many times." Antonio slapped his knee on that one.

"Fuck you, asshole, you know I'm right," replied Chris.

"Yes, in most cases that would be right, however, I didn't have a beef with Shakes or his crew. My thoughts were he wanted to bring me in on some action because I knew the racket or hustle. That immediately changed when I entered the apartment and saw what looked like a young beautiful Native American girl next to a big white boy with a shaved head surrounded by Shakes and his boys, Frankie, Lefty and Bates and all but the white boy had guns out by their sides."

"Shakes tells me about the girl who couldn't be older than sixteen. Her story was that she was brought over by the white boy as part of a debt payment from a mark that owed him. He wanted me to help the girl get back home to a hick town outside of Pittsburgh, Pennsylvania."

Chris jumped in, "How the fuck did she get from Pittsburgh to Manhattan?"

"Same question I asked. She told him that members of a local biker gang snatched her on her way home from school. They brought her to some house out in the middle of nowhere with other young girls. She told Shakes that all the girls except her were raped by the bikers and were told that they would be sold into prostitution. The only reason she was not touched was as the leader pointed out to her she would fetch top dollar as a virgin Native American girl. I asked him what he wanted me to tell her family. He just said get her home and give them the information on the biker gang. That's what I did, left her with one of the guys in a nice hotel until I found her family."

Chris enthralled with the story so far interrupted and asked, "What happened to the skinhead?"

Antonio snorted, "What the fuck you think happened Chris. He was fed a lead sandwich. You should be asking about the girl," laughed Antonio.

"I know but I was hoping the bastard wouldn't be given a chance. OK, tell me what happened with the girl," replied Chris.

"I asked her for her parent's phone number but she gave me her brothers instead. She told me her mother would be worried but it was her brother, who lived outside Philadelphia, that would be searching for her. She added that her brother was someone people did not mess with and who had a soft spot for those not able to defend themselves. She stopped talking after that and I figured she was still in shock. I called her brother and told him that I had his sister." Antonio took a breath reached out for his cup of coffee and donut.

"Really, you're fucking taking a breather now before telling me about her brother. Shit, you really love breaking my balls," whined Chris

"Easy, Handsome, when you get irritated wrinkles form around your pretty, blue eyes and you know once that happens your looks start to fade." Laughed Antonio

"Kiss my ass. So what happened?" Chris asked with a smile.

"Well, her brother asked me a bunch of questions most of which I didn't know the answer to but I walked him through how I and Shakes fit into his sister's story. The guy was so emotional over the phone especially when he heard his sister's voice that he cried and, to be honest, I told myself some fucking tough guy he turned out to be," explained Antonio as he sighed.

Chris took that pause to comment, "Now you feel like shit because you're going through the same thing and you could relate making you feel guilty for even questioning his manhood. Am I right?"

"Hit it right on the nail, Chris," replied Antonio.

"As long as you realize it then you could chalk it up to a lesson learned. Can we stop feeling sorry for you and get back to the story," smiled Chris.

Antonio didn't have a comeback so he smiled and continued, "The brother asked if it would be possible to meet him in Jersey so he could pick her up. I told him of course and gave him the address to Biggie's place; I figured eating a cheesesteak and fries while we waited would help fill the time. That man-hauled ass because he made it up from Philly in just under an hour. When he walked into Biggie's, he made a beeline for his sister. He picked her up off her feet and held her tight as they both cried."

"You know, Chris, that I'm a good judge of character." He lifted his hands and told Chris not to say anything about that, "He gave off a good vibe. He's about six-one well-built, black hair, brown eyes, and olive-colored skin. If I didn't already know the sister was Native, I would have guessed him to be from somewhere in the Mediterranean. When he stopped hugging his sister, he stepped away from her and carefully looked her over. Then he started asking questions, and let me say he didn't beat around fucking the bush."

"Why do you say that?" asked Chris

"Well, for one, he asked if anyone including me had sexually assaulted her but he prefaced it with a comment to please don't take offense to his question. I told him no offense was taken and added that we may be criminals but not savages. He laughed at that comeback and proceeded to probe his sister about her abduction and captivity."

Chris sighed, "Touching story the only thing I learned is that the brother is Dean and he went through something similar to what we're going through. However, you still haven't given me enough to prove to me that this character can find our Sofia. Shit, he couldn't even find his own little sister."

Antonio shook his head and matter of factly added, "Well, hate to break it to you Mr. FBI but you and I haven't exactly done a good job in finding our own niece."

"Touché, you are exactly right, sorry," replied Chris rather sheepishly.

"Sorry, didn't mean to be a douchebag. And just so you know, I did say the same thing. His response actually made sense. He said when you're close to the missing person, your emotions will cloud your judgment and decision making. Which he said happened to him and he's pretty sure it's doing the same thing to us," stated Antonio.

"Makes sense," replied Chris.

"Agree now listen to this. Remember that biker gang that snatched his sister?" asked Antonio.

"How could one forget," replied Chris.

"Well, he found out that they were from Greensburg, Pennsylvania. They were affiliated with the Pagans biker gang headquartered in Pittsburgh. A week after bringing his sister home, the biker's clubhouse and garage burned to the ground with their leader and twelve of their members inside," explained Antonio.

"Fuck," was the only response Chris could give.

"I know but here's the first reason I chose him, his determination to get a job done. When cops sifted through the ashes, they found thirteen skulls. Each skull had a bullet hole behind the right ear," stated Antonio.

"OK, where is the determination in putting a bullet in someone's head?" asked Chris.

"Simple, he made a promise that those involved would be found with a bullet behind their ear. The determination factor was he found them and shoot them less than a week after bringing his sister home," exclaimed Antonio.

Chris shook his head in disbelief, "Shit, that is crazy determination."

"Exactly but that wasn't the most important reason why I chose him," replied Antonio.

"Could you please stop being so fucking dramatic and just come out with it," laughed Chris.

"What and miss the chance to bust your balls, fuck that," chortled Antonio.

"Alright, uncle, tell me the main reason," shouted Chris.

Antonio simply stated, "Shakes getting whacked."

Chris's eyebrows knotted in confusion, "You lost me."

"Then let me get you back on track. You see, Dean was enraged that someone had the nerve to whack Shakes, after what he did for his sister. He wanted me to find out who did the hit and who ordered it. I told him we were also surprised but I was able to find out who put the hit out but the identities of the shooters were proving elusive. I offered to bring law enforcement, you, to take care of the person who contracted the hit but no one was talking about the shooters. He agreed for me to bring you in and promised me that he would handle the shooters. That's when I turned the information over to you which in turn helped you arrest and convict Sammy and John Constantine for putting the contract out on Shakes. You remember when you arrested Sammy and John, they were in bad shape."

"That's right, it looked like ISIS got to them," replied Chris.

"I'm sure they would have preferred them to Dean. He tortured them until they gave up the shooters," explained Antonio but was interrupted by Chris.

"That's right, we couldn't figure who the fuck did the number on them and they would not say who did it to them actually they thanked us for arresting them," Chris responded shaking his head.

"That's because he spared them on two conditions, give up the names of the shooters and serve their sentence without appeals," explained Antonio, "and before you ask what would make them keep the deal, he showed them pictures of their kids. That's all it took no words just photos."

"Shit he must be something, those assholes didn't scare easily. But wait didn't you tell me that you didn't know who they hired for the job?" asked Chris.

Antonio waved him off and smiled, "When I told Dean that the Constantine's put the contract out on Shakes for stealing their product, he had a shit fit. He told me that he would make them pay for regarding his sister as product. Afterward, he told me that both Constantine's were pussies and gave up the shooters within ten minutes. He assured me that their pain lasted longer than that."

Chris laughed, "Don't worry I'm not mad you lied to me. Who were the shooters?"

Antonio stuck his middle finger at Chris and continued, "You remember two Irish boys from Queens, Ed and Tim O'Leary?"

37

Chris nodded his head, "Yep, couple of Irish thugs. Their bodies were found in Gateway National Park in Queens. Eddie was hanging from a tree with his brother next to it with a bullet in his head and gun in his hand. NYPD closed that case as a murder–suicide based on the suicide note left at the scene written by Eddie. In it, he apologized for being part of an escort service that damaged the lives of teenage girls and their families. What now you are telling me that they whacked Shacks and Dean did them?"

Antonio nodded his head, "That's what I'm saying exactly. Dean tracked them down and waited outside their home until they were together. When he knew they were both home, he called them on the number given to him by the Constantine's. They answered thinking it was their bosses but it was Dean telling them to come down and get into his car."

Chris jumped in, "How the fuck do you get two tough Irish motherfuckers to just get in a car with someone they didn't know? They would have shot him, right?"

"No doubt they would have made a play but for one thing they did not expect Dean to hold," answered Antonio.

"OK, don't fucking leave me in suspense, what was the one thing?" shouted Chris.

"He had their only niece in the back seat with him. Fucking balls, he had but it worked. They dropped all their hardware where they stood and slipped into the front seat without a hitch," continued Antonio.

Chris's face turned ashen, "He used a young girl, how's that gonna convince me to use him now?"

"Come on, Handsome, did you really think he would have hurt her after what his sister went through," sighed Antonio.

"Still fucked up if you ask me and how did he get her into the car especially since she didn't know him," asked a skeptical Chris.

Antonio nodded his head and continued, "He told her that he was asked by her uncles to pick her up and bring her to them. She got in the car with no problem, I'm sure she was aware that no one would be stupid enough to mess with her uncles. He made them drive to the niece's school where they dropped her off. Her uncles told her not to worry they had some business with the man but once done, they would take her out that night to eat. Dean told me she looked at her uncles and knew they were not coming back. He told me that it was a sad affair but they made their choice in life now they had to pay the consequences."

"Damn, this fucking guy is like ice," was Chris's response.

"Let's not forget, it was all about his sister," replied Antonio.

Chris nodded his head for Antonio to continue, "He dropped the niece off at school with no issue. He continued onto the park where they all exited the car and walked to a cluster of trees not visible from any walking paths."

"They must have been shitting in their pants," a somber Chris stated.

Antonio nodded his head in agreement, "I stated the obvious also and Dean acknowledged again that they would have done anything as long as their niece was left alone. We both know about that kind of love."

Chris had to admit he did, "You're right, if I had to choose between myself and Sofia dying, it would always be me."

Chris looked as though he would start crying but held it in and asked Antonio to continue, "He made Timmy do a hangman's knot with the rope he brought with him. His brother was made to take out a folding chair from the truck and bring it to the tree. Once they were both under the tree, he made Eddie place the rope around Timmy's neck and helped him onto the chair."

Chris sat dumbfounded, "That is some cruel shit."

"No, this is the cruel piece he had Eddie kick the chair from under Timmy's feet. After doing that, he made Eddie write the murder–suicide note. Once the note was done, he helped Eddie put the gun to his head and watched him pull the trigger. Before you ask, Dean had a gun trained on him as a safety value in case he changed his mind."

Chris sat speechless for a moment and could only utter, "Jesus Christ."

"My thoughts exactly, he reminded me that he did it for Shakes. It was a debt owed and paid back. Afterward, he gave me his phone number and told me my debt was still unpaid. He said to call him whenever I was ready to call it in," replied Antonio.

"I take it you called in your marker?" asked Chris.

"Yes, I called him a couple of days ago and told him that my goddaughter was missing. He told me not to worry he would find her. I stopped him and told him that you would have to be the final word on whether we use him. He respected that and was willing to meet with you and assure you that he could do the job," answered Antonio.

Chris lost in thought turned to his close and dear friend, "Against my better judgment especially after hearing the truth about the O'Leary's, it sounds like this Dean character might be able to do what we haven't, so let me meet him." And with that, he kissed Antonio, walked out ready to meet Dean.

Chapter 7

"Top of the fucking morning, Wyatt Earp, heard you collected another notch in your belt," shouted Desk Sergeant, Peter O'Malley.

"Kiss my ass, you fat fucking leprechaun. The asshole thought hands up meant let's shoot us a cop," laughed Duncan as he strode pass the front desk of the sergeant and added, "Any messages?"

"Yeah your new girlfriend, Dean said he'll pass by later and fill you in on what happened downtown," laughed O'Malley.

"Beats having to go to those rest stop bathrooms you visit for your intimate date nights," cracked Duncan back.

The Sergeant's girth around his stomach moved like Jell-O as he laughed, "Don't fucking knock it till you try it, no one bitching for you to take them out for dinner beforehand."

Duncan just smiled, shook his head and climbed the stairs to the second floor where the Detectives Unit was located. The room was an open area containing ten cubicles. Six were located in the center of the space with the remaining four-lined alongside the windows. Duncan along with the three other First-Grade Detectives earned the right to the window cubicles with their promotions to First-Grade. As he walked to his cubical a three by five cellblock as he usually referred to it, several Second-Grade Detectives gathered around the room's only watercooler.

"Hey, fellas look its King Midas," cracked Eddie Lewinski.

His straight man Ricky Sanchez threw back his line, "Why's that Eddie, because everything he touches turns to gold."

"Naw, Ricky, Midas for Duncan means MI DAS well shoot the motherfucker, doesn't matter if they're innocent or guilty," laughed Eddie with Ricky and Dominic Bonaduci next to him cracking up as well.

Duncan smiled and shook his head heading for his spot, "Pricks, and you wonder why you're still Second-Grades. Maybe some newer and funnier material would help you in your mediocre rise to fame."

The collection of detectives hooted and hollered simultaneously while disbanding. Duncan almost made it into his cubicle before Captain Mary Ellis Campanini stepped out of her office and called him over into her office.

"Morning, Cap, what's up?" asked Duncan as he walked into her office.

He liked the captain; she like him had been in dicey situations when she was on the streets first as a patrolwoman then as a First-Grade up in the Bronx. She had been involved in several shoot-outs with some badass motherfuckers. Each time, she came out alone earning her instant credibility with the rank and file. That also helped her rise to the rank of Captain, which was usually given to assholes that were part of the old boy's network or to men who knew how to kiss ass. His only knock on the Cap was her insistence to rules. She did not take kindly to those that would bend a rule for an advantage. Which was contrary to his style of law enforcement, he was a proponent of enforcement but with a physical component attached. He couldn't complain though because she hasn't interfered with his physical methods so far.

"Just heard from Internal Affairs, they are classifying the shooting as justifiable," she replied.

"Nice to know, they can take my side for a change," laughed Duncan.

"Well, correct me if I'm wrong but you've been involved in more shootings then I have fingers," she stated.

"That seems about right," replied Duncan.

"And let's not forget those complaints this department gets from detainees and members of the community who say your 'tough tactics' should be addressed," explained the Captain.

"Now, Cap you've been out there and know there are elements on the street that would love nothing better than to off a cop. It's our duty to make it known that those ideas are a no-no. Plus, if the community isn't bitching about our tough tactics then we're not doing our jobs," smiled Duncan.

"Can't argue about that, forget it. What about this Dean character the Superintendent told me to assign you to, I heard you worked with him before," she asked.

"I wouldn't say I worked with him. It's more like provided backup when he needed it. Judging from both those times, he definitely needs it," laughed Duncan.

"You've been here for an eternity, Duncan. I know you have sources all over the department so what's the buzz on him," asked the Captain.

"Strangely, nothing exciting, he had helped a prominent member of a wealthy Pennsylvania family. Supposedly, the individual had some problems with local criminal elements and he put a stop to it. It may seem small to us in the big city but that little favor allowed him to get an open carry permit anywhere in the U.S.," Duncan was explaining when the Captain chimed in.

"Sorry, but it has to be more to it than that. I don't know anyone that can carry like that except maybe the Secret Service."

"You would think so but the wealthy family he helped has a nephew in the U.S. Senate, so it wouldn't be such a stretch if strings were pulled to get him that permit. That job also put Dean on the map, for those who were looking for discretion when wanting a problem solved without the help of law enforcement," explained Duncan.

"Fucking sounds like this guy watched too much Equalizer to me," cracked the Captain.

Yep, he did like the Captain she knew what and how to state the obvious. "Nice you just dated yourself. I told him something like that as well and he laughed it off. He told me it was simply doing favors for those without the resources to do it themselves. I asked him how he was going to make money if it was all charity. You know what his fucking corny response was?"

"Let me guess," the prick probably said, "Their happiness is all I need, right?" she sarcastically responded.

He had to clap his hands with that one, "no but shit that was funny. Try this fucking on for size, everyone, especially those that are not finically capable needs justice."

Shaking her head, "You got to be shitting me; he's not a doer but a do-gooder. All right, maybe I'll bring him in later to get the real lowdown. Meanwhile, tell me about the asshole that tried to take you out."

"His name was Freddy and he was a frequent visitor to many of our fine caged institutions. His rap sheet runs the gamut from drug possession to assault. He just served two years for assault and battery. His victim was his ex-wife whose testimony helped send him on his vacation upstate."

"Sounds like a piece of garbage," replied the Captain.

Duncan laughed, "You mean sounded past tense. He was released several weeks ago, should have gone off, and started a new life. However, you know some assholes pride is a virtue. In his fucked-up mind, he needed to right the wrong of his ex-wife testifying against him."

"Please this fucking story is as old as ice, he found out her new place, waited for her to come home, beat the shit of her and told her not to tell or else she would die," stated an exasperated Captain.

"Damn talk about cutting to the chase. How about I finish the story, it's quite entertaining especially my small role in the storyline," responded Duncan.

The Captain moved her arms towards her signaling him to continue. "Since Freddy's been in the system, he has made hundreds of acquaintances including some Aryan asshole that ran guns. He aptly took the opportunity to purchase one from the assholes associates on the street. Dean told me that after purchasing the gun Freddy made his move on the ex-wife. Her name, by the way, is Margaret."

Duncan remembered Dean telling him what happened to Margaret in such a way that it made him feel as though he was actually witnessing the assault.

As Dean described the day of Margaret's assault, Duncan pictured it. Freddy lying in wait for Margaret in the alleyway of her friend Julia's apartment building. He saw her walking towards the alley then passing by the entrance. At that very moment, he saw Freddy's hand reach out, grab Margaret by her arm, and jerk her onto the floor of the alley. Duncan could not explain it but Dean's description of Margaret's fear at that moment sent him a chill as he listened.

Dean said that Margaret told him that she looked up and could only stare, as she was stunned at the attack. She was about to scream but stopped immediately as she noticed the barrel of a gun pointed at her face.

She screamed, "Please God, don't hurt me, take my purse and leave I swear I won't say a thing."

"Still fucking lying, you can't help it huh, bitch," Freddy told her and moved more into the light so that his ex-wife would know it was he.

The look of pure unadulterated fear passed over her face as she recognized her past tormentor. "Ah, that makes my heart flutter knowing that you recognize your husband. If I wasn't so disgusted with the fact that you betrayed me, I would have suggested some sucking action on your part." She trembled uncontrollably and he leaned down towards her placing the barrel of the gun on her forehead and whispered gently into her ear.

"It's your lucky day, baby, I just wanted to reintroduce myself to you. I'm going to let you live another day so that you can remember the good times. Then I'll come back to slit your throat."

She started sobbing uncontrollably and loudly, "Go have dinner with your lesbian bitch but fucking say a word to her or the cops and I'll cut her throat as well."

He leaned in and kissed her on her neck. She closed her eyes and counted to twenty before running out of the alley and into Julie's apartment building.

"Duncan, hey, Duncan, snap out it," the Captain shouted.

"Sorry, went off to dream world, where was I?" asked Duncan.

"He purchased a gun and made a move on his ex-wife," came her reply.

"That's right he followed her to her friend's house where he accosted her in the alley of the building. He told her that he was going to slit her throat later in the week. He also warned her that if she told her friend or the police then he'll have to gut her friend as well," explained Duncan.

"Fucking gentleman, so how's Dean mixed up in all this?" asked the Captain.

"This I forgot to tell you about Dean and his work. The way he gets work is simply word of mouth. Margaret's friend Julie had just hired him to help her son out of jam with the neighborhood gang. He actually wanted me to contact him when those gang members were back at their hangout. Shit, I forgot about that, once I'm done with you Cap, I'll check it for him," explained Duncan.

"That still doesn't help me, how did Julie know to call Dean?" asked the Captain.

Duncan was smiling and nodding his head, "You are right it doesn't. When Julie went to the police station for help with the gang issue, she was told since she or her son didn't have evidence of an assault or intimidation, there was really nothing they could do about it. As the officer was telling her this a desk sergeant overhead the exchange and approached Julie on her way out of the precinct. He told her that he knew of someone who helped those in need that were turned away from the police. She was skeptical at first but had no other choices. She called the number the sergeant gave her which surprise, surprise happened to be Dean."

"Shit talk about being in the right time and place. What are the odds of that happening?" she shook her head in amazement.

"After working with him those odds are a sucker's bet and just an FYI, don't bet against him," smiled Duncan.

Chapter 8

"Hello, can anyone hear me?" she shouted as she tried to shake the cobwebs from her head but the movement hurt like a bitch. She took stock of where she was and it wasn't good. It was some kind of walk-in closet but she couldn't differentiate the size or much content because of the lighting. Someone did provide a small reading lamp on the floor alongside a mattress she had been sitting on. The light was turned on but had only enough ambient light illuminating from it to cast a murky scene before her eyes. She looked around and had the sense as if she was participating in some kind of horror movie. At that thought, her blood turned cold and the hairs on her arm stood on edge.

"What the hell am I doing here?" she whispered to herself, "Why can't I remember anything?" this last question brought her to the point of hysteria.

She stood and shouted as loud as she could, "Help me, someone please help me," all the while banging on the door as hard as she could. No one came or responded to her outburst and actually, it had a different effect; it became eerily quiet once she stopped hitting the door. She sat back down on the mattress pulled her knees up under her chin and placed her hands on her face. When she touched her left cheek and jaw, her body flinched with pain. She probed along her jawline and cheek slowly with her hand. It was swollen and tender to the touch. She sobbed then stopped realizing that she needed to focus and concentrate on how and why someone had her locked up. Closing her eyes, she started to take deep breaths to help her focus. It began to work, the haziness crowding her mind slowly dissipated giving way to images and voices.

She remembered standing in front of apartment 2A and could make out loud music permeating from behind the door. She knocked and waited for someone to open it. A young Hispanic male opened the door and gestured her into the apartment. As he walked with her, he began to speak to her.

She smiled inwardly as this information came back to her. She actually remembered their conversation.

"Hey, glad you could make it," the man moved forward and gave her a peck on the cheek just like someone she would have known and liked.

"Come on in make yourself comfortable, drinks are on the table and there's some food in the kitchen."

She remembered reciprocating his greeting and thanking him as she walked into the apartment. Just remembering the loud music renewed the throbbing in her head. She remembered looking over the apartment just as most people do when entering an unfamiliar space. It was actually quite spacious being a loft of course. She could make out just about fifty people mingling around the space each holding a drink and talking. Obviously, she was invited to the party and it seemed as though the host knew her. However, she could not place him or the event.

She needed to refocus. As she inhaled, she counted to ten and slowly exhaled all the while concentrating on both the host and event. The exercise worked and she was again transported to the event.

"Hey, let me introduce you to Rebecca. I would like her to be my new canvas but she's on the fence. I thought maybe you could talk to her and show her the piece I did for you. Seeing that work of art would change any naysayer," laughed the nice-looking host.

She saw herself laugh and nod in agreement with the host. She turned her attention to the girl Rebecca.

"Jesus could not stop talking about the piece he did for you. He told me that it was a favorite of his. You think I could see for myself maybe it will change my mind about letting him work on me?" laughed Rebecca.

"Of course, you can but it's on my hip. I don't' want everyone to see it. Let's go over to the bedroom away from the crowd," she answered. They both walked over to what amounted to a cubicle but to the realtor that sold the place to Jesus probably listed it as a bedroom. When they were both away from the crowd and in the room, she lifted her shirt and pulled the waistband of her pants slightly down to provide Rebecca with a clear view of her tattoo.

"That's the most beautiful and lifelike hummingbird I've ever seen. Especially the way the wings appear to be in motion," stated Rebecca in admiration.

"That's my favorite part of the piece," she countered.

"Did it hurt? Because that's the main reason I'm leaning towards not doing it," added Rebecca.

"Shit yeah, it hurt but after ten minutes you'll be numb to the pain. Afterward, you'll be glad you endured those first ten minutes of pain just to see Jesus's exquisite body art," she laughed then added, "Make no mistake if an artist like Jesus believes you to be a good enough canvas then you should not hesitate to let him create. And if he hasn't told you yet, let me be the first. Anytime he chooses someone to be his next canvas, the artwork is free. The

only price you pay is when he asks you to be his advertisement, you oblige. That happens usually at his parties, like tonight. Once you've been inked, you'll be doing what I'm doing with you to other potential canvases."

She can't remember whether this Rebecca decided to get the tattoo but talking about Jesus did help her jog her memory about him and the event she attended. The party was usually a monthly affair in which Jesus tried to drum up business for his tattooing side business. He would invite his female canvases so that they would show prospective clients his creations. That night she just happened to be one displaying at the event. She also remembered meeting someone else at that party.

"Wow, you are one beautiful woman, may I introduce myself," he was good-looking in a surfer kind of way. However, as she thought about him some more there was also something else about him that did not sit well with her.

She tried to focus more intently on him but she thought she heard someone walking towards the door. She got up quickly and began to shout and kick at the door, "Help, Help, please I'm trapped in here."

Chapter 9

Chris decided to wait for Dean at the far end of the bar with his back to the wall and in full view of the entrance. He had contacted him on the phone after meeting with Antonio earlier and told him to meet him at a particular bar.

Whenever Chris worked a case and needed to meet with someone, either a witness, confidential information or a person of interest, he would dictate the logistics of the meet such as the day, time and location. This particular meet he decided would be a bar.

Chris desperately needed help looking for his missing niece and since he was going to use someone like Dean, it had to be as her uncle and not as a member of law enforcement. Nevertheless, as a cop, he knew anyone missing for three days usually meant that they would never be found again. He sighed and pondered about his niece.

"Alright, Sofia, if someone grabs you from behind what do you do," asked Chris.

"You yell for your Uncle Tony and I'll come running and rip the piece of garbage's head off," shouted Antonio.

Sofia started to laugh, "Come on Uncle Tony, Uncle Chris is trying to teach me self-defense."

Chris saw her wink at her Uncle Tony as she said this. Twelve and that kid had the presence of mind to not only appease me but also acknowledge her criminal uncle's humor all the same. He started to feel a little choked up.

The bartender placed his beer on the counter snapping Chris out of his daydream. He slipped him a hundred-dollar bill and told him to use it to cover any drinks he and his guest would be ordering. He had arrived at the bar early, a habit that stemmed from a tragic incident involving his first murder case with the bureau.

He remembered canvassing the neighborhood in which the murder had occurred and identifying a witness to the shooting. However, the witness was scared and reluctant to talk to the police. He didn't know how but he convinced him to talk to him about it but the eyewitness whispered to him to find an area outside the neighborhood where they could talk. He told Chris once he found a good place; he should call him giving Chris his phone number. The witness made it known that he would tell Chris everything on the condition that he would not testify in court. Chris remembered being fine with that deal. It was his first murder case and he just wanted the shooter's name and the reason for the killing. He laughed thinking about it and how friggin cocky he was, no naïve would be a better description.

Chris immediately drove to the park he passed earlier adjacent from the neighborhood from where the murder took place. He found a spot and decided to conduct the meet at 6:30 pm the next day. He reasoned that the sun would go down at that time coupled with foot traffic increasing with people either returning from work or beginning their evening workout. This he told himself would provide them with some cover.

He contacted the eyewitness but when he initially called the number provided, no one answered. He decided to try again and leave a message if they didn't answer. However, it wasn't necessary, the witness's sister had answered the phone. She told Chris that her brother went to the store and forgot his phone. She then asked Chris if he would like to leave a message. She didn't mind passing it on to her big brother.

As he thought about it, he felt it was fine for a family member to pass on a message. Shit, he thought the witness wouldn't be mad if his sister answered his phone and took a message. Therefore, he obliged and told her to tell her brother that Agent Gates would meet him tomorrow at 6:30 pm in Prospect Park in front of the boat basin. He thanked her and reminded her that it was important that her brother get the message. She responded as though she was offended and reminded him that she made the offer.

The next evening at 6:20, Chris parked his unmarked Crown Victoria about a hundred yards from the boat basin giving him a direct line of vision to his witness. He saw his eyewitness standing in front of an Oak tree situated in front of the basin smoking a cigarette. He dressed like a typical teenager from the inner city, baggy jeans, Jordan sneakers and a black hoody over his head as he smoked. Chris could see him looking back and forth like he was following a tennis match. He was also moving his legs side to side as if he had to use the restroom. There were people walking, jogging and riding bikes all around him.

Chris remembered that it was a tranquil setting. He was on the verge of getting that first big break needed in solving his first murder case. Unfortunately, as in life, it did not go as he had hoped or planned. As he pondered his good fortune there in the car, he noticed from the corner of his eye someone on a mountain bike coming within fifty-feet from his eyewitness. It wasn't unusual to see a mountain bike among the many bikes that were in the park especially at that time in the evening. However, what caught Chris's attention was the biker's attire, black jeans, and black sweatshirt with a Raiders cap on his head. Gut instinct took over pushing Chris out his car and running towards his eyewitness all the while yelling for him to run. The only thing that happened was Chris's warning alerted the potential threat to his presence. When that happened, the biker raised his right arm directly at the witness. The whole scene in front of Chris played out in slow motion. He could see the surprised look on his eyewitness's face as he realized death was coming. The flash from the gun and gore that blew out the back of the witness's head as he fell backward into the Oaktree left a lasting impression on the FBI rookie.

In that thirty-second timeframe, Chris had a dead witness, discharged his weapon for the first time, killed a suspect and learned a painful lesson. One could never divulge information about a possible eyewitness to anyone including to his or her family.

Chris later found out that his killer happened to be the sister's boyfriend. The very sister Chris left the message with and decided that her love for her boyfriend was deeper than the love of a brother. The encounter also ingrained in him to arrive at a meeting point earlier than the scheduled time to scout the area for potential risks. And to think that was the saddest day of his life and career until his niece went missing several days ago.

Chris heard the bar's front door chime as it was opened. A tall man entered the bar. He was about six feet even and about 180 pounds making him look sinewy but not skinny. He walked right towards Chris. Using one of his sister's sayings, the man had an aura about him, not menacing but capable and willing if need be. His vide told those in his presence that he was easy going and in a good place but it also warned you if you wanted to dance with the devil, he would gladly oblige.

"Do you always meet potential clients, in some fucking dive gay bar in the middle of the village?" asked Dean.

"I wanted to put you in a situation most men would feel uncomfortable in but seeing that you are not fazed by men staring at you like some piece of meat, I guess you don't shake easily," Smiled Chris.

Dean sat across from Chris at the Meat Market Bar on the corner of Hudson and Grove streets in downtown Manhattan. Chris continued, "Thanks for taking the time to come down here and meet with me. I don't know how much information, Antonio provided you but it has to do with my niece. Let's get the fee out of the way before I tell you anymore?"

Dean put his hand up as to say stop, "Let me first say outright that there is no cost."

Chris was about to interject but Dean put his hand up again and smiled, "What Antonio did for our family bringing my sister home unharmed was something I may never be able to repay but I will always try at no cost to him. Now he doesn't need to hear that because he's still a crook. You and I know if you give a crook an inch, he'll try and take a foot. Of course, I mean no offense to you or your family."

Chris already knew once he came through the door that he was going to like this kid but hearing his sense of humor sealed it. "None taken, shit I asked for the truth. I can't deny the fact that my best and dear friend is definitely a crook. You know even to this day whenever that prick hugs me I check to see if I still have my wallet," Chris snickered.

"He called and asked if I would help find your sixteen-year-old niece and his goddaughter. It was a no brainer for me. I will do everything that I could to help your family and at no cost. This job would be just a small token of my appreciation for Antonio's good deed."

Chris smiled and shook his head from side to side, "Alright Antonio said that you would say that exact thing and being pressed for time, I accept your offer. However, let me stress that whatever resources you will need, legally, of course, you will have including any backup, computer services, or anything my agency can provide. I'm sure Antonio offered you the resources that we at the agency certainly will not provide."

"Yep, he sure did but I'll make sure to use him sparely and when I deem it necessary. May I suggest a couple of drinks to help forge our new partnership," stated Dean.

"Yes, of course," replied Chris.

Dean raised his hand and looked in the direction of the bar where a young male waiter who couldn't have been more than twenty-one but whose fake I.D. probably said differently, was standing.

Chris saw the waiter smile as though he just won the lottery. He walked; no thought Chris sashayed towards Dean. Once there he squatted down like a catcher in a ball game alongside Dean and asked in a throaty voice, "Hey, big man, how can I be of service to you."

Without missing a beat Dean gave the waiter a million-dollar smile and whispered loud enough for Chris to hear, "May I please get a Cock Sucking Cowboy."

Chris almost lost it. He knew the waiter heard of the drink but it was the waiter's look that had him. The waiter was staring at Dean with a look that radiated please let me be that cowboy. Chris smiled broadly because he also knew Dean was busting his fucking balls for a reaction to his drink choice. He needed to turn the situation back onto Dean, so he tried one, upping him with his drink request.

"Shit that sounds delicious but I'll stick to my regular, Anus Burner, please," countered Chris. At that moment, they both burst out laughing and the waiter had no choice but to join in.

It was time to talk business and Dean knew it would be difficult for Chris to discuss personal matters with a stranger. He decided to make it comfortable by initiating the conversation, "When Antonio called me to collect on the debt I owed him, I was surprised. A person as resourceful as him could find or get anything, take for instance the return of my sister. Then I put myself in your shoes and remembered I was powerless to find my own missing sister."

Dean could see that he had Chris's attention and continued, "You see, what I learned from that ordeal was that I was too close to the case because it involved family. My senses were clouded by pain and rage. It took someone not related to me to help bring my sister home. Antonio sees that and, in some sense, I believe you do as well."

"You are not far off with that assessment," replied Chris.

Dean nodded his head knowingly, "Not to change the subject but I know you must have done some preliminary research on me, right?"

Chris responded, "Of course, I started through my official channels. I put your name through our National Crime Information Center database and you came up clean. That information would have satisfied most field agents but I'm not like most field agents. I put your information into our Violent Criminal Apprehension Program database, which you also came up clean. Although, you were clean on both fronts, I needed more assurances that you could be trusted."

Chris could see that he had Dean's full attention and continued, "So I met with Antonio today and was told that you were some 'doer' from some hick town in Pennsylvania who had helped law enforcement several times in locating missing persons in the past. He also said something I didn't believe."

Dean's eyes widened, "Really and what was that?"

Chris laughed, "That tracking and locating missing people was in your blood."

Dean smiled and nodded his head as Chris continued, "I asked him what the hell did that exactly mean and his response was that you were a descendant of Native American warriors from a tribe out west and was known at the reservation to be the best tracker."

Dean laughed, "At that point, you probably thought Antonio was crazy to think that some Indian could track a missing person in the city, right?"

Chris smiled guiltily, "It did cross my mind but you can't blame me. The closest I got to an Indian was a couple of kids named Patel from the neighborhood. Plus your type of Indian came from TV shows that showed your people scalping women and children."

"Shit, that is so racist that I'm not going to comment on it but since we're on the subject of Indians let me know if you heard this one before. There was an Indian on a street corner with his hand up and palm out and every time a beautiful woman walked by, he would say aloud, 'Chance.' A couple of women walked by and again he would say aloud, 'Chance.' Finally, this one woman walked up to him and said that she thought Indians always said, 'How,' he smiled and replied, 'Lady, I know how all I need is a chance.'"

Chris almost pissed his pants slapping the table and laughing, "That is fucking hilarious but if I had to guess, I would say you look more like an Arab or Turk than Native American."

Dean nodded his head, "I get that a lot and actually both Arabs and Turks belong to their own set of tribes."

"Just goes to show you that you learn something new every day," countered Chris, "Now I'm curious about how a bona fide Indian from out west grows up in some Pennsylvania hick town then decides to move on to the city of brotherly love."

Dean looked at Chris and knew that he was in the presence of someone that was going to be a friend and trusted soul once this ordeal was over and with that thought; he began to tell Chris more about himself.

Chapter 10

She could see the doorknob twisting and the door easing open. She stepped back from the door and waited. She didn't know what to expect but it definitely wasn't what stood before her in the open doorframe. She was stunned and speechless, and before she could utter a word the person in front of her spoke with a carefree and comforting tone.

"Now, now baby, you have to keep it down. I could hear you from outside the hallway. You're lucky my neighbors think I own a dog. If they knew it was a young girl pounding on the door, they would have called the cops. If that happened you could kiss both our asses' goodbye," explained the young beautiful teenager no older then seventeen standing before her.

The whole scene was bizarre and surreal. She looked at the girl again and for a fleeting moment thought about shoving her aside and running out of there. But she could not bring herself to move and couldn't understand why. Maybe it was the way the girl smiled at her. It was not your friendly, how can I help you smile. The girl's smile radiated a menacing feel with confidence and a touch of violence attached to it. Although she wanted out bad, she also wanted to live. At that moment, she decided that she had to outthink her captor and figure a way out. However, to do that she would need to get more information. She saw the teenage girl watch her as she moved closer to her. She tried to speak but it came out as a stutter, "Um, who are you, where am I, why am I a prisoner here."

The teenage girl calmly and slowly put up her hand to signal her to stop. She then smiled and politely answered, "My name is Hailey, you are in my apartment and you are not, repeat not a prisoner here."

"Alright, then why the hell was I locked in this room?" she replied.

Hailey shook her head, "You were not locked in the room."

"Don't you fucking tell me I wasn't locked in? I tried opening the door and it was locked," she shouted.

Again, Hailey smiled and put up her hand, "Please there is no reason to curse. And yes, the door was locked but that was for your safety."

Dumbfounded, she, replied, "How the hell is being held against my will considered safe?"

Hailey facial features changed slowly towards a serious nature as did her tone, "I guess you don't remember what happened after you left the party."

"Party, do you mean last night's party at Jesus's apartment?" she replied.

"Yes, but not last night try two nights ago," Hailey responded.

She shook her head back and forth as to say it can't be. She just woke up. Hailey could see her going through her thought process seeing the anger dissipating and being replaced with confusion and uncertainty.

"Maybe I could help you remember. Do you remember leaving the party with someone?" asked Hailey.

She shook her head back and forth slowly, "I remember Jesus introducing me to many people throughout the night but not leaving the party with someone."

"Let me give you hint, the person you left with wasn't female," winked Hailey.

It suddenly came back to her transforming her back to the night of Jesus's party.

"Wow, you are one beautiful woman. May I introduce myself," asked a good-looking in a surfer kind of young man.

Although she knew his "woman" comment was meant for him to justify his interest in a minor, she thought he was good looking and not much older than she was so she played along, "Thank you and you may."

He smiley devilishly, "My name is Hunter and who do I have the honor of speaking with."

She smiled, "Sofia, are you here alone, Hunter?" My god, she couldn't believe that she was being that forward with a guy.

"Matter of fact, I am," was his reply.

Shit, she was suddenly mortified and immediately tongue-tied but it didn't last long because he saved her with a joke.

"I'm with me, myself, and I," he laughed loudly at his own joke. She smiled and laughed with him for saving her any further embarrassment.

"So how do you know Jesus?" she asked.

"He's my star tattooist at my Harlem shop," was his reply.

She was a little surprised, "You own your own business. Sorry, didn't mean to be rude. It's just you look so young to own a business."

He laughed hardily, "Well, thank you and none taken, as for age I just turned twenty-one. Since we're asking about age, how old are you?"

55

She thought to herself if she told him sixteen, he would excuse himself and she didn't want that because she was interested in him. So she decided to fudge the truth a little, "Just had a birthday, the big one-eight," she laughed.

He looked satisfied, "Well, happy birthday, let's have a toast." He stopped for a second and added, "Is it to forward for me to think you would be drinking?"

She laughed, "Isn't that what you do at a party," she laughed and added, "Green Apple Martini, please."

She remembered being with him for over an hour and in that time the party's attendants grew in numbers to a point where it was hard to carry a conversation. He suggested a boat at the marina he was currently renting. At first, she wasn't sure but relented when she figured he was young and rich, plus how cool was to live on the water especially in New York. She consented but not before telling her friend Jesus who she was going out with and where.

"It looks like your remembering what happened to you," Hailey stated as she saw Sofia in deep thought.

Sofia nodded her head, "But it still doesn't answer why you have me locked in here."

"Again, it's for your safety. I think you have to go further in your memory to understand why. Do you remember being at the yacht, yet?"

She indicated not yet and began to focus on that night again. Her memory came back to when she was standing on the dock with Hunter looking directly at the yacht.

"Oh my god, it's beautiful, I can't believe you can afford a yacht," she told him with a disregard of grace.

"Yes, believe it or not, tattooing is big business and if you have someone like Jesus, who has the reputation one needs in the business, money will come," he laughed, "and for the record, this is a modest houseboat but is cheaper than renting anything on in New York."

She remembered walking up the gangplank and onto the yacht. Her mind fast-forwarded to when she entered the Captain's bedroom where neither could keep their hands off each other, hot and heavy kissing, touching, the undressing of clothing.

It was at this point that she stopped for a minute and looked at Hailey. She heard Hailey egg her on about that night, "Go on, from the look on your face I think you're about to learn the reason why I'm protecting you."

He slowly drew away from her mouth and with his two hands cupped her face, "remember you asked how I could afford this place and I told you that it was the tattoo business."

She nodded her head but was a little confused especially when that was not on her mind at that moment.

"Well, what I didn't mention was it was also because the majority of our clients are high school girls," he told her.

Now she was confused which immediately killed her mood as she pushed away from him, "What are talking about. I don't understand how high school girls can help you pay for your houseboat?"

"They like you are willing to have sex with older men..." he couldn't finish his sentence because she jumped up from the bed.

"Fuck you! How dare you say that we haven't had sex," she shouted.

"Calm the fuck down. You were about to, look at yourself in just your bra and panties with someone you just met who by the way is older than you." He raised his voice for the first time.

Now she suddenly realized how vulnerable she was alone and away from everyone, "Listen, I met and liked you and wanted to be alone with you. But you have to understand that this is a first for me, being alone with a man," she tried to appeal to his decency but didn't want to rely on it. She needed to get out of there without upsetting him.

He smiled then chuckled and tried to calm things down, "I figured that and I'm sorry if I came across harsh. You just struck me as an adventurous type. I was going to see if you would be interested in something those high school girls are doing for me."

She has to keep it so he thinks she's interested but she really needed an out, "And what is it that these girls are doing for you?"

"Well, they earn some money on the side and get to meet some very powerful people that can help later in life after college," he replied.

She again looked at him strangely, "Earn money? What do they have to do for the money?"

He stated it as matter of factly, as if it was no big deal, "Have sex with them, of course."

She stepped back a little further from the bed and closer to the door, "Fuck you, asshole, I'm no prostitute. What fucking balls you have..."

She did not have enough time to finish her tirade as she stopped mid-sentence when she saw him leaped off the bed and swing his fist. It was coming towards her jaw but it looked and felt like slow motion. She saw the blow come into her vision clearly. She tracked it with her eyes as it violently and forcibly opened her mouth as it landed. Her lower jaw felt as though it was unhinged and she felt herself begin to tilt towards the floor. All she could think about was how powerless she was at that point. She couldn't even stop herself from falling to the floor. She hit it with a sickening thud.

"Aghhh," was all that escaped from her mouth as she began to fade into blackness.

She didn't remember how long she was out but she could hear another female's voice. She tried opening her eyes but they felt heavy but after a couple of tries, her eyes slowly opened to reveal that she was laying on the bed in the Captain's room. She felt weak and sick to her stomach but she was able to turn her head towards the doorway and saw Hunter talking with another young girl. She must have been out a while because it seemed he found another girl to recruit but that thought changed when she saw them both walking towards her.

"Shit, did you have to hit her more than once," the new girl shouted to Hunter.

He shouted back, "She wouldn't shut the fuck up. What else was I supposed to do? Anyway, you have to help me get rid of her. She knows about the girls."

The new girl looked at him with disgust, "That's only because of your stupidity. You should stay away from my side of the business, asshole."

He raised his hand as though he was going to strike the new girl but she stood her ground with a look that invited him to try to hit her. He nervously laughed lowered his hand, "Just fucking get rid of her or we're both dead."

"Alright, dick weed, get the fuck off the boat and untie it from the pier," she replied.

"Where the fuck are you going with the boat?" Hunter asked.

"What's it look like. I'm getting rid of the body. You didn't say where. What better place to rid a body than the ocean? The fish and hopefully a shark would eat the evidence for us," she laughed.

He just shook his head, "You are one sick fuck, Hailey."

"You should talk, you fucking pedophile," was her reply.

The girl heard it all. She could do nothing but simply sob and pray that she would get the opportunity to see her mom one last time before she died.

The girl, called Hailey, walked up and knelt down beside her, smiled at her and simply said, "Oh, don't cry baby, this will be over before you know it. I promise that you will not feel a thing. You know it's not your fault, you just happened to pick the wrong man for your first night out in the big bad city." And with that, Hailey plunged a syringe into her arm sending her spiraling down into a black hole.

Chapter 11

Still at the bar and sitting across from Chris, Dean opened up about his life, "My parents came from Arizona. My mom was from Phoenix but is originally from New York City and was born in Dublin, Ireland. Her parents, my grandparents had immigrated to Ellis Island in the early 1930s, settling in the Upper West Side neighborhood of Hell's Kitchen. They lived there until 1965 when my mother was twelve, her parents decided to move from New York to Arizona."

Chris didn't say a word just nodded his head urging Dean to continue.

"They made that decision based on the escalation of the war in Vietnam. It was a tumultuous time when major cities experienced widespread violent anti-war protests which usually resulted in protestors and police being harmed or killed," stated Dean.

"My parents used to tell me stories about the violence during that time. It wasn't bad in affluent neighborhoods but in inner cities like Newark and Trenton, it was commonplace," countered Chris.

"My grandparents worried that my mother would be hurt either going or coming from school because she traveled on the subway. It was their belief if they moved to a smaller city that was not near metropolitan areas like San Francisco or New York there wouldn't be as many anti-war protests or demonstrations and in essence, lessoning the chance of violence."

"OK, but why not Butte, Montana instead of Arizona?" laughed Chris.

"That would have been funny if I was a fucking cowboy but seeing that I'm Native not so much," laughed Dean.

"Oops, forgot about that small detail," smiled Chris.

"My grandparents picked the city of Phoenix because according to my mother most residents were senior citizens that either served in WWII or the Korean War," explained Dean.

"That's actually smart, they probably figured people in Phoenix would be pro-military and wouldn't start any anti-war protests," countered Chris.

"You hit the nail right on the head and my mother said that they were right about it. However, what they didn't realize was that people were not only pro-military but nationalistic with a racist bent," stated Dean.

"OK, how so?" asked Chris.

"Let me give you an example, one day during my mother's high school freshman year, she was returning home. That day, she decided to take a shortcut through the city's downtown area. The route took her to the bus terminal where she noticed a couple of Native American children with two adult Native women. The women were asking people for food to feed their children but were having no success. Not one person stopped to help. She even saw white mothers with children of their own pass them as though they were not present and several older men told them to go back to their country," explained Dean.

"I'm surprised the women didn't tell them that they were in their country only it was stolen from them," remarked Chris.

"I agree but you and I both know those women would not say a word but my mother was so ashamed and disgusted by the scene she decided to do something about it. Although she didn't have any food or money at that moment, she told the Native mothers to stay there until she returned. Twenty minutes later, she returned with groceries and clothing. She later told me that the experience forever changed her life," Dean smiled proudly.

Dean stared off to the right of Chris as though he was reliving his mother's anger at people's racist indifference to other human beings, "She told me that her heart broke because no one would acknowledge the hunger and pain of those Native children. I have to tell you that my mother was not naïve about what your government and its citizens did to our people but to experience it close and personal lit a fire she didn't know was dormant in her soul. It burned with veracity and from that point on my mother dedicated her life to the Native American people."

With that, Dean attempted to take a sip of his drink but didn't have a chance with Chris shouting, "Come on, don't keep in suspense tell me how she dedicated her life to Natives?"

Dean laughed, "Shit can a brother catch his breath."

"Of course, after you finish," laughed Chris.

"Alright, alright, she waited until dinner that night to speak to my grandparents. She informed them that she was going to college to become a social worker and work specifically with the Native populations living on the reservations," explained Dean.

Chris again interrupted, "Were they surprised? Did they try to persuade her to change her mind?"

Dean smiled, "Surprisingly, no but she did say that they were not enamored with her choice of college majors. They like most immigrants parents wanted their children to assimilate into being an American. Their idea of an American was working hard and going to school to become either a doctor or lawyer. Those positions exuded success and wealth, not a social worker."

Chris could see pride in Dean's face and posture as he began to talk about his mom and her college career.

"My mother is a woman of her word. She was accepted and graduated from Arizona State University in 1974 with a double bachelor's degree in both social work and American Indian Studies. Her first and only job was the social worker for the local Indian Clinic on the Tohono O'odham Reservation in Southern Arizona."

Dean could see confusion on Chris's face, "You look a little confused, Chris."

"That's because I've never heard of a Tohono O'odham Indian. That name sounds more like it is more native to Ireland then North America," chucked Chris.

Dean liked this man. He laughed with him, "I agree and I get that all the time. People see me and mistake me for an Apache, Comanche, Sioux or Cherokee. I have to explain that there were over 500 tribes living in the Americas before the United States came into existence. Our people settled and populated the Sonoran Desert lands of Arizona and present-day Mexico. Their known as fierce warriors, expert trackers, and hunters of antelope and other wild game. It was on the reservation where my mother met my father, a young male Tohono O'odham Indian named Michael Stanton."

Chris look perplexed again and stated, "Your father's name sounds more like someone born in California or New York and not on an Indian reservation."

Dean nodded his head, "His parents decided to give him an American name as a way for him to easily assimilate into American and its culture. My parents did the same to my sister and me. My father's Indian name was Matunaagd which meant, he who fights."

Chris smiled, "Now that's a fucking great Indian name. What's yours and don't say little Matunaagd."

Dean laughed loudly, "Asshole, you wouldn't believe it if I told you. I was named, Ahanu, which means, he who laughs and fools around."

Dean already knew it was coming and was not disappointed when Chris started to crack up then shake his head and state, "No fucking way, well Pocahontas the name suits you to a tee."

Dean laughed again, "My father named me that because as soon as the doctors delivered me and slapped my ass I laughed instead of crying."

Chris looked at Dean and smiled, "I believe it. What about your sister's name?"

A shining glow came across Dean's face as he invoked his sister's name, "My beautiful and headstrong sixteen-year-old sister's full tribal name is Cha'kwaina, which means 'one who cries.' She hates the meaning but loves the sound of it when it is pronounced. However, many people outside the res have trouble saying it so she lets them call her Cha."

"It's actually a beautiful name and I would agree with her about the meaning. But your mom probably named her that because she was the opposite of you instead of laughing, she cried," replied Chris.

"That's correct but there is actually more to the story. You see my sister was adopted," stated Dean. He could see Chris's eyes open wide as they conveyed shock.

"Are you serious, call me naïve and sorry for the dumb question but there's adoption in your culture?" asked Chris.

Dean nodded his head, "I'm sure you've heard this phrase, there are no dumb questions, as a matter of fact, that is a great question. Our culture does not consider it an 'adoption' per se. If a native-born child's parents die, members of that tribe would raise them as their own. It would have been different if my sister were not native-born. In that scenario, my mother would have to go through tribal elders for permission. If it was granted then the child would go through a rebirth ceremony in which they are bestowed a native name. In my sister's case, she was already native so she just assimilated into our tribe as though my mother gave birth to her."

Chris looked on with amazement, "That is really something, no, incredible. But what happened to her mother and father."

Dean was about to answer when Chris cut in, "Sorry, I just thought of this, and how did she end up with your mother and father. OK, I'll shut up now."

Dean laughed, "All good questions but then again, you are an investigator."

Chris waved both his arms away from his body, "Enough kissing my ass, you already got the job, just finish the story."

Dean again had to laugh, "Remember that my mom was not native. However, tribal elders witnessed her commitment to the betterment of their people and her love for our tribe and traditions. They decided to bestow upon her the greatest honor a tribe can give to someone outside the tribe. They made her a tribal member. She was taken aback by such an honor and accepted it with pride. A ceremony was performed at an evening bonfire, which was surrounded by all members of the tribe. My mother was given her tribal name and all those in attendance chanted it. Elders anointed her with the smoke of sage and introduced her to the tribe and welcomed her into her new family."

"Damn, that's a fucking beautiful story. What name was she given?" asked Chris.

"Oh, sorry, she was presented to the Tohono O'odham as Makawee. It means one who is generous, abundant, freely giving and motherly."

Chris sat there for a moment looking at Dean with appreciation, "You know those tribal names are truly wonderful as well as accurately deserving. I'm curious though does your mother use her American name like you or does she go by her tribal name?"

"Another great question and I'll answer in this way, when natives are in your world and by that, I mean outside of our reservation, we tend to use our American names. It's safer and causes less hassle for our young ones. Unbelievably, there still is rampant racism towards my people especially in the Southern and Western parts of the states. Once we step back onto our plains, we revert back to our traditional names which each of us holds sacred," explained Dean.

"Makes sense but it's a shame that we still have ignorant people amongst us. What happened to your sister's birth parents?" Chris asked.

"It was a typical tragic story with a happy ending. You see Cha was given a second chance to live even before she was born," Dean explained.

Chris's eyebrows knitted, "What the hell does that even mean?"

Dean cracked up, "Sorry, I was trying to be philosophical."

"Well, don't, it'll just confuse the hell out of me," laughed Chris.

"Alright well, Cha's birth mother, a Hopi Indian named Sihu and her birth father, Mochni also a Hopi were driving home from a doctor's appointment when their car was struck by a drunk driver."

"Aw shit, that fucking blows," was Chris's immediate response.

"It does and unfortunately alcoholism is my people's albatross that doesn't seem to want to go away. When the accident happened, Sihu was eight months pregnant and Mochni had just become the Shaman of his tribe," explained Dean.

Dean started to laugh because he just saw Chris raise his hand as if he were in grammar school.

"What, I have manners. You just said Cha's birth parents were Hopi Indian, why did your reservation have another tribe living on its land?" asked Chris.

"They did not live on our reservation. The Hopi reservation is about an hour west of us. They were my parent's best friends. My mother and Cha's birth mother met at Arizona State and both graduated with social work degrees. As for Cha's birth father, he was close to my dad. They served in the government together. Hopi elders would have wanted Cha to part of their clan but realized the type of bond formed between my parents and Cha's birth parents and felt it would be most beneficial if she became part of our clan. And as they say, the rest is history," explained Dean.

Chris could only shake his head, "Wow, that is some story. Does Cha know it?"

"Yes, when she turned ten my mother told her. At first, she was crushed as most children who find out they are adopted. The abandonment issues, their sense of drifting not knowing if it was their fault somehow that they were given away, it was a difficult year, to say the least, but my sister is one tough bird and was able to come to terms with it. As a matter of fact, I believe it strengthened our bond as siblings."

"What about your father, you said earlier that he worked for the government. What exactly did he do?" asked Chris

Just as Dean was going to answer Chris, his phone rang. "Sorry, Chris let me answer this call real quick and I'll get back to my dad." Chris waved him off and told him to go ahead because he had to use the restroom.

Dean nodded his head, and then answered his phone, "What's up, Duncan?"

"You remember you asked me to tell you when those gang bangers were back at their base," replied Duncan.

"Yep, they all home now?" asked Dean.

"Yes, including that kid fucking with your client's son," replied Duncan.

"Great, once I'm done meeting with my new client, I'll head up there and have a heart to heart with the little bastard," countered Dean.

"You need some backup. I'm almost done here," offered Duncan.

"For a couple of punk ass kids, shit if I need help with kids I shouldn't be out here offering my services anymore," laughed Dean.

"Alright, have it your way. Don't be pissed if you get your ass handed to you because you refused my help," responded Duncan.

"If I need the help, I'll be sure to call you," chuckled Dean.

"Fuck you, tough guy. I won't be answering any smoke signals from you. I offered but you declined," was Duncan's response as he laughed and hung up the phone. Dean had to nod his head. Everyone had an Indian joke, as he walked back towards Chris.

Chapter 12

"I don't know about this, Hailey. Maybe we shouldn't have skipped afternoon classes to come here. Look at those people standing on line. They seem to be much older than the both of us combined," Megan commented nervously.

"Oh, come on, Megan, just follow my lead," countered Hailey.

"And look at the way the women are dressed and made up. The men that are with them are prettier than us," Megan retorted.

She and Hailey were standing on the corner of 72nd and Central Park West parallel to the historic Dakota Apartments. They could see limousines with other expensive cars lined up along the sidewalk leading up the Apartments. There was a bright red Tesla parked in front of the valet stand by the entrance. They both watched as a tall beautiful woman with Nordic features was helped out of the passenger side door by the valet. As she stepped up onto the sidewalk her male companion an equally stunning tall man with blonde hair, wearing a suit that must have cost more than the car itself took the woman's arm and walked towards the Apartments.

Megan followed the couple until they reached the security checkpoint, "And look at those guards?" Megan whispered gingerly.

"I see them. But I already told you, stop worrying," an exasperated Hailey stated as she could feel herself getting annoyed at this teenage girl.

"Oh, that's just fucking super just tell me not to worry. OK, miss calmness, would you like to tell me how the hell we are past that security checkpoint?" whined Megan.

"Jesus, Megan, stop acting like some fucking little kid with all that bitching and moaning. Is this your way of telling me that you were full of shit about being rebellious," Hailey said with a low voice laced with disappointment.

Hailey knew that her disappointed tone would get the teenager, to react apologetically. She understood that teenagers especially girls never wanted to disappoint their peers for fear of rejection. She remembered clearly, when it happened to her at ten years old.

"Hailey, you think your mom could take us to the park after school. She's the only mom that doesn't work," asked Barbie a classmate.

"She can't ask her mother Barbie, because her mommy does work, didn't you know that?" replied the class bully, Christina.

Hailey just stood there watching as they talked about her mother. She really wanted to go to the park with Barbie but she knew she would disappoint her since she could not count on her mother to do anything for her.

"What kind of work does you mom do, Hailey?" Barbie asked.

Again, Hailey was petrified and could not move a muscle, which enabled Christina to continue, "My mom says that Hailey's mom is a streetwalker for hire."

"What does a streetwalker do?" Barbie asked innocently.

Hailey started to feel hot under her clothes and beads of sweat started their way down the back of her neck.

"Well, my mom says they walk up and down the street waiting for daddies and other boys to stop and talk to them. She says they go with the daddies and other boys and do favors for them. My mom told me that those mommies are also very lazy because they work lying down. She also told me that I should stay away from kids that have mommies that are streetwalkers because they carry cooties. Since Hailey's mom is a streetwalker, you shouldn't hang around her." And with that Christina grabbed Barbie's arm and proceeded to move away from Hailey.

"I still don't understand Hailey but if Christina's mom told her that then I have to believe it. She is an adult and goes to the same church as my mom. I'm really sorry, but maybe you could go to the park with someone else," replied Barbie as she walked off with Christina.

All Hailey could do, was storm off in the opposite direction. She was thinking about how much she hated her mother for not being there for her and always putting a strange man ahead of her.

"Hello, Hailey, are you even listening to me?" whined Megan again.

"Yea, yea, don't be such a fucking pain in the ass. I told you already not to worry," snapped Hailey.

"Alright, shit, you don't have to be so fucking nasty," a wounded Megan, replied.

Hailey knew she had to calm down or she'll lose the girl, "Sorry, Megan, didn't mean to snap like that but come on already. Who bought you that smoking low-cut Black mini-dress you have on?"

She then pointed at Megan's shoes, "And who took you to that hidden shoe spot in the East Village to buy those sick Jimmy Choo's to match."

"You did," replied Megan sheepishly.

"How about your hair and makeup?" she added.

Megan showing her age just nodded and pointed at Hailey.

Hailey had her on the ropes. She just needed to throw the knockout punch, "You've done everything I asked in order for us to get you into this party. Now walk with your head high and strut with confidence. We'll pass those losers on line and walk right into the party," smiled Hailey.

Hailey could see Megan nod her head in agreement but also saw some moisture around her eyes. "This is no time to second guess yourself, embrace the fact that you are about to enter a world of fun and games usually reserved for adults. Now, wipe your eyes before your mascara runs," Hailey stated with an air of confidence.

Hailey had to continue her charade of someone who was in complete control of the situation and confident in her abilities. If these girls knew the reality that Hailey was a guilt-ridden seventeen-year-old girl that was always on the verge of a mental, physical and emotional breakdown they would have run far away from her. She saw in Megan and the other teenage girls she recruited into the club, the genuine reason they gravitated towards her, acceptance, love and sense of personal belonging. She sighed inwardly knowing regrettably that it was those very idealistic things that lead her to becoming who she was today.

Chapter 13

Chris returned from the restroom and sat across from Dean pointing at the phone on the table, "Everything good?"

"Yea, that was my NYPD contact telling me about some punk kids I got to deal with after I'm finished here," replied Dean.

"Anything, I could help you with?" countered Chris.

"Nah, it's related to another case I got going but don't worry it'll be wrapped up tonight. That way, I could start fresh tomorrow on your case," replied Dean, "where were we?"

"You were going to tell me about your father before you got the call," replied Chris.

"Yes, that's right. It's a sad but vital story that shaped me into who I am today."

"A little melodramatic but go on," laughed Chris.

Dean smiled and proceeded, "My father worked for the federal government when he met my mother. At the time he could not tell her his occupation or which agency because he was bound by confidentiality. It was also a way to protect himself and his colleagues but she didn't care as long as it was steady legal work."

Chris chimed in, "Practical thinking coming from an intelligent woman."

"Yes, and thank you for the compliment, but remember she wasn't born native. In our culture, anything to do with the federal government was suspect especially its employees. As with everything in life, there were exceptions. In our world, there was a group more hated than the government," explained Dean.

Chris sat dumbfounded, "What could be worse than having a tribal member working for the federal government?"

Dean responded simply, "Drug and human traffickers."

"I don't understand," replied Chris.

"The stereotype of the American Indian over the last fifty years has been that most are alcoholics. Unfortunately, that is not a stereotype, alcohol is still a problem but tribes saw a more dangerous scrounge encroaching our lands.

Drug cartels began to trespass on our native lands and sacred burial grounds to smuggle drugs and people into the United States."

Chris interjected, "So members of the tribe were fine with your father working for Uncle Sam as long as he didn't work for any drug or human smuggling ring."

Dean laughed, "In a nutshell, yes. Our elders understood that he and the agency he worked for were trying to stem the drug cartels from using our sacred lands."

Chris interrupted, "What part of the government did he work for?"

"At that time no one, including my mother, knew which agency. It was only after marrying her did he disclose his job and the agency he worked for."

Chris put up his hands, "OK, enough with the buildup. I'm interested, now, what did he do?"

Dean sat up straighter and stated in a strong and proud voice, "My father was a 'Shadow Wolf.'"

Chris took a second to take in that name, smiled and shouted, "What the fuck is a Shadow Wolf and what the hell does it have to do with the government?"

Dean looked at Chris with a stare that conveyed total seriousness that prompted Chris to apologize, "Sorry didn't mean to interrupt, please continue."

Dean with pride explained, "Shadow Wolves were an elite tracking unit within the United States Department of Immigration and Customs (USDIC). They were considered the best human trackers in the world. The unit consisted of twenty-one Indian warriors comprised of several Native American tribes including the Tohono O'odham, Navajo, Hopi, Lakota, and Blackfoot."

Dean paused, looked at Chris, saw that he was fully engaged, "My father had been a Wolf since its inception back in 1972. On the USDIC website, a Shadow Wolf is described as an individual known for their ability to track not only animals but also human beings. That skillset enabled them to track and arrest drug and human smugglers crossing the borders into the United States."

Chris interrupted, "Why were they called Shadow Wolves?"

"It referred to the way the unit hunted, like a pack of wolves. When a wolf corned its prey, it would wait until the rest of the pack was there before killing it," responded Dean.

Chris saw the pride illuminate off Dean as he spoke about his father. "Damn that is some fucking cool shit, man. That is why Antonio said a finding person was in your blood. But that doesn't explain how you got started doing the things you do," said Chris.

Dean replied, "It'll become clearer, once I'm done explaining my story. Back in 1982, my birth year, the Columbian's began their rise to power in the illicit drug trade. The United States decided they needed to take action and deployed the Wolf unit. Their task was to patrol Native reservations and stop the cartels from trafficking drugs and human cargo. They easily and immediately began to disrupt the drug cartels shipments of both drugs and human cargo. They set up and conducted ambushes, seized large drug shipments and arrested smugglers and their associates."

"They must have pissed off a lot of Columbians messing with their product," responded Chris.

Dean laughed, "Now that's an understatement if I ever heard one. My father's unit cost the cartels millions of dollars in product and human cargo. However, that's not what was driving the head of the cartels crazy."

"What else could possibly get them upset?" asked Chris.

"They could not identify who these men in uniforms were because the unit was deemed classified. The handler and the USDIC Director only knew it. It was purposely designed that way to protect its members."

Dean could see Chris shake his head and heard him say, "Something like a CIA Black ops unit."

Dean nodded his head, "Exactly, and it almost neutralized the cartels until…"

Chris did not let Dean finish by cutting in, "A fucking mole. Someone on the inside let the cat out of the bag."

Dean laughed, "Good analogy and correct. At the time, the government did not realize the amount of money changing hands on a daily basis it was millions and all the cartels were making it but at the time, there were three vying for supremacy in the region. The money turned out to be the game-changer."

Chris retorted, "The root of all evil is greed, power, and most importantly, money."

Dean shook his head in agreement, "That's right and the cartels had more than enough to go around, which happened. They flooded local municipalities with cash enabling them to have in their back pockets from your everyday citizen to your local politicians and law enforcement including members of the USDIC."

Chris could only say one word, "Holy, Fuck."

Dean gave Chris a pained expression, "Fuck is right. You wanted to know why I do what I do, right?"

Chris just nodded his head affirming the statement.

Dean continued, "Back in 1982, two events forever changed my father. The first was my birth which we both know was the most important event of his life."

"Humility isn't your strong point, I see," countered Chris.

Dean laughed loudly, "I'm kidding but I was important. The second event happened when he was a wolf. A couple of months after my birth, his unit made the biggest bust in U.S. Customs history when they seized the largest ever shipment of Columbian Cocaine along the border of Nogales, Arizona."

Chris nodded his head, "Yes, in Quantico they talk about that raid as the government's first introduction to Pablo Escobar and his budding drug empire."

Dean smiled, "That's right and to be honest my father didn't care who it belonged to just that his team stopped it. However, someone did care, it just so happened to be the unit's handler. At the time of the bust, neither my father nor the rest of the wolves knew that the handler was a drug addict or that he was accepting cash from Escobar's operation."

Chris shook his head back and forth, "He had to be giving something good to get that cash, what was it?"

"Great question, you must have conducted an investigation or two," laughed Dean.

"Well, dipshit, you must have forgotten that I am a bigwig for another fed agency," snorted Chris.

"OK, ok, it was the handler's job to gather intelligence on prospective drug operations and other targets like human traffickers. The handler had to do this job because his unit had to remain anonymous in order to surprise those in charge of the criminal activity," explained Dean.

"And how did the handler gather this information?" asked Chris

"He would cultivate it from confidential informants, mainly, low-level drug dealers and coyotes that guide individuals through the desert and across the border."

Chris raised his eyebrows, "Why would they trust a cop especially if they didn't know him."

"Agreed, but what if you were snatched off the street, blinded folded and taken to an undisclosed location by masked soldiers?" asked Dean.

"Now that's different. You bet your ass that I would shit my pants then give up my own mother," smiled Chris.

Dean almost fell over with that response, "Not far from the truth my friend. The dealer or coyote would wake up bound to a chair with a hood draped over their head. The hood is removed and the person would see the handler sitting across from them. He would tell them that they had a choice die where they sat or flip and become an informant. At first, they would argue that the cartel would cut their heads off and shit down their necks."

"I would feel the same way but you're going to tell me that something changed their minds," smiled Chris.

"Give that man a prize. The handler not only offered immunity to any criminal charges, except murder and rape, but they would be able to keep conducting business with impunity," explained Dean.

"That seems a little much don't you think?" asked Chris.

"Not really, because they knew not to go too far or the wolves would take care of them. Once they got with the program, the handler would ask for small items. It could be something as simple as who in the community was buying. Then the handler would ask about the suppliers. The handler was so successful he was able to acquire quality information on cartel drug shipments and identifying those taking payouts. Initially, the cartels could not figure out how this information was being obtained," Dean sighed and continued, "that, however, changed when the handler began to use the very same product his team was seizing. It didn't take long before his addiction became unmanageable and unaffordable. The only way he felt he could feed his addiction was to go to the cartels with a proposition."

Chris looked puzzled, "The cartels, you mean he actually approached them?"

Dean nodded his head, "Yes that is exactly what he did."

Chris was exacerbated, "And they didn't put a bullet behind his ear?"

Dean shook his head no, "Remember above all else it was a business and what they saw with him was an opportunity to manage the flow of their product. You have to give them credit or in this instance, Escobar. His plan was to keep the handler in place so that he could control his shipments into the US. And so no one would be the wiser, he would sacrifice a smaller shipment to the wolves in return the handler would let two larger shipments into the US uncontested."

Chris nodded his head, "Fucking hate to say it but the asshole knew what he was doing because it kept the unit's reputation without them the wiser. Were any of the units compromised?"

"No, because the handler needed that leverage, and before you ask how the cartel permitted him the leverage, he initially told the cartels that those units were comprised of state S.W.A.T teams and only state officials knew the teams. His function on the federal end was to advise state officials when and where shipments were entering their states. To his credit, the cartels believed him plus the arrangement was working smoothly," explained Dean.

"So you could say that the handler had a 'handle' on the situation, sorry for the pun," laughed Chris.

"You should be that was too easy, I expected more from you," smiled Dean.

"The handler did this for several years without incidence or injury to the unit."

"Impressive, especially since it was undercover work," replied Chris.

Dean turned somber, "Unfortunately like all good things it came to an end."

Chris interjected, "I figured it wouldn't end there we didn't get to your role in this yet. So go on tell me why it was too good to be true."

"My father and his unit were unaware of the handler's drug habit or the cash payments he received from the cartels. As I told you, the handler not only had the cartels fooled but his own unit as well. The wolves continued to seize drugs, arrest both dealers and smugglers as usual but that changed when the unit seized a particular shipment of Escobar's that was not slated to be taken. That shipment contained the largest quantity of cocaine ever attempted to enter the United States. Escobar actually gave up two smaller loads to the handler prior to sending his historic shipment. But my father was not aware of the deal made by the handler and the rest, as they say, is history."

Dean could see that he had Chris on the edge of his seat, "What happened, did the handler get a conscience so he let the unit take it down?"

Dean shook his head back and forth, "No, but I wish that was the case. That particular seizure made national headlines, was on every television news program, and made every newsstand. News agencies identified it as the largest narcotics shipment ever seized. They also identified it as belonging to the new up and coming cartel boss, Pablo Escobar. When the handler awoke the next day from his drug stupor and turned on the news, he knew what was going to happen to him. Remember, he knew that he had not given any order for a seizure that night. The first thing he did was rush to the office and summoned my father. It was a testy meeting in which the handler wanted to know who authorized the operation."

Chris stopped Dean with a hand wave, "Aside from the handler being a scumbag, the question he asked your father was a legitimate one in that situation."

"I agree until I was told the reason it went down, that night my father was on duty when he received an anonymous tip. The tipster told my father that a large cocaine shipment was making its way towards Nogales, Arizona. It would hit the border within the next 45 minutes. My father tried for over twenty minutes to reach his handler but could not get him. Since he was the team leader, if the handler was incapacitated and did not respond to a call, any decision would need to be made by him. Since the handler was AWOL, he made an executive decision. By all accounts, it was the correct decision. The Shadow Wolf's job was to stop the cartels from bringing in drugs and human trafficking. As he told the handler at that meeting, the operation was a no-brainer and a win-win situation. My mother later told me that my father thought the handler was upset because he wanted the credit for the operation that cost the cartels approximately five million dollars of product."

Chris put up his hand to stop Dean from continuing, "I don't want to sound like a dick and put a damper on your father's big bust but five million dollars doesn't seem like a large haul to get from someone like Pablo Escobar."

Dean smiled, "Sorry, at that time it was big but if you put the numbers in today's terms, it would have been like losing one hundred million dollars in one night."

"Jesus, that's fucking unbelievable and a major blow for someone trying to make a name for himself in the drug world," replied Chris.

"Exactly, but my father was unaware of the situation. However, the handler was shitting bricks because he knew Escobar would be calling for him. It wasn't even the money that scared him, most was the fact that Escobar was embarrassed in front of competing cartel bosses."

Dean gave a painful sigh, "The handler knew he was as good as dead if he didn't' give Escobar something to make up for the fiasco. The only thing of value was the identity of the men who did the seizure."

"I don't like the sound of this," replied a pissed off Chris.

"Neither did I as I was being told," Dean continued, "Two weeks after making the nation's largest drug bust the handler calls my father into his office and tells him that he received another anonymous tip about another big drug shipment."

"And your father bought it?" asked a skeptical Chris.

"Why not, you and I know the story but to my father, it was another chance to put a dent in the cartels' operation. But what really convinced my father not to suspect anything was the handler said it would be Escobar's replacement shipment for the one that was captured."

"Do you know whether or not your father at least questioned that information?" asked Chris.

"In a nutshell, no, because he was told that the source happened to be a rival boss, looking to put a stop to the rising cartel leader."

"Plausible, then what happened?" asked Chris.

Chris noticed a somber look come over Dean's face, "On December 15, 1982, six months after my birth my father and his unit went out into the Nogales Desert with the intention of possibility shutting down a budding cartel leader but what happened was I and many other native children became fatherless."

Chris was stunned and looked on in horror, "Shit, I'm so sorry for your lost."

Dean gave Chris a slight nod, "Thank you."

"May I ask how the families knew they were dead? Escobar could have hidden them and no one would have known but the handler."

Dean nodded, "That would have been the smart thing to do. However, you have to remember, Pablo Escobar's ego was in play here. After looking weak and foolish for allowing his shipment that was supposed to be protected to be seized, a message needed to be sent out. The unit was his message. Escobar knew the government would send some other unit to try to locate them. They did and it was the remaining wolves. They went out every day until they found their brethren. It was several days later when they found the bodies on the Mexican side of the Nogales desert. Each wolf showed evidence of torture that ended in a single bullet hole placed behind each ear. It shook the remaining wolves so badly that after retrieving their brother's bodies and conducting traditional burials for each member, they unceremoniously left USDIC. The government had no choice but to shut down the program."

Chris put up his hands and asked, "Wait, what about the handler?"

Dean smiled again, "Hold on I'm getting to that part. The remaining wolves were led by my godfather a Blackfoot Indian aptly named Bear."

Chris laughed, "You're shitting me, right. If that isn't a fucking Hollywood name then I don't know what is."

Dean cracked up as well, "If you saw him, you'll understand. He's six-seven and weighs two hundred ninety pounds all of which is pure muscle. If you rile him up, he'll stand straight up and grunt like a fucking grizzly. However, that's not the best part about my godfather. What makes him cooler than anyone's godfather was that he is a direct descendant of the great Indian Chief, Sitting Bull."

Chris looked at Dean with awe, "That's the fucking coolest thing I've ever heard. Is he still alive?"

Dean responded with pride, "Yes, and I felt the same way growing up. I tell you what once we're done finding your niece, I'll invite to the reservation where I'll introduce you to him."

Chris nodded his head, "I look forward to it. Can I ask you a quick question?"

"Sure, what do you want to know?" countered Dean.

"Was it your godfather that told you about your old man? I know your mom told you a lot but I'm sure she didn't know the day to day workings of the units," replied Chris.

"Yes, most of what I'm telling you came from my godfather. I also got the info from all the surviving wolves in addition to whatever my mom provided," replied Dean.

"What happened after your godfather and the other members left government service and whatever happened to the handler?" Chris shot off two rapid questions.

Dean shouted, "Whoa, one question at a time. In truth, the wolves did not disband; they only left federal government service. As a point of reference, reservations are recognized as separate sovereign nations so the unit became the reservations tribal force against the drug cartels. Same concept as before but no need for informants because our lands were patrolled day and night, if they encountered any smugglers, tribal justice was meted out. As for the handler, consensus from the remaining wolves was that the handler had to face tribal justice for his crimes."

Chris jumped in, "Does tribal justice mean what I think it means?"

"Of course it does. Members of the unit including my godfather concluded that the handler betrayed them. They also felt if the handler had been native, the murders could not have been conducted."

Chris again jumped in, "Wait, wait, you can't make an assumption that the reason the handler betrayed you was because the unit was Indian. The man had a disease, addiction, it doesn't discriminate between race, color or national origin nor does the victim control his or her actions."

Dean nodded his head, "I agree but hear me out. Autopsies were done on each murdered unit member. The report indicated that each one was tortured and shot once behind the ear. It is safe to say that the only information important enough for someone to torture would be the names of the remaining members of the unit."

"Wait, that's another assumption. How would Escobar know that there might be more members of the unit? Didn't the handler only give up the unit that made the seizures?" countered Chris.

"You have to remember that Escobar was putting out two smaller shipments the day prior to the larger one. He knew there was more than one unit because it took two to stop those shipments," explained Dean.

"Alright, I can see it now. That means those that were tortured did not give up the others since your godfather and his unit are alive," stated Chris.

"That is exactly right and it also shows why I believe the handler if native would not have provided any information on the units," replied Dean.

"Because of the tribal bond between all native peoples, right?" asked Chris.

"Man, you are smarter than you look," laughed Dean.

"Yeah, yeah kiss my ass," stated Chris.

Satisfied with Chris's deductions Dean continued, "Damn can't you take a compliment. Well, the remaining wolves wanted proof that the handler had betrayed them. So they decided that they would conduct a 'snatch' operation on the handler, ironic because it was the handler's go-to method in recruiting confidential informants. It took several months to gather information on the handler before it could be run. He was forced to retire from USDIC after no other native warrior would join the unit after his betrayal."

Chris chimed in, "If I was native, there would be no fucking way I would have trusted the federal government."

"Exactly, now my godfather told me two days prior to the snatch, they watched his patterns to make sure his routine stayed pat. On the third day, they ran the operation and successfully snatched him off the street in less than two minutes," stated Dean.

Chris laughed, "Shit that is impressive."

"I said the same thing. He was thrown in a van and driven over eight hours to the very spot in the Nogales Desert where their brothers were executed. They dragged his ass towards a bonfire that was burning. They had removed the hood that covered his head during the trip," explained Dean.

Chris cut in, "Let me guess those guys threw him in the fire and roasted his ass."

"What, get the fuck out of here, we're not savages," laughed Dean.

"Sorry, it's what I would have done," smiled Chris.

"Well, that's not what happened. What the handler saw once his hood was removed were fourteen native warriors clad traditional wardress, black paint, shields made out of rawhide and brass tomahawk pipes," Dean proudly explained.

"That must have been one scary sight, although for someone not in the asshole's predicament, it would have probably been a majestic one," countered Chris.

"Agree, when my godfather described it to me, it made the hairs on my body stand on end and pride pulsated in my veins. He told me that the handler almost shit himself and would not take his eyes off their tomahawk pipes," replied Dean

Chris gave Dean a quick smile before interrupting, "Come on, a tomahawk pipe?" He laughed and added, "What after you kill the motherfucker you grab a smoke of tobacco?"

Dean shook his from side to side, "The weapon had a dual purpose. Warriors used it as an accurate close-quarter weapon in hand-to-hand combat. But it also served as a symbol of peace."

Chris interrupted respectfully, "In what way would that weapon represent peace?"

Dean explained, "Think back early 18th Century when three-quarters of your America belonged to the natives. Tribes went to war with one another for land and when the time came for the warring tribes to make peace, a neutral site was chosen for the peace talks. The tomahawk pipe would be present at those talks. If the talks resulted in a mutual peace between tribes, the pipe portion of the tomahawk is filled with tobacco and lit. The pipe is passed and smoked between representatives of both tribes as a symbol of peace and unity. After both representatives had smoked from the peace pipe, it would then be taken outside and buried. Your people stole our symbolism for peace and made it one of your famous metaphors."

Chris tried to deduce which metaphor, "Sorry, which famous metaphor are you talking about?"

Dean laughed, "What happens when you decide to make amends with someone you're having problems with; both sides decide to bury the hatchet, which is just another word for tomahawk."

"Crazy, how one never knows where a saying comes but now it makes sense," said Chris, "So what happened after the handler saw the twelve little Indians?"

"Fourteen, you prick. The group passed down a guilty verdict and my godfather told the handler his punishment. They decided that he would be giving his life to the mother. Before you ask, in our culture Earth is considered the mother because it nourishes all living creatures and without it, we do not exist," explained Dean.

"OK, I get that but how does one give their life to it?" asked Chris.

"In our culture, when a member of a tribe has taken a life for no reason, other than they could, elders would punish them by digging a horizontal hole equivalent to the condemned warrior's height from foot to neck. The individual would be placed in the hole and buried up to their neck leaving the head exposed. They would be left alone with no water, food and most importantly protection. After the first day, the person is thirsty, hungry and is both sun and wind burned," explained Dean.

"Fuck that is terrible, so they die of starvation, right?" asked Chris.

"If they are lucky but what usually happens is that predators would smell death in the air and make their way towards the burial site. My godfather would tell me that if the coyotes didn't get the person then mountain lions would enjoy the prize," stated Dean.

"Shit, that a fucking disturbing thought," replied Chris.

"My godfather said once the handler understood his punishment he cried for his mother and begged for his life," explained Dean.

"A well-deserved consequence for his betrayal," stated Chris.

Dean smiled, "No argument here but it did little good for me because I still did not know my father. The saving grace if there was any, was that my mother felt it was important for me and my sister to grow up native. She made the very difficult decision not to live in Phoenix with her parents and instead remained on the reservation near my godfather Bear and his Blackfoot family. It was he that taught me the ways of the Tohono O'odham, Blackfoot, Navajo, and Lakota."

Dean looked at Chris smiled, "Because of my mother's decision both my sister and I were able to live and learn among our people."

Chris looked on in awe, "Man, you just gave me fucking goosebumps."

Dean lifted his middle finger again and pointed it at Chris, "Fuck you, asshole. By the time I was fourteen, I knew how to fight in hand- to- hand combat, hunt, and track and spoke four separate native tongues."

"Damn, at that age, all I did was play second base on my town's little league team," replied Chris.

Dean laughed, "Don't get me wrong, learning all the time wasn't my choice. I wanted to play games and fuck around like a normal teenager but I also wanted to be like my father. It was a tough education, especially because my teachers would physically push me around and purposely try to get me angry. It got so bad that eventually one day, I lashed out and told them that I was done with it all. That same night my godfather sat me down for a lesson in humility. He pointed out that my father's friends who were teaching me pushed and pulled on me out of respect and love for who and what my father was to them."

"How the hell is bullying someone a way to show respect and love?" jumped in Chris.

"That's what I thought at the time but here's what my godfather told me. Those very warriors saw and felt that I had the same qualities as my father. However, they also felt that I could be stronger, more fearless, committed and a better all-around leader than him. Hence the rough treatment it was their way of not letting me become conceited and squandering the gifts they did not possess but I was given."

Chris cut in, "That doesn't sound like you at all. I mean I haven't known you long but from what I've heard from Antonio and listening to you now that's not how I see you."

"I said something similar to that to my godfather. His response was no matter who you are; admiration from one's peers, unchecked could lead to one losing their true nature. So, to balance that out the unit needed me to understand hard work, commitment and a dash of humility in order to become the warrior they believed I had in me."

"I can understand that now," answered Chris.

"As I did that night, but here's the kicker. My godfather told me that I was given more than my father's warrior spirit. I was gifted with empathy from my mother. That night, my godfather told me that he had a vision the night I was born. The ancestors spoke to him and prophesied that I was given my gifts as means to help those in need who did not have a voice, both native and non-native peoples. It was my destiny to become the champion of those voices."

"Visions and helping the less fortunate, how fucking cliché is that," laughed Chris as Dean gave him the two-finger salute, "but all kidding aside, learning who you are and sitting in your presence has confirmed what Antonio already knew, you are the one that can help us find Sofia."

Chapter 14

"You better fucking take care of this Abraham. It was your shit for brains assistant's fault. He said the fucking girl was sedated and wouldn't move no matter what I did to her. I should have known the piece of shit didn't know what the fuck he was talking about," shouted the American Ambassador to Saudi Arabia.

"Calm down and tell me what happened," asked Abraham.

"The bitch fucking woke up that's what happened. She started yelling for the police. What was I supposed to fucking do," the Ambassador shouted again.

"Simple, follow the club's most important rule; if in trouble, hit the emergency button on the side off the dresser. Someone would have gotten here in less than two minutes. But let's be honest Mr. Ambassador have you ever had to do that?"

The Ambassador swallowed hard, "No."

"And do you know why, because that 'shit for brains' is the same guy that has been handling the girls you handpicked for your visits. So excuse me for not taking your fucking side on this one. It wasn't him that grabbed a vase and struck the girl over her head. You should have pushed the emergency button or better yet, slapped her and told her to shut up. The only one to blame is you," retorted Abraham.

"Watch how the fuck you speak to me, Abraham. It would be wise of you to know your place. Let's not forget that I could easily put a stop to this shit and have you sent back to place you really belong," shouted the Ambassador.

Abraham's face turned a deep purple crimson, "Let me say this once, Mr. Ambassador, you may be in a position of power but threaten me again and you'll find yourself in a world of hurt make no mistake about that."

"Just do your fucking job and clean this mess up. I want it so that she was never here and this didn't happen. We on the same page?" replied the Ambassador without the previous superiority.

Abraham stood up straight which put a good three inches of height over the Ambassador. He gave him a look that conveyed his hatred and contempt for the short, weak man "Do us all a favor and get the fuck out of here. Oh, and don't come to any more parties for the next two months. My girls and I need a break from you."

Bravado came back to the Ambassador after that remark, "Don't worry about me coming back to one of your shitty parties Abraham." And with that, the Ambassador stormed out of the room and party.

Abraham looked down at the body of young Megan and knelt alongside it. He placed two fingers on her neck. He didn't know why he checked her pulse for the second time because it didn't change from the first time when it confirmed that she was dead. That must have been some fucking blow the Ambassador administered.

He shook his head and thought what a waste of such a beautiful girl. Abraham always felt bad for the things his girls had to endure as part of the White Lily Club, but he felt they brought it upon themselves.

Abraham snapped back to the moment, what a colossal fucking mess this night turned out to be. The party was still raging downstairs, the majority of bedrooms upstairs were occupied by clients and club girls. He thought to himself, with all of this activity, how was he going to get Megan's body out of the Dakota without being noticed. Moreover, he had to try to make her death look like an accident. He breathed a little easier knowing Hunter had drugged her probably leaving traces of narcotics and alcohol in her bloodstream. That deadly combination could be used to his advantage. He would need to brainstorm with Hunter and Hailey to figure it out the best way to do it.

Abraham stepped out of the Ambassador's room and closed the door behind him. He walked up to his close associate, Michael and told him that no one was to enter the room unless he approved. He walked down the corridor to the duplex apartment's library room. This was his favorite room in the apartment because of its ambiance and elegance. Each wall had bookshelves that started at the base of the floor and rose up to the ceiling. A railing surrounded the entire room just below the ceiling. It had a beautifully sculpted wooded ladder on a set of wheels attached to the railing. If one wanted to, they could push off the floor and ride the ladder all the way around the room. There was not a space in that room that did not hold a book. The library had over ten-thousand books in its collection and included many subjects and genres. The room itself also had two brilliantly trimmed high windows with a fireplace between them.

He opened the door to the library and saw Hunter sitting in a smokers chair in front of the fireplace looking pale and deathly. Hailey sat on the floor next to one of the windows with her knees tucked under her chin. She looked up as he closed the door and when he turned to face them and she simply stated, "Dead, right?"

"What the fuck you think, Einstein? You went in after the Ambassador called Hunter for help and saw for yourself," he snapped.

"That fucking coward didn't have to strike her with a vase. A simple slap and she would have shut the fuck up," Hunter stated in a shaky cracked voice.

"Well asshole, he didn't do that and now you and Hailey have a body. So it's up to the both of you to get rid of the girl," his voice carried with it a threatening tone.

"She had a fucking name, asshole, it was Megan," shouted Hailey.

Abraham took two quick steps with his hand raised to deliver a slap but before he could Hunter cut across the room and stepped in front of him. "Come on, Abraham, she's just distraught and in shock. She doesn't know what the hell she's doing at the moment," Hunter pleaded.

"You're fucking lucky, bitch that I could be an understanding man sometimes. I'll forget your transgression this time but do it again and I'll make sure you swallow a fucking closed fist, understand?" Abraham stood over Hailey with a raised fist.

She nodded although she knew that she could easily grab her blade and swipe it across his fucking throat. However, she had to play the part of a weak and frightened teenager useful only because she was good at recruiting new girls for the club. So she flinched and let tears flow freely from her eyes but inwardly she laughed.

"Alright, stop fucking crying and let's get this fixed," he shouted.

"Just tell us how you want it done," replied Hunter.

Abraham calmed down and gave it some thought, "How about you wrap her in that rug there by the fireplace and load her into a laundry cart. You guys with the help of Michael take the cart to the freight elevator and unload her into one of our vans and take her body to her parent's apartment building."

"Whoa, hold on, it sounds like you're setting us up to take the fall on this one. How do I know once Hailey and I are in the van driving away you won't drop a dime with the police and bam we're left holding the bag, literally," whined Hunter.

Abraham didn't get excited this time he just put his hand palm out, "Calm the fuck down. Listen, if I wanted to set you up, it would be easy. Let me tell you how easy, first I would drug you and take your body back to your apartment. Then I would call the cops anonymously, and tell them that I heard muffled cries of help coming from your apartment. You wouldn't be able to open the door when they came so they would have no choice but too forcibly enter. Surprise, there they would find you with Megan's body. Come to think about it that actually sounds like a better option."

Hunter jumped up, "Come on man, I was just nervous is all. No need to take offense and put me in that situation."

Abraham had to laugh, "Jesus, Hunter, I was only joking. You need to learn to control your ADHD. That shit is going to drive us all fucking nuts."

"OK, OK, you win, now help me to understand what happens when we get the body in the building," asked Hunter.

Abraham continued, "You guys take her body to the roof of her building and roll her over the ledge and let gravity do its thing."

Hailey shook her head in disagreement, "First, no one would believe that she jumped off a building because all that knew her knew she was afraid of heights. Second, prior to her 'death,' she showed no signs of depression and as a matter of fact, she was always smiling and ready to have fun."

"Since when did you become a fucking therapist? If you have something better, I'm all ears," responded Abraham.

"As a matter of fact, I do," was Hailey's response.

Abraham stood up and walked towards the empty seat by the window and sat, "That's what I'm talking about. Hunter, you should take notice, Hailey's showing some initiative, and maybe you could learn a thing or two from a girl."

If Hunter's look could kill, both Hailey and Abraham would have dropped dead immediately. However, his look did not deter Hailey who continued with her plan.

"She was not a suicidal person, like I said earlier Megan was the opposite, full of life and always ready to have fun. She had told me that her parents would bring her along to their evening dinner parties and allow her to drink socially at the age of fourteen. She even said they expected her to drink behind their backs since she was a teenager."

Hunter not liking the fact that Hailey spoke with such confidence tried to break her flow, "So she was allowed to drink with her parents, how the fuck does that help us?"

Abraham ignored Hunter's childish outburst and just listened for he knew Hailey was building up to her plan.

She smiled and continued, "Her parents are at an event held by one of their friend's downtown this evening. That leaves the parents duplex empty. We get Megan inside the apartment and take her up to the top of the second-floor landing. We hold her up facing the bedroom, and then do, as Abraham asked to let gravity take over. She will fall down the stairs, snapping her neck in the process and presto, a simple accident for someone that had too much to drink."

"That's fucking stupid and ridiculous," shouted Hunter.

Abraham started to clap his hands stopping Hunter before he could berate the plan further, "Bravo Hailey, now that is what I call ingenious. Let's get it done, ASAP."

"We could get caught in that apartment, then what?" pleaded Hunter.

"Easy, don't get caught and if you do, I'll make sure you die in custody," responded Abraham casually.

Hunter looked like a deer in headlights. "Snap out of it, Hunter, give Michael twenty minutes before he brings you the cart in the meantime go ahead and wrap her body in the rug. Once you've done with Megan, go home and carry on as though nothing happened."

Abraham pointed at Hailey, "When the school finds out about Megan, they'll inform the students and might offer grief counseling for anyone who may need it. It would look good if you took them up on the offer, and it might give us an opportunity to learn what students are saying about her death. If you hear anything of importance, call me right away." with that Abraham walked out of the library

Hunter stood up walked right up to Hailey and said in a menacing voice, "Who the fuck you think you are? You were trying to make me look stupid in front of Abraham?"

Hailey was getting tired of this asshole but she again remembered her role, "Look you fucking prick, I wasn't trying to do that. Maybe you forgot but I know my girls better than you do and Abraham put together. Let us not also forget that I put my ass on the line with Abraham helping you out. If he found out that you tried to recruit a girl without his permission and that I got rid of the body, both our fucking asses would be passed around at the next party. So cool the fuck down and let's get this done before he changes his fucking mind."

She didn't see it coming but sure as hell felt it when Hunter's fist caught her in her flush on the cheek knocking her down to the floor. She considered him a coward and pussy so expecting him to throw a punch was not on her radar. Dazed and in pain she raised her hands and arms in defense all the while tasting the iron in the blood filling her mouth. She looked at him and knew she had to take his shit for now. But in the back of her mind, she knew he would pay dearly for striking her. In due time, she thought. She waved her arms back and forth and pleaded for him to stop, "Please don't hit me again."

He didn't but he sneered and gave her a look of triumph, "Let that be a lesson to you to stay in your fucking place bitch. Now, go fucking wash up."

That punch actually made her nauseous but she wouldn't give him that satisfaction of her throwing up. She tried to walk past him towards the bathroom, but he stepped directly in her path and gestured with his hand to stop, "I just remembered something. Tomorrow you're taking me to the spot where you dumped that girl's body."

That request came out of the left field and it startled her. However, she recovered quickly enough for him not to notice, "Why would you want to do that? I already told you that I took care of it."

"Is there a problem with my request?" questioned Hunter.

"Of course not, but if anyone sees us in that area it could be a problem. And do you really think her body is just floating on the water, give me more fucking credit than that, I weighed it down," shouted Hailey.

"That's the problem, you are fucking smart, and it seems your using that to get more attention from Abraham. Which would mean you're trying to push me out of the equation," countered Hunter.

"You're joking right. You don't think it's enough that I have to recruit, befriend then watch all these fucking prima donnas walk around as though they are entitled to everything. Where the fuck would, I have the time to do your job. Even I'm smart enough to know it takes a lot of work to run a business and organize these pedophile parties. I was just making sure Megan's body doesn't come back on us," explained Hailey.

"I understand that but I still don't fucking trust you. The only way you can change my mind is to at least take me to your apartment so that I can see for myself that you have no evidence that could link that girl to me," countered Hunter.

She stared at him for a moment then smiled, "Of course, if that what it takes for you to leave me the fuck alone then you can come over but for now can we hurry this shit up."

Hunter stood there as a chill enveloped his body; it came first from Hailey's stare then her smile that she just gave him. He should have been satisfied that she acquiesced to his demand but instead he felt fear from the aura of violence radiating from Hailey. She scared the shit of him; of course, he would never admit that to anyone especially her. He then slowly turned and walked away.

Just outside the library, Abraham could hear Hunter attempting to intimidate Hailey and it made him laugh inside since he knew as did Hunter that Hailey was someone that had no problem with violence aside from him. She was the smartest of his employees. He understood why his boss chose Hailey as the recruiter for the White Lily Club. The girls she chose all came from the same background, rich white teenagers whose fathers were in positions of power. They all were young, beautiful and virgins. He had once asked Hailey how she was able to recruit them. She told him that they all possessed a trait that was easily manipulated, their egos. These girls came from a world in which their every whim was catered to whether it be related to food, drink or material items. They asked and they got simple as that. He still wanted to know how one's ego would let them sleep with older men. Her response was modest; she explained that they felt that they were so desirable that they could do almost anything including having the power to control men. That's how she ultimately got the girls to do the things they did at the parties. She challenged them to do just that, control the men at the party. Abraham smiled to himself and at Hailey's skill in manipulating the girls to think that they were in control of their situations.

Hailey would go on to explain that the girls were told in order to become a member of the club they would have to attend a party and choose a man to be their "mark." She would give them until the end of the night to convince the mark to do two things, first buy them a drink then, more importantly, have them offer to take them on a trip. Both must be done without the promise of sex. Hailey had told him that it was the thrill of the challenge that made them stay and play along. Once that happened and they were at the party, Hailey would wait for the right moment before slipping a sedative into their drinks. Once the girls were drugged, their marks would go to an assigned bedroom where the girl would be brought and placed naked on the bed for their enjoyment.

Abraham shook his head at the thought of the girls waking up in those rooms from a drug-induced stupor naked lying next to some fucking relic that could have been their grandfather. He remembered he saw a video with audio of a girl waking up in one of the rooms. That video displayed Hailey's talent. Man, he thought it was some fucking Oscar-worthy shit.

"Shhh, it's going to be alright. I'm here now, no one is going to hurt you, baby," Hailey whispered in Samantha's ear.

"Hailey, I don't remember coming to this room or getting undressed. I think the fucking bastard drugged and raped me. You have to call the police," shouted Samantha.

Hailey took Samantha's face into her hands and looked directly into her eyes, "Sorry, Sammy we can't call the police, it'll just cause me a headache."

Samantha slapped Hailey's hands away from her, "What the fuck do you mean it'll cause you a headache. I was raped dammit and fuck you. I'll call them myself." Samantha quickly got up from the bed and walked over to her clothes laid on top of a chair. Hailey also got off from the bed and followed Samantha to the chair. She watched as Samantha dressed and as she was about to step to the door, Hailey blocked her way.

"Hailey, get the fuck out of the way. You can't stop me!" Samantha shouted.

"I can't let you go to the police, Sammy and anyway why would you want to. You just passed the test to be inducted into the White Lily Club, congratulations," smiled Hailey.

Samantha looked at Hailey in disbelief, "You're fucking out of your mind, Bitch."

Hailey's smile quickly disappeared as she lifted her right arm above her shoulder and swung it with speed and veracity. The palm of her right-hand connected flush with Samantha's left cheek sending her down to the floor in a heap.

"The next time you call me a bitch, I'll make sure to cut your fucking tongue out," seethed Hailey at a Samantha who had curled into a fetal position sobbing uncontrollably. Hailey walked over to her purse on the bed, removed twenty crisp hundred-dollar bills, and walked back to where Samantha lay.

"This is how it's going to work, Sammy. You are going to take these two thousand dollars and do whatever you want with it. Tomorrow, you and I will head out to Harlem to Hunter's Tattoos and get you marked with the White lily. Once done, we will head down to the village for some clothes shopping. Now go wash up, your gentleman friend wants to buy you another drink." She tossed the crisp bills on top of Samantha and walked out of the room.

Abraham remembered being impressed with the rage that came out from the teenager. He thought it was that violence that keeps them from going to the police, she disagreed. She told him it was something else entirely that stopped them from turning. Embarrassment, once they realized that they never had control of the men or the situation their egos deflated. They would never let anyone know what happened because it would paint them as weak and pathetic. They did not want that so they continued to play along. Abraham again had to admit Hailey was one fucking shrewd badass who knew exactly how to play these girls and anyone else who didn't know her for that matter.

Chapter 15

Dean walked with Chris out of the bar towards his car parked on Hudson Street, "You need a ride?" asked Chris.

"Thanks, but whenever I'm working in a big city, I like to take its mass transit," smiled Dean.

"Haven't you been told how unreliable big-city mass transit is especially the New York City subway?" laughed Chris.

Dean laughed as well, "I know their unreliable, asshole, but it beats having to dodge these fucking cabbies every ten feet."

"Can't argue with that one, where are you headed now?" asked Chris.

"Uptown, that call I got from my NYPD contact, Detective Duncan was about a couple of gang members I'm interested in talking to. He gave me the heads up that they were outside their 'HQ,' which is a brownstone uptown. I'm going up there for a heart to heart talk about not picking on kids," laughed Dean.

"Alone?" asked a surprised Chris.

"Yep, don't be so surprised. These are just some misunderstood teens that need some fatherly advice," smiled Dean.

"You shouldn't go uptown alone especially to deal with gang members on their turf. You're a stranger in their neighborhood that might make them feel threatened. Trust me they'll try and make an example out of you," replied a worried Chris.

"Don't worry, I'll be very careful, plus, it's still daylight with plenty of witnesses around," joked Dean.

"Have it your way. Oh, hey, if you don't mind me asking, what's the job you are doing that concerns gangs?"

"I don't mind at all. I was hired by a woman, Julia Westen, to help her seventeen-year-old son, Mark, who's having difficulties with those same boys," answered Dean.

"What's the name of the gang or 'boys' giving the kid trouble?" asked Chris.

"Don't fucking laugh, but the crudely and highly offensively named, Young Savages," smiled Dean.

"Now that's fucking ironic but I'm familiar with those clowns, a couple of ragtag teenagers trying to put together a respected crew. Their territory is relatively small about a square mile. Our gang unit has them under light surveillance to see if they're interested in expanding outside that mile. So I agree with you, you'll be able to handle it but nonetheless, watch your back, you don't want to be scalped," smiled Chris.

"Prick, like I didn't know you were going to say that but thanks for caring and giving me permission, pa," cracked Dean.

Chris laughed, "Asshole, so what happened to the kid, they rob him?"

"Yes and no, tried to, but weren't successful. The kids a highly sought-after senior at the local high school. He's been heavily recruited by Ivy League colleges because of his outstanding academics and extracurricular activities. The kid's a fucking boy scout, literally earned his Eagle ranking at 16 with a four-year GPA of 3.95. He was offered four Ivy League college scholarships and, in the end, he chose the only one that would give him the full ride, Duke University (Pre-Med)," replied Dean.

Chris stopped him, "Holy shit, Duke is no joke but I'm confused. Why is the gang messing with him? He's not going to be around the neighborhood come this fall."

Dean responded, "To put it bluntly, the kid is 'school smart' but 'street dumb.' He made the mistake of telling his friends that he was going to be getting paid to attend Duke and they mistook that to mean that Duke was going to pay him to attend."

Chris snorted, "Why the fuck would anyone believe that a college would pay its students money to attend. Shit, even college athletes don't get compensated."

"I know but kids nowadays lack common sense. One of those students who heard about it was the sister of one of the Young Savages, a douchebag, named Dupree. Dupree heard his sister talking to one of her friends about it. Genius figured it would be easy money for him and his boys. So the next day, he and a couple of his crew approached the kid, his name, by the way, is Mark, to shake him down."

"Who probably did not know what the hell the gang was talking about right," jumped in Chris.

Dean nodded, "Exactly, he vehemently denied that he was going to get money from the college. He tried to reason with them by telling them that the only thing the college was going to give him was a lunch card but it involved no cash. Of course, the assholes didn't believe him and felt he needed an incentive to pay up. So they beat the shit out of him and told him he had two days to come up with some cash. And if he didn't have the money then, they would beat his ass every day until they got their money."

"Jesus, why didn't he press charges?" Chris stated angrily.

"They threatened to kill his mother," Dean replied.

"Fucking animals, listen if you don't want my help, let me call Antonio. Those motherfuckers will be paying his crew for protection," laughed Chris.

Dean put both hands up, "No, that's alright. I'm going there now to have a talk with this scumbag, Dupree. I'll make sure it's done in front of his crew so if they don't agree with my terms, I can kill two birds with one stone, sorry meant to say beating two birds with one stone that is."

Chris smiled, "Man how I would like to see that playout. Alright, you want to meet up in the morning?"

"Yeah, that sounds like a plan, I'll meet you here at the coffee shop, say around eleven," Dean replied.

"Done, see tomorrow, take care and be careful. If you need anything, you already have my personal cell number, feel free to use it," was Chris's response before getting into his car and driving off.

Dean turned south and walked up Chambers Street on the way to the local number 4 uptown Bronx train. Dean was telling Chris the truth about his love of using big-city mass transit, especially in Chicago and New York. What he didn't tell him was the reason why. That's something he shared only with three people in his life, his mother, sister, and godfather. The only reason for that was he felt no one but a native would understand how it felt to ride those trains.

He was sure most Native Americans in the city felt the same way. It happened after leaving the reservation for his first case in New York City. Back then, he was naïve and didn't' know what to expect from visiting and working in one of the most populated cities in the United States. Prior to going east the biggest city he visited and worked was Phoenix. That city dwarfed his reservation with triple the amount of dwellings and population. However, unlike New York, a Native American would not feel entirely alone walking in Phoenix because one could always bump into another tribal member since many lived and worked there. When he got out of the taxi cab for the first time in the middle of Times Square, a feeling of isolation quickly spread throughout him, it was as though he was insignificant in an ocean of humanity.

He remembered it like it was yesterday. The moment his foot hit the Times Square pavement, his first impulse was to immediately return to the reservation. Thank goodness, he didn't listen and made the decision to soldier on with his assignment. To do that he had to something else that was unfamiliar to him, taking the subway. He took those steps downward to the underground trains and was again thrust into a hectic and chaotic scene with many of the same crowds he encountered on the streets above. He readied himself for that feeling of isolation but to his surprise, it simply dissipated when he boarded the train. That feeling never came because of the multitude of native peoples sitting and standing on the Bronx uptown train. The feeling of isolation dissipated as many of the white passengers disembarked in Manhattan leaving him and his brethren alone to end their travels in the Bronx. After completing his task in the Bronx, he returned to his hotel room and scoured the internet for a reason why there were so many natives not only on the train but also in the Bronx.

Dean learned that the majority of native people worked in Manhattan but could not afford to live there so they settled in the only area affordable and available, the Bronx. This borough, as he learned on Wikipedia was home to many tribes, including Aztecs, Incas, and Taíno but many non-native people didn't refer to them by their tribal names but instead by their countries of origin such as Mexico, Peru, Ecuador, Guatemala, and Puerto Rico.

Dean laughed when he remembered his godfather saying he wasn't surprised about the Bronx having native tribes living there. He would get on his soapbox and preach to Dean that every country on Mother Earth has had native tribes displaced because of the government and America was no different. However, what did surprise his godfather was that the Taíno tribe from Puerto Rico which was an island and not a state but whose population were American citizens. Dean smiled at remembering his godfather's response, "only in America."

"Now arriving 116th street, please watch your step leaving the train. This is the number 4 train uptown, next stop, 125th street."

Dean snapped out of his daydreaming in time to exit the train walk up the steps into the neighborhood, called Spanish Harlem. In his internet research, he learned that this neighborhood was technically part of upper Manhattan although many white non-native Manhattanites would disagree.

The night before Dean scouted this same location for potential problems as well as possible escape routes should his plan not go accordingly. Walking across 116th street towards the Taft housing projects just off Fifth Avenue, he ran through his mind the three alternate routes of escape chosen the night before. Two of the three routes had him running towards either Saint Nicholas Avenue or Second Avenue with the third leading him back to Lexington Avenue and the downtown Brooklyn #4 train. His best chance at escape would have been hail a cab from the main street but his research revealed that taxi drivers did not venture past 96th street since it became more of a brown and black city then they preferred, fucking racists he thought. The irony in that was the majority of taxi drivers were black or brown.

Dean walked pass the Taft housing projects and came upon a two-story brownstone house with three young men sitting on its stoop. A fourth young male was at the top of the stairs and by the photo; Julia provided, Dean could see that it was Dupree. Dean stopped about ten feet from the stoop and faced the young men.

At first, all four boys watched in bewilderment as he approached then stop in front of them. They probably were thinking that this stranger must have been lost and crazy to stop in front of them without their permission. In their minds, the stranger did not fit the normal profile they were used to when selling their trade. He wasn't thin, withdrawn and dirty. An addict would keep their head held downward in submission when approaching them knowing if they did what Dean was doing, eyeballing them, it was a sure way to get a good old-fashioned beat down. They also figured that he wasn't a cop, since he didn't take out a shield.

Dean saw them trying to decide whether he was a threat. It took them only a minute to decide he was not. That moment they decided that he would be a victim and simultaneously rose up off the stoop. They were only able to descend one-step before Dupree stopped them with laughter, "Whoa, let's not get too excited boys just yet. Why don't you sit down, watch and maybe learn a thing a two?"

Dupree approached Dean with both his fast tightly balled, arms pointing downward towards the sidewalk, his back straight and head held high. Dean did not stare directly at Dupree's face. He focused on the peripheral essence surrounding him. On the reservation, Dean was well respected and revered because of his gift of special insight that enabled him to see one's true essence reflected in his native realm. That essence would form as translucent animal shapes, each representing a different meaning. In Dupree's case, the essence that currently surrounded him was serpents. Such a representation to natives would mean that the person represented chaos, corruption, and darkness. This information confirmed to Dean that this Dupree and the antics of his crew would need to be quelled.

Dupree continued to stride towards Dean with confidence and menace. It was his way of signaling to those in sight that he was the alpha male in this scenario. It was at that point Dean knew that Dupree's inflated confidence would assist in a terrible lesson of tough humility for him.

"You fucking lost white boy?" shouted Dupree in the most menacing way possible while continuing to walk directly in front of Dean.

Dean laughed loudly, "White boy, shit you either must be one fucking blind idiot or your mamma didn't teach you the colors of the rainbow."

Dean knew it even before it happened. The second he finished his insult, a looping right haymaker was unleashed from Dupree accompanied by colorful commentary, "Fuck you, bitch."

Dean sidestepped the punch with the grace of a cat and countered with a tight right cross connecting on Dupree's right cheek producing a sound like a newborn baby's ass being slapped a doctor. It was such a quick and violent move that Dupree did not have the time to appreciate the beauty of the punch. The only thing he felt was his face exploding with pain and agony. Before his brain comprehended the strike, the ground approached his face with an equal amount of speed. All anyone heard was a loud thud as Dupree's head hit the concrete. It took a couple of seconds before Dupree had the strength to open his eyes.

When he did, the pain hit him like a freight train, "Fuck," was all he could muster. His brain was foggy, face hurt like hell, and he not have the strength to get up. Dupree looked over at his friends and wondered why they haven't jumped in to help.

He then looked up at the man that just knocked him out with one punch and saw him lift his shirt exposing an automatic as if saying to his crew, mind your business or get popped. The man bent down, kneeled by his ear, and whispered, "If you or your punk ass friends go near Mark again, I'll come back and slit your throats."

Dupree nearly shit his pants at the threat but knew he had to save some face. He decided to spit on Dean's face and definitely shout, "Fuck you, white boy!"

Dean calmly wiped the spit and blood from his face, reached in his pocket came out with a pair of brass knuckles, gave a quick look at his friends, saw that they were not moving, pulled back his arm and swung it at Dupree, "No you piece of shit, fuck you!"

Dean struck him two more times in the face breaking his nose and jaw. He was about to finish with a gut shot but became distracted when he heard other people yelling and running towards him. He went for his gun but hesitated when he saw them abruptly stop in their tracks. For a minute, Dean was confused at why they stopped. It couldn't be his gun because it was still holstered. He turned away from the gang and knew immediately why their sudden reluctance to attack. Standing across the street leaning on an undercover unit with his NYPD Detective Gold shield dangling from his neck and his hand on his weapon was Duncan.

"I told you, I didn't need any help!" shouted Dean.

94

"Shit, your welcome first of all and second I just happen to be in the neighborhood and decided to pass by is all," replied Duncan.

"That's bullshit and you know it. Now, why are you here?" Dean asked with a calmer tone.

"Man, you got to learn to relax a little and yes, I purposely came around to make sure nothing happened to you. Wait before you say anything, it wasn't for me the Captain was just protecting her ass. She thinks if you get hurt or worse, killed, it'll ruin her chances for an office over at One Police Plaza," laughed Duncan.

Dean nodded his and smiled, "Talk about cold, she doesn't give a shit about my well-being. She wants to make chief someday. How about you for a moment I thought you just cared."

Duncan smiled, "Not a bit, now what do you want to do with these assholes?"

"Just give me a couple of minutes with them, and then you could drive me back to my hotel," replied Dean.

Meanwhile, as the two talked, the group of Young Savages slowly walked over, lifted Dupree off the ground and proceeded to back away from both Dean and Duncan. They stopped gruffly when they saw Dean put up his hand, palm out indicating for them to stop.

He walked over not concerned for his safety, now with Duncan backing him up. "Listen carefully, and you might just live to see another day. As I told your boy, Mark and his family are off-limits. In fact, if you see him or his family walking down the block, you cross to other side. If I have to come back here, it'll be to drop bodies, understand."

The three Young Savages nodded in agreement simultaneously and disappeared into the brownstone carrying the bleeding Dupree.

Duncan laughed, "That's the first time I've seen gangbangers look like they've been scolded by their dad. Look they even sulked back into the building."

Dean smiled, "That's the problem with these wayward kids, no father figure to kick them in the ass from time to time. You ready to take me back to my hotel?"

"No problem, but let's get some coffee first. That show you put on bored the hell out me, need to wake myself up again before I get behind the wheel," joked Duncan.

"Prick, if I knew there would be an audience, I would have hammed it up a bit more," laughed Dean.

"Come on, I know a bodega that serves the best *café con leche and pan con mantequilla*," replied Duncan.

"What the hell is that mean?" asked Dean.

"Sorry, that's Spanish for store, coffee and bread, and butter. This is a Puerto Rican neighborhood, so coffee with bread and butter is a staple here," smiled Duncan.

"Alright, sounds good, I could use some coffee," replied Dean.

"So, now that you've put the fear of God in those boys, you're going back home," asked Duncan.

"No, probably have to stay longer but don't have an idea how long," replied Dean.

"Does it have to do with your federal escort downtown this morning?" asked Duncan.

Dean nodded his head, "Yep, I'm going to do some work for the New York Special Agent in Charge. You know him?"

"Only by name, don't forget I just a peon on the force. He's been around the precinct on some other cases but usually works with the Captain," replied Duncan.

"What's she say about him?" questioned Dean.

"That I can't tell you because she's never spoken to me about him. However, I have worked with members of his team and they rave about him. They say he's one of them, came up the ranks and earned his stripes the old fashion way," replied Duncan.

"That's the feeling I get, genuine and a man of his word," countered Dean.

"What's he want you to do?" asked Duncan.

"Now come on, you know I can reveal any information. I'm a stickler for confidentiality," smiled Dean then continued, "But even I'm smart enough to know that I'll probably need you or someone you know on the job to help me. His niece has been missing a couple of days now. He wants me to find her."

"Shit, he has the entire fucking federal government at his fingertips why not marshal them up and send them out to find her?" Duncan countered.

"His sister doesn't want him to do that just yet, she's hopeful that the kid is with friends or a boyfriend but he's thinking something bad may have happened to her. In an effort not to upset his sister, he's trying to use outside help to find her." Dean thought about adding the information about Antonio but decided to keep that part of the equation to himself.

"Where did she live and go to school?" asked Duncan.

"She's from New Jersey but goes to a high school here in the city. Actually, I think it's close to here but I'll know more tomorrow. I'm going to meet the mother in New Jersey tomorrow. Once there I'll get all the information and give you a call maybe you could help with the New York stuff," explained Dean.

"Not a problem would be glad to lend a hand. Here's the bodega, let's get that coffee and bread," smiled Duncan.

Chapter 16

"Please, oh god, no more, I swear I never saw that girl before," sobbed the man, "I'm just trying to make a living." The man sat on a lone wooden chair, arms tied behind his back, hood over his face. Joey looked down at him with disgust; the man had pissed and shit on himself. He shook off the disgust and threw a savage punch into the man's kidney. The man lost his voice midstream as the air rushed out with the punch. A couple of seconds passed before he started coughing uncontrollably. He was able to get back under control by taking short quick breaths but he still sobbed only this time he kept his mouth shut.

Joey who stood to the man's side leaned down and whispered, "Listen, you fucking pervert, don't give me that I don't know bullshit. Word on the street says you set your fucking coffee and donut cart in front of grammar schools by the projects so that you can offer young poor girls free donuts but we both know it's not free right, you piece of shit."

More sobbing from the man, "Yes, I do offer free donuts to the kids from those schools but only to those that don't have the money, I swear."

Joey walked to the opposite side of where he just punched the man. He picked up a baseball bat from the floor and took a lefty batter's stance. "Now you fucking know that's not true, the things you give those young girls are not free."

The man nodded furiously, "Yes, yes, I swear, they don't have to pay."

Joey swung the bat downward onto the kneecap of the man, "You lying sack of shit," the man did not hear that last comment for he screamed with hoarseness and pain not known to a human being. After a couple of minutes of screaming the man dropped his head to his chest and began praying and crying at the same time, "Oh, God, please help me, I don't know what I've done."

Joey laughed at that last statement, "Really, you sick fuck; you don't know what you did. How about asking those ten and eleven-year-old girls to show you their stomachs for a donut, or how about when you pat them on the ass while you jerk off under your apron. You sick fucking piece of shit."

The man cried louder, "No that's not true, all lies."

Joey laughed, "Oh, don't fucking deny it, I watched you do it yesterday, scumbag. You know the sad part of all this, their parents don't even know that it's happening. What's even worse is those girls won't rat you out because that's probably the only meal they get, you fucking lowlife..." Joey was about to hit him again when his cell phone buzzed.

"Hey, Boss, what's up?" asked Joey.

"Did he recognize Sofia's picture?" questioned Antonio.

"No, he claims not to and for what it's worth, I believe him. But not all is lost; he'll give up one of his sick friends for me. Once I got another name, we'll have a talk with them as well," countered Joey.

"Alright, see if you could do it quickly the longer she's missing..." Antonio choked up a little but his crew knew and loved him so Joey gave him an out.

"Stop that shit already, boss. I told you we'll get her back to you and Chris. We just have to keep pushing," replied Joey.

Antonio smiled at the phone, Joey grew up with him and Chris, and was counted as a true friend, "Your right Joey and just to keep you in the loop, I talked to Chris, he hired someone to work the case as well," answered Antonio.

"Why, I thought we were doing this because law enforcement has to wait a week before a person is considered missing," asked Joey.

"Yea, that's right but he's paying for the extra help as a private citizen. It just means that we have another avenue to help us find Sofia. Enough talk Joey, get that piece of shit you have there to give us name," replied Antonio.

"You got it, boss. I'll call you after I'm done here," responded Joey.

Antonio sat on the park bench lost in thought after hanging up the phone with Joey.

"Pop, why do we have to leave Chicago in such a hurry?" asked a young Antonio.

It was the middle of the night when his father woke him from his sleep and told him to start packing his clothes. He saw his mother behind his father under the bedroom doorframe holding a tissue in her hand. She had been crying, he could tell by the redness and moisture in her eyes.

"Listen, kid, you know I've always been honest with you including telling you that my job is not like any job your friends' fathers have, right?" asked Salvatore.

"Yeah, pop, I know you work for the family and many of the things you do are not on the up and up and you do these things because the government and guys with businesses won't hire you because you're Italian. Is the government

after you because of your job, pop? Is that why we have to leave now?"
inquired Antonio.

Salvatore smiled at his son then at his wife. He loved his wife more than
anything in life not only because of who she was but because she also blessed
him with a son. "No kiddo, it's the family that will be coming for me. You see
I did something wrong tonight, not on purpose, but it was still done. They
expect me to pay for it but the price is too high. So we have to move away and
start over."

"You mean I have to leave my friends and school?" whispered Antonio.

"I'm sorry, baby, I didn't mean for this to happen but it has. It's a great
lesson. Sometimes you have to do things you don't want too but in the end, it
will work itself out. I promise you kiddo that you'll meet new friends who will
become your new family," Salvatore stated confidently.

Antonio felt his hand shake as his phone buzzed. He thought Joey must
have gotten the information faster than he would have thought possible. When
Antonio opened the phone, it wasn't Joey's number on the screen but Chris's
instead.

"Hey, Handsome, any good news?" asked Antonio.

"I wish, just letting you know, Dean, and I will be going over to sis's house
tomorrow. You going to be around?" responded Chris.

"No, I'm still working the streets, but I'll stop by later, I told her I would
bring some Fiore sandwiches and chips with me for lunch," replied Antonio.

"Shit, I haven't had their ham, mozzarella and roasted red pepper sandwich
in ages, get one for me so I could have it for dinner. By the way, did your boys
find anything on the street?" asked Chris.

"No, but I just got off the phone with Joey. He's entertaining some piece
of shit pedophile as we speak. He got his name from one of his deadbeats as
payment," replied Antonio.

"You thinking our girl is caught up in the street?" asked a worried Chris.

"Come on, Chris, you remember my pops telling us that honesty makes life
difficult but easier to live through."

Chris smiled, "I loved your old man, fucking too honest sometimes."

"Yea, he loved you as well. But he was right, although you're an agent and
I run my own crew, doesn't mean we're immune to the streets. So it makes
sense for me to run this angle," explained Antonio.

"As much as I hate to say it, you're right. Keep me informed on Joey's
progress, talk to you later," replied Chris.

"More times than not, asshole. Once Joey has something, I'll call you,"
laughed Antonio.

Joey moved across the room back towards the man in the chair, "Come on already, stop fucking crying. Grow a pair of balls. Look, it's no secret that I'm killing you tonight. You might as well make peace with whatever god forgives a child rapist."

The man continued to sob and murmur, "I didn't rape any child, please. You have to believe me."

"Pleading your case is the least of your worries. The thing you should be concerned about is how I'm going to do you. If you give me the name of one of your child molesting friends, you'll die without pain. However, if you keep lying then you'll get the car battery treatment. Trust me that shit will make you beg me to put a bullet in your head but I won't. You have sixty seconds to make your choice before I turn on the battery," Joey explained as he lifted the hood of the man.

The man's eyes adjusted to the light in the room. He had to squint in order to get his focus back but when his eyes cleared, he immediately wished to be hooded again. In the corner of the room was a car battery on a table with cables running down. As his eyes tracked the cables to the floor, he noticed a bucket filled with water alongside it.

"Ah, I see you understand what I meant by battery treatment, good. This picture I'm showing you is my boss's goddaughter. Her name is Sofia, she's not the age you prefer but I'm guessing you know someone who might be. All you have to do is whisper their name and it's over."

Joey quickly placed his finger over the man's quivering lips, "Shhh, it sounded as though you were going to utter another, I don't know statement, before you make that painful mistake. Hear this carefully, if the next word out of your mouth is not a name, your feet are going into the bucket, understand?" asked Joey.

The man affirmed by nodding his head, "Good, once you give me the name, I will do as I said and put a bullet behind your ear. Trust me it won't hurt," soothed Joey.

The man sobbed uncontrollably until Joey smacked his face, "Stop the fucking blubbering, and give me that fucking name."

The man must have concluded that death was inevitable because he hung his head and whispered a name to Joey. As he was thanking the man, he was also pulling the trigger of the gun already held behind the ear of the man. "BAM" was the only sound heard in the basement as the man's brains were scattered all over the table holding the car battery and cables.

Chapter 17

"Morning, Pocahontas, you want some breakfast, maybe a ham, egg and cheese sandwich or a buttered roll."

Chris put up his hand.

"No, sorry, just remembered that you come from the desert, so maybe tumbleweed on cactus," snorted Chris. Chris was sitting at a table in the back of the coffee shop where they met yesterday.

"Blow me, flatfoot, just coffee, thank you," chuckled Dean.

"How did it go yesterday with those punk kids up in Spanish Harlem?" asked Chris.

"As you could see, no harm done and I got my message across quite easily," smiled Dean.

"No shit, they didn't come at you," a surprised Chris asked.

"The scumbag, I was there to see tried but I introduced him to my new favorite band, "the Brass Knuckles,"" hooted Dean.

"Holy fuck, they still make those things," laughed Chris, "What about his crew, they just let you walk into their spot and fuck up one of their own without lifting a finger."

"They were about to try but something stopped them dead in their tracks," replied Dean.

Chris shouted, "Ha, you did need my help. Some fucking tough warrior you are, bringing a gun to a fistfight."

Dean smiling and shaking his head back in forth, "No, you prick. I didn't have to pull out my gun because the Lone Ranger was behind me scaring the shit out of them."

Chris's eyebrows went up, "Lone Ranger, what the fuck does that mean?"

Dean shrugged his shoulders, "Detective Duncan was fucking watching the whole scene play out without me knowing. When he saw the rest of the gang charging me, he opened his trench coat revealed his gold shield and shoulder harness which stopped them dead in their tracks."

"Why the hell was he there? Didn't you tell him you didn't need any help?" asked Chris.

"Just like I told you and Antonio but his excuse was that his captain wanted to make sure nothing happened to me," replied Dean.

"Why, you know his captain?" countered Chris

"Nope, and I told him as well. His explained that she wanted to occupy the corner office down at Police Headquarters in the future and didn't want my death to squelch that plan."

"I still don't understand. She doesn't know you so why care?" asked a confused Chris.

"Fuck, that's cold even for you," laughed Dean.

Chris smiled, "Come on, you know what I mean."

Dean laughed, "I know but Duncan told me she knew that I had helped both Philly's Chief of Police and one of their state senators. She probably thinks, she keeps me safe and it makes her look good with the brass and gets her a feather in her cap," replied Dean shrugging his shoulders.

"I think it's a stretch. My two cents are that she's keeping tabs on you while you go around her fiefdom," countered Chris.

"Na, you're just suspicious by nature, most cops are. I get it she wants to move up so she needs to make sure nothing happens on her watch that could come back to her or the department," answered Dean.

"OK, if you're alright then I'll drop it. Since you don't want anything to eat you want to head out to my sisters?" asked Chris.

"Yep, come on," responded Dean.

They both got up from the booth; Chris left money for the food and tip and walked out into the street towards his car. Chris unlocked the car so that Dean could get into the passenger seat. Once Chris settled into the car, he drove several blocks North of Canal Street towards the Holland Tunnel and into New Jersey. Driving through the tunnel, Chris asked Dean, "You ever been to my hometown of Hoboken or New Jersey in general."

Dean laughed, "You mean if I've ever crossed the armpit of the United States, the answer is yes but thankfully just to get to the city."

"Go to hell and just so you know, when you drove through my hometown, you were passing through history," Chris laughed.

"How so?" asked a doubtful Dean.

As the car emerged from the Holland Tunnel into Jersey City, Chris made a right on Henderson Street and drove about five blocks before entering into the town of Hoboken.

They drove along Observer Highway, which separated Hoboken from Jersey City towards its main street, Washington.

Chris proceeded to tell Dean a little about his hometown. "Hoboken is famous for many things but the two that will always be mentioned in conversations is it's the birthplace of America's national pastime, baseball and the second and most important in any Italian household worth its salt is that it was birthplace of the greatest entertainer ever to carry a tune, old blue eyes, himself, Frank Sinatra."

Dean laughed, "Have you lost your mind, it would be more believable if you said this was Einstein's birthplace and Polio vaccine was developed here. But a fucking mobster lounge singer and a sport stolen from my own people being historic, no way man."

Chris could only shake his head, "Spoken from someone who's fucking tribe gave up the island of Manhattan for a couple of beans, corn, and chance to sit at the table for some turkey."

Dean shouted with approval and pleasure on that comeback.

Chris continued, he told Dean that his family lived in Hoboken since 1918 when his great-grandfather left Naples, Italy for New York City. Back in the old country, his great-grandfather was a dockworker. His decision to leave his home and country predicated on the danger he and his family faced daily from living during the Great War. After the first two years of the war, he decided in order to keep his family alive they needed to move to America. It turned out to be the smartest thing he ever did for his family.

Dean stopped him for a moment, "I thought at that point, America joined in the war effort?"

"Yes, it was at that time when they entered into the Great War but remember no fighting took place here on our soil. What we were doing was sending our troops and equipment to Europe. That created a shortage of manpower in labor. It was my great-grandfather and immigrants like him who capitalized on that labor shortage by filling the void. Companies competed with one another for any able body man and at one point, it became so competitive that companies had to start offering housing to men as an incentive to come and work for them. The offers varied from state to state. In New York, for example, men were offered apartments with more than one bedroom. That was unheard of at the time but New Jersey's package was even better."

Dean gave Chris a surprised look, "That couldn't happen today especially with the costs associated with living in the city."

Chris nodded his head, "No question, but here's what made my grandfather special. He knew that living in New York City meant apartments in tenements that were already crowded. He already lived that type of crowded life. What he wanted was the deal that others in his family received from New Jersey. Companies offered workers a small home instead of an apartment."

"Using a home as compensation, that must have a radical idea at that time," responded Dean.

"Very much so, it gave immigrants the opportunity to own real estate in the outlining cities surrounding New York. The best opportunities were in towns closer to New York like Hoboken. Here living across the river was considered being in the boonies and most people felt it was too far. Not my great-grandfather, he thought it was perfect enough to purchase a three-story brownstone in 1919 located on fifth in Washington Street for a little over eight hundred dollars."

"Man, that doesn't sound like a lot, what was he earning at that time?" asked Dean.

"He worked at the Jersey City Dixon Pencil factory. They paid him $80 per month which at that time was an excellent wage."

Dean put up his hands, "Hold on, how was he able to purchase a house that was ten times his salary?"

Chris laughed, "Ah ha, you are paying attention. That was part of his package. The company would take out $10 a month to pay off the house. It was a way of assuring that they had him locked into their company over the next ten years."

"It sounds like both parties win. Is that house still in the family?" asked Dean.

"Yep, my sister and I happen to be the proud owners of that Brownstone. Although when my sister got married, she purchased her home about three doors from me and across the street from Antonio's place."

"If you don't mind me asking, what is your home worth today?" asked Dean.

"Not at all, if my sister and I decided to sell, it would bring us a cool three million," replied Chris.

"Holy shit, that's crazy," smiled Dean.

Chris slowed the car down and parked in front of the sister's building. He turned the engine off and turned to face Dean with a serious expression on his face, "Listen, I didn't tell you much about my sister because I wanted you to get a clean first impression of her. I was also very vague about my niece because my sister knew her the best. She could good give a more accurate picture of the situation. Once you've spoken with her and you decide you need to know more than I will try and fill that void," explained Chris.

"Alright sounds like a good plan but why tell me this?" asked Dean.

"My sister is not your ordinary mother or woman for that matter and although, she's been through a lot in the last year, she's got a big heart and matching personality and she means the world to me and Antonio." That's all I was trying to say.

Dean responded with a genuine smile, "I have no doubt that she is an incredible woman. She's had to deal with you and Antonio all her life which to me speaks volumes."

"Fucking prick, come on Elizabeth's expecting us," laughed Chris.

They walked up to the second-floor landing of the Brownstone, knocked on the door and waited for a response. The door was opened by a woman about five feet four weighing around hundred thirty-five pounds, not skinny in the warped American sense but well suited for the body frame that was presented in front of Dean. He noticed a keen resemblance to Chris with eyes that shone with a sharp and vivid green color that conveyed warmth, friendliness, and comfort. Dean also sensed that she was cautious but protective. She also carried a heavy fog that surrounded her and if you looked at her closer, you could feel a repressed sadness. It was as though she wanted help but was too proud to ask, it made her more endearing.

"Oh my, Handsome told me you were an American Indian but I thought he was just messing around with me," smiled Elizabeth.

"Handsome, are you shitting me, is that your nickname," laughed Dean looking over at Chris.

"Alright, forget you ever heard that name. Liz, I told you not to use that name around people I work with," replied a pained Chris.

"Come on, you know I love that name. It reminds me of growing up with Antonio and his mom." She smiled at Chris who nodded his head as a form of surrender.

Dean laughed, "May I ask how did you and your family come up with Chris's nickname?"

"That name was given to Chris by Antonio's mom. When Antonio moved in across the street, he and Chris became inseparable. Before that, on the actual first day, Chris met Antonio. He introduced him to his mom. She took one look at my brother and proclaimed to Antonio and his father that Chris was so handsome. She said Chris reminded her of Frank Sinatra, who like Chris was born in Hoboken. Once Antonio heard that, it was all over. He started calling him that in the street and in school, sealing his fate as Christian 'Handsome' Gates."

That elicited a grunt of a laugh from Elizabeth and a scowl from Chris.

"May I call him handsome?" laughed Dean not serious but still getting an answer from Elizabeth.

Chris immediately jumped in, "No way, Liz, Antonio would pee in his pants if he heard him call me that."

She put up her hands, "I think the name suits you as did Antonio's mother. I think it brings great joy for Antonio to use it as it reminds him of his mother.

So, Mr. Dean, if you grow tired of calling my brother, Chris, then, by all means, you call him handsome."

Dean started laughing, "Although it would give me great pleasure to call him that, I have to disagree with it because it's not remotely true."

Chris stuck his middle finger up at Dean. Elizabeth motioned for both of them to follow her into the living room, "Please come and sit. Can I get either of you something to drink or eat?"

"No, thank you, I just finished eating lunch with handsome over here," he looked over at Chris who quietly mouthed off a curse, "If you don't mind though, can we go ahead and start talking about your daughter?"

Dean saw her deflate a little while sitting forward with her elbows on her knees. He noticed immediately that her eyes began to mist. Most times, Dean's natural native gift of seeing a person's true essence came from those with evil hearts but on some rare occasions, he would see the essence of pure souls, as was the case with Elizabeth. It happened in her living room when several female deer surrounded her. In the native world, the deer represented gentleness, grace, and survival.

"I don't mind at all. In fact, I truly appreciate you taking the time to listen to me. You know Chris and Antonio wanted to bring in both law enforcement and the families but I'm afraid," she stated.

"Of what?" Dean asked.

"If she's been harmed, both my brothers would kill all that were responsible and I would have to carry another burden of guilt for involving them. That's why I'm glad you are here. This has been a difficult time for me more than when my husband was killed." She put her head in her hands. Dean could hear her sob and saw Chris lean over and put his arm around her. She took a deep breath and apologized.

Dean smiled, "Please no need to apologize, your pain is real and keeping it inside just makes it harder to confront."

She nodded her head, "That's true, and in life, one must always confront reality. Unfortunately, my reality is that my daughter is missing but in the eyes of the law since it hasn't been seven days, they don't consider her missing. Believe me or not, I also have a gift, it is what we moms call a mother's intuition. It says that my baby is alive but not out of danger. If I told Chris and Antonio to find her, it might do more harm than good. Does that make any sense to you?"

"Perfect sense, especially to me," Dean laughed and continued, "You also proved to be cautious and trustful by agreeing to meet with me. I could also see that you carry great composure and intellect."

Elizabeth provided Dean with a genuine, warm smile, "Compliment accepted. I could see why my brothers trust you. Are you confident that you could find my daughter?"

"Without question, but it starts with you answering some questions," replied Dean, "May I proceed?"

"Of course, what would like to know," she replied.

"Let's start off with Sofia's father, what happened to him?" It was a fleeting moment but one nonetheless, her eyes misted again then she refocused.

"He was murdered last Christmas," she answered in a painful hollowed voice.

Dean did not see that coming. He could count on his hand the number of times he was surprised by someone's answers to his questions. He would now have to add her answer to his hand. Dean could also see from the corner of his eye, Chris staring at the wall directly behind Dean. He held a look of sadness that amazingly also contained contentment. Dean made a mental note to ask Chris why he felt contentment at hearing about his brother-in-law's murder but it would have to wait until they were alone.

Chris for his part didn't notice Dean looking at him from the corner of his eye. Once his sister mentioned the murder of his brother-in-law, his mind drifted back to January of last year.

"It wasn't me, I swear," cried Peter.

"Listen to this fuckin pussy, crying and begging. Did my fucking brother-in-law, Lou cry and plead for you not to blow, is fucking brains all over the floor and wall," Shouted Antonio as he slapped Peter's face with an open hand making a loud crashing sound.

"Oh god, oh god, I told you I didn't fuckin shoot him. It was supposed to be a straight-up robbery. I wasn't the stick-up man just the getaway driver," sobbed Peter.

"Tell me, who the fuck the shooter was? If you don't, I swear to god I'll fry your fucking balls," yelled Antonio accompanied by a punch to the side of Peter's head knocking him and the chair sideways to the floor. Antonio bent down and in one swoop lifted Peter and the chair back into position. Peter tried to catch his breath through sobbing.

"Jimmy. Jimmy. Jimmy Rivera set the whole thing up. He came to me with a plan to rob Lou after he made his monthly collection from the Longshoreman's union steward. He never said anything about shooting him. Jimmy told us that the union steward was a good friend of his named Kenny. Kenny called Jimmy about a score. Kenny told Jimmy that Lou would pick up the monthly payoff from him and take it to the boss. The next pickup was the

biggest ever paid out, over twenty-five thousand cash. Jimmy said it would be a quick ten-minute job, in and out," stuttered Peter.

Antonio walked by Chris who was standing to the side of the scene by a table parallel to the chair that Peter was tied to.

Antonio looked down at several instruments on the table including an ice pick. He picked up the ice pick walked towards Peter. Peter began yelling for Antonio not to kill him. Antonio paid him no mind as he plunged the ice pick into the soft tissue under his collarbone eliciting a savage and primal scream. After several minutes of sobbing, Peter again pleaded for mercy.

"Now listen carefully scumbag. The answer you give to this next question will determine how you die. The truth gets you a quick death but tell me a lie and it will take me days to put you out of your misery. Now tell me where Kenny and Jimmy are," asked Antonio.

"Jimmy's grandmother's house out in Teaneck, we're supposed to lay low there for a couple of weeks before going about our business," answered Peter on the verge of passing out.

"Good job, Peter, you earned the right to die quickly," responded Antonio as he stepped away from Peter allowing Chris to walk to Peter's side place a gun to his temple and pull the trigger blowing blood and brain matter clear across the room and putting the piece of shit out his misery.

"Did you find out who killed him and why?" Dean followed up with Elizabeth.

He could see her straighten up and with a trace of pride say, "It was a robbery gone badly, three boys from the neighborhood robbed and killed my husband when he came out of the Longshoreman's Union office. I heard, he told them to go home and forget about robbing him because he was a made-man in Antonio's crew. He knew they were young and probably didn't want to hurt them but the leader of the group some kid named Jimmy popped off at my husband and shot him. My brother's found Jimmy and his partner Kenny bound gagged with their eyes cut out in the back of their getaway car. The third kid, Peter, the driver was found in a barrel floating on the river with the back of the head blow out."

"Did the police ever find out who killed them?" asked Dean.

"No, they chalked it up to street justice. Which was fine by me, they got off easy if you asked me," replied Elizabeth.

"How did Sofia react to losing her father?" asked Dean.

At the mention of her daughter, Elizabeth went back to a state of despair, "Like any child that loses their father, depressed, angry and rebellious. She had just graduated from grammar school and was enrolled at Manhattan's Berkheart High School Academy when it happened."

"Manhattan, really why did you enroll her in a New York high school instead of New Jersey one?" asked a surprised Dean.

"Sofia was a genius and I don't say that because I was her mother. Her IQ at twelve was 130. My husband and I researched high schools in the tristate area and Berkheart ranked first in academics. It also had a who's who in alumni who they shamelessly used for funding, potential employment or references."

"Is that an exclusive and expensive school?" remarked Dean.

"Yes, but in our 'family' both my husband and Antonio brought in enough money to pay for it. But that changed when he was killed, that income was no longer coming in so there was a point in time when I was going to transfer her to our local high school."

"But you somehow got the funds right, because she never transferred?" asked Dean.

"That's correct, when my husband was killed, my brothers collected the funds owed to him from that robbery and the rest of the family kicked in donations to help pay the entire tuition," replied Elizabeth.

Dean smiled, "That is what I call a family. Now tell me a little about her rebellious stage."

"She would attend overnight house parties in Manhattan hosted by seniors from her school. I was in no shape to oversee her during that time, depression and anger issues ruled my life. As long as she returned the next day, all was forgiven and she would always return." She paused took a deep breath for a moment she looked like she was about to cry again but regained her composure, "add to it that she still pulled down a 3.9 GPA, there was no reason to be concerned. During that time, she also started to hang out with school girls that had piercings and tattoos which struck me as odd because before her father was killed, she didn't think too highly of girls with either one of those things."

"Behavior changes are usually a coping mechanism and that's what she used with the death of her father. Nothing abnormal about that, you did the right thing to let her vent off the way she did," responded Dean.

"Come on, Liz, don't beat yourself up, it's been a rough year for all of us. You need to realize that your one hell of mother," countered Chris.

Elizabeth eyes watered but did not leak, she smiled touched her brother's face with her left hand, "Thank you, handsome, I could always count on you to bring me up."

Dean smiled inward as he could see Chris melt at the touch of his sister's touch and love. She then turned her attention back to Dean.

"I remembered that a couple of weeks ago a friend of hers took her to get a tattoo. I wasn't happy but I was in no shape to say anything."

Dean cut it, "What type of tattoo did she get?"

"She had gotten a bird on her inside hip. She told me that it represented her father lifting her out of her depression," she looked at both Chris and Dean, "how someone responds to that?" asked Elizabeth.

"You don't, it was her way of remembering him. Do you happen to know the name of the girl who took her for the tattoo or the person that actually did the tattoo?" asked Dean.

"Her friend's name is Carol Mears. I believe I have her address and phone number." She grabbed her purse from the table by the couch and reached into it. "Here it is. Go ahead and take it. As for who did the tattoo, sorry but I didn't think to ask her that," she replied.

"No problem, how about the tattoo? Did it look like a professional did it?" Dean asked.

"To be honest, I'm not a fan of tattoos but it actually looked like a work of art. It had asymmetrical lines, sharp brilliant colors of red and black, two of her father's favorite colors that made it look like a bird in motion flying towards heaven," replied Elizabeth in a breathless manner.

Dean went over and laid his arm around her shoulders, "Thank you; you've actually given me a great lead to follow up on."

"I'm glad I could help a little," replied a saddened Elizabeth.

"I will find Sofia, Elizabeth that much is true. However, I will be honest, there is no promise that she will be alive," whispered Dean.

Elizabeth shuddered, nodded that she understood and began to sob. Chris, who kissed the top of her head, immediately embraced her "Don't worry, Liz, we'll find her."

Dean touched her back, stood up and asked Chris to take him to Carol Mears's home. Chris leaned in, kissed his sister on the cheek got up and walked to the door with Dean. They climbed down the stairs of the Brownstone and got into the car in silence. Chris backed out of the driveway and headed south on Washington Street towards the viaduct that would take them to the Mears house located in Jersey City.

Chapter 18

Hailey stood over the girl as she stirred in her sleep. She finally had the time yesterday after sedating her to look through her purse. She found her school I.D. and that pissed the shit out of her because it made clear that Hunter was more of an idiot then she could have ever imagined. The young girl's name was Sofia Elizabeth Romano of 325 Washington Street, Hoboken, New Jersey. Her I.D. had her birthday, which indicated that she had just turned sixteen. She is a sophomore at Berkheart Academy located in upper Manhattan. Hailey seethed at the fact that Hunter picked up a girl from the very school they ran the operation. Hailey would have to tell her boss that Hunter just jeopardized the White Lily operation.

She shuddered at the thought of doing that, her boss was one cold son of a bitch and would be infuriated that a nothing like Hunter just cost the operation millions of dollars not to mention the leverage her boss had against those in power. She already knew that she would be the one tasked with making it right and had no qualms about having to take out both Hunter and Abraham. Her problem was staying off the boss's shit list. She had to keep Sofia under wraps until she came up with a plan to introduce her to her boss. It didn't take her long before a plan started to materialize in her mind. It didn't fully set because her thought process was interrupted by Sofia.

"How long have you been standing there?" Sofia asked.

Hailey smiled down at her, "Just a minute, I came in to bring you some breakfast."

"You think it's possible to get some aspirin, for some reason my head is killing me," replied Sofia in such a soft and innocent way that it brought back a faded family memory from Hailey's past.

"Hailey, can I ask you something?" asked Hailey's six-year-old sister, Mila.

"Of course, pretty girl," replied Hailey as she stroked her little sister's porcelain white cheek with the palm of her hand.

"Why does mommy know so many mean boys and why do they always have to be in the house?" Mila asked in a hushed conspirator tone.

"Well, baby, mommy is very popular with the boys because she helps them feel better," explained Hailey as she squeezed Mila's cheek.

Her sister giggled and asked, "But how does she make them feel better?"

Hailey in a voice she always used when she played the big bad wolf, "By making them feel big, strong and important. Now get to sleep, we have to get to school in the morning, pretty girl."

Hailey could see a tear coming down her little sister's cheek as she decided to press a little further, "Is that why she lets the mean boys push and hit her."

"Oh, pretty girl, that's part of it but you shouldn't have to worry about those things, that's mommy's job to worry. Your job is to keep working on your dream of becoming an astronaut and flying to the moon," she whispered on the verge of tears herself. "Now, get some rest, and in the morning, I'll make your favorite breakfast."

"Nutella pancakes," squealed Mila.

"Of course, now it is time for night, night."

Hailey kissed Mila again, stood up stared down at her beautiful little sister and smiled sadly before turning off the lights.

"Hailey, hey, Hailey, you alright?" questioned a worried Sofia.

Hailey snapped out of her moment down memory lane, "Sorry, I was just remembering a time in the past. And of course, you could get some aspirin. Just give me a minute to get them."

Hailey walked out of the room closing the door and locking it behind her. She returned five minutes later with the aspirin. As she was given the aspirin, Sofia noticed that anytime Hailey looked at her she did so with a fondness as though she reminded Hailey of someone she might have known. Sofia thought she could use that to get out of her predicament. She just had to get her captor to realize that it would be helpful to let her go and be with her family.

"Hailey, may I ask you something personal?" asked Sofia purposely in an innocuous manner.

Hailey gave her a soft smile, "Of course, what is it that you want to know?"

"Several times, you've looked at me as though I reminded you of someone. Do I remind you of someone?" asked Sofia.

"Sorry, if I might've creeped you out with my staring," replied Hailey.

"No, it's not that, I was just curious because those looks conveyed some type of happiness that's all," countered Sofia.

"That's because you reminded me of my younger sister, Mila," responded Hailey.

"Ah, I knew it had to be someone you cared for," smiled Sofia, "how old is she?"

"She would have been thirteen this month," replied a morose Hailey.

Shit thought Sofia this was not going where she thought it would. Now she had no choice but to ask the obvious question. The problem with that was she does not know if it would shut Hailey down and any chance for her to sympathize with Sofia's plight. Then again, what choices did she really have, "Hailey, you just said would have been. Does that mean Mila passed away?"

Sofia could see Hailey's eyes moisten a bit, "Yes, my little sister died a couple of years ago."

Sofia moved her hand quickly towards her mouth, "Oh my god, Hailey, I am so sorry for your loss."

Hailey shook her head back and forth and along with her hands, "Listen, I told you it was alright to ask. And before you ask, you probably want to know what happened, right?"

Sofia was taken a back for a moment because that was going to be her follow-up question, "I'm not going lie that was my next question. So, what did happen to your sister, Hailey?"

Hailey gave Sofia a wide grin, "I killed her."

Chapter 19

"Once we get past this corner Carol Mears's apartment building should be in the middle of the block," Chris told Dean.

After leaving his sister's home, Chris drove uptown on Hoboken's main street, Washington, towards 14th street and the viaduct that connected Jersey City to Hoboken.

"How do you want to approach Ms. Mears interview, good cop bad cop?" asked Chris.

Dean couldn't help himself but laugh, "First off, I'm no pig, second from the feeling I got from Antonio and your sister you could easily be both."

"Funny, asshole, you're sure it wasn't your fucking great-grandfather Geronimo whispering sweet nothings in your ear about me," countered Chris.

"Look, we both know that you'll get pegged as a cop once they lay eyes on you but with me there is no such vibe," explained Dean.

"Yeah but with you, they'll be scared that you'll scalp them," Chris cut in with laughter.

Dean stuck his middle finger up and smiled, "Just let me go in and ask Ms. Mears if I could talk with her daughter. I'll tell her the truth that I was hired to look for Sofia by Elizabeth and according to her Carol was the last person to be seen with Sofia. If by any chance she refuses to talk to us then you could rough her up a bit."

"Douchebag," Chris shouted just as Dean slammed the car door shut.

Dean got out of Chris's car, walked down the street, and onto the stairs of a two-family home located the corner of Hancock and Central Avenue.

He decided to play the private investigator role since he already carried credentials similar to what the FBI usually flipped open to show people. It wasn't a crime to have credentials with a picture I.D. and the words 'Private Investigator' embossed on it. But it sometimes made him feel like a heel because people always assumed credentials meant federal agents and no one ever questioned a G-man. However, that assumption was needed in some situations to get someone to open a door. He stopped at the front door and knocked.

Dean heard someone shuffle towards the door but not open it. He stood there a good five minutes before a woman called out from behind the closed door, "Who is it?"

Dean responded, "Morning Ms. Mears, my name is Dean Stanton. I'm an investigator investigating a missing person, Sofia, Elizabeth Gates daughter."

The door opened swiftly revealing a petite good looking in a homely way, middle-aged woman with a warm smile and eyes that showed concern. "You said Sofia was missing," Ms. Mears responded in a worried tone not even noticing that Dean had also flipped his credentials.

"Yes, mam, Sofia's mom, Elizabeth hired me to locate her daughter."

Ms. Mears responded, "You sure she's missing and not just with a friend."

"Ms. Gates told me that her daughter sometimes went out with friends and would come back the next day but it's now been more than three days since she last saw her," replied Dean.

"Oh, my, that doesn't sound like something Sofia would do. She's such a thoughtful, kind and respectful girl. You know I've always been grateful to her for choosing my daughter, Carol as a friend."

Dean smiled, "May I come in so we could talk more privately?"

Ms. Mears moved aside to let Dean through the threshold, "Now where are my manners. My apologies and of course, come in."

Dean entered the hallway and waited for Ms. Mears to close the door. She led the way to the living room where she gestured him to sit in the recliner as she took the sofa.

Dean sat down and gestured with his hand for her to proceed, "You were saying that you were grateful that Sofia befriended your daughter, may I ask why you were grateful?"

"My daughter had a hard time adjusting to high school especially making new friends at first but I noticed after a couple of months she was feeling better about school. I asked her what changed. She told me that she met a new friend, named Sofia, who she could relate to," beamed Ms. Mears.

Dean asked, "Was she more specific about why she could relate to Sofia."

Ms. Mears responded, "Oh, yes, of course. She told me that they were both from immigrant families, hers from Italy and ours Poland. Both girls grew up in blue-collar neighborhoods and unfortunately suffered the same heartbreak."

Dean could see her eyes moisten, "Which was?"

Ms. Mears dabbed her eyes with a tissue she grabbed from an end table alongside the couch, "Their fathers were both deceased."

Dean's face softened, "I'm sorry for your loss. May I ask how your husband died?"

Ms. Mear's demeanor took on soft side, "My Frankie was a hard-working longshoreman. He worked his butt off to provide for our family, especially his little girl but in the end, he couldn't beat the big C. God rest his wonderful soul."

"How did your daughter take the loss," Dean asked respectfully.

"How do you think, Mr. Dean, it broke her heart. The only saving grace was he was able to see her graduate and be accepted into high school before he died. She walked around in a fog those first three months of high school. Until the day, Sofia entered her life. She was also struggling with the loss of her father. She was a godsend because my little girl didn't feel alone anymore. It was Sofia's friendship that brought my little girl from her dark abyss."

Dean was speechless and touched, "Both girls are amazing," was all he could muster. He decided to change the subject so the conversation didn't turn to morose, "May I ask the name of the school your daughter attends?" asked Dean.

Ms. Mears smiled, "Well, I don't know if you know anything about private high schools here in our area but she was accepted to one of New York's if not the entire country's most exclusive school, Berkheart Academy located in Upper Manhattan."

Dean nodded his head and smiled, "Please don't take offense to my next question but isn't it also very expensive, how are you able to send Carol there?"

"No offense taken. I can see where you would be confused being that we live in a modest home in a deteriorating neighborhood," explained Ms. Mears, "but each year Berkheart conducts a lottery for families that can't afford the tuition. They receive over ten thousand entries for only eighty freshman slots. Now this is not your run of the mill lottery where you put the entries in a large drum and have someone pick out twenty-five names, no sir; the school had a strict criterion in order for a name to be entered."

Dean responded, "Such as?"

"Well, for starters each child had to have an IQ over 110 which meant that your child would be classified in the IQ superior intelligence range," replied Ms. Mears.

"What was Carol's IQ?" asked Dean

"My daughter's topped out at 133 near the genius level of 140. The second criteria were the student's computer skillset would have to be on par with current technological advances," replied Ms. Mears.

"How would they know the student was 'on par' with current technology?" asked Dean.

"Student had to pass a specific computer exam tailored to the student. In Carol's case, she had to try to enter a private company's computer network without being detected. I really don't understand what that means but my daughter told me that school administrators instructed her to access the computer network of a mock private company and obtain the social security number of an employee without leaving a trace behind that the system was compromised," explained Ms. Mears.

Dean interjected, "I don't think I understand what that means or even how to attempt to understand."

Ms. Mears laughed, "Don't feel bad, I was in the same boat."

"Was your daughter able to do it?" asked Dean.

"Yes, she told me that the school had placed a software program specially designed to track any intrusions into the company's computer systems. However, students were not told this. Carol successfully entered the computer system and retrieved the information," smiled Ms. Mears.

"OK, she completed both criteria, what was her next step?" asked Dean.

"The final step was an interview with school administrators to determine whether the student was suitable for the school. If you were successful, your name was entered into the lottery. That's what happened to my daughter her name was placed in the lottery," Ms. Mears responded proudly.

Dean clapped his hands together, "Wow, congratulations, your daughter definitely deserved to get in even without the lottery."

"Thank you for your complimentary words," replied Ms. Mears.

"And you said there were over ten-thousand entries for those eighty slots?" asked Dean.

"That's right," replied Ms. Mears.

"That's crazy, you should have also played the state lottery the moment the school called," laughed Dean and followed up with another question, "How did you know about the school and for that matter its lottery?"

Ms. Mears looked at Dean for a moment before answering, "I didn't know about the school but my brother, Tommy did. He was a Captain in the New York City Police Department. He was stationed at the 19th precinct on 67th and Park Avenue. The school is located a couple of blocks south of the station. He worked that beat when he was in plainclothes early in his career and had established relationships in the neighborhood with shopkeepers, teachers, students and their parents. When the time came for us to decide on a school for Carol, he asked his contacts about the school. They in turn told him about the lottery and the requirements. He already knew his niece's IQ, which he relayed to the school's administration. They told him to go ahead and put in an entry form and as they say the rest is history."

Dean tilted his head to the side as if pondering a thought, "Did you say your brother is with the 19th precinct?"

"Was and yeah, why?" asked a perplexed Ms. Mears.

"What a small world, I work with a detective for the nineteenth, Detective Michael Duncan. Do you know him?" asked Dean.

"Get out of here, of course I know him. You have to understand cop culture, Mr. Dean. A station house is like a fraternity. Everyone is like family, looking out for one another. My brother came up in the nineteenth with Duncan both as detective third-grades. They weren't partners but like I said they were all brothers under the same precinct number. Tommy eventually decided to get off the streets and into management. Duncan, I believe, did not want to leave the streets and stayed on as a detective making it to the highest rank, first-grade. My brother got as high as a Captain," she replied.

"Damn, what were the chances," was all Dean could say at what he just heard.

"Many people outside tristate area believe that living in New York you're isolated. That's far from the truth, men and women on the force once they pass probation move to the outer boroughs and Jersey. It's their way of not wanting to police the same neighborhood they live in. And as I said, it's like a fraternity and officers usually move into neighborhoods that have retired members living in them. Jersey City is no different, I know of five other men who worked the 19th living in this neighborhood."

"Amazing, and plausible, I guess. Can you tell me more about your daughter's tough time adjusting to the new school?" asked Dean.

"Sure, I don't know if you remember going to high school but in my experience, it was a difficult transition, especially if you are going to a school, not in your neighborhood. Add to the equation, the majority of students are from money. Go a little further and think about those students believing that you were one of the token picks from the lottery. Kids, Dean are cruel and my daughter was ostracized for not being from money," replied Ms. Mears.

"Are you saying she was being bullied or picked on?" asked Dean.

"I wish, then that would mean that she was being acknowledged. No, it was worse than that. She was completely ignored as though she wasn't alive. I believe Sofia saw in Carol the pain and sorrow she was feeling at the time since both lost their fathers. However, unlike my daughter, Sofia was popular in school. If you saw Sofia, you would see a tall, thin and strikingly beautiful girl. Don't get me wrong my daughter is just as beautiful just not to the girls at school. To them, Carol was a hick, an outsider, a person that did not belong to their group. Sofia was the opposite of Carol. She was not only beautiful but also stylish like some trendsetter, the very style every conceited Berkheart student strived for but couldn't achieve. Since they couldn't be Sofia, they could at least be associated with her so they welcomed her into their fold. But that angel would not agree to be part of any clique unless Carol was included. And that, Mr. Dean, is why Sofia will always mean the world to us."

Dean was about to ask a follow-up question when he heard the door open and slam accompanied by a female voice, "Mom, you won't believe what happened to one of our students last night," shouted Carol as she rounded the corner of the hallway that opened into the living room where her mother and Dean were sitting.

"Oh, sorry, mom, I didn't know you had company." Carol eyed Dean suspiciously, as she approached them.

Dean could see how Carol would have a hard time fitting in and it wasn't because of her weight. It had more to do with her style. She was not short but also not the tallest for her age group. She had some weight to her that would exclude her from the anorexia of her teenage brethren but not to the eyes of some oversexed teenage boys. Her dress and hairstyle Dean summarized as today's Gothic trend. She was tattooed and pieced in both ears and above both eyes. Dean thought girls her age might have grown out of that t-shirt and jeans faze but on her, it showed confidence and independence.

She walked up to her mother gave her a kiss on the cheek all the while keeping her eyes on Dean. Her mother touched her cheek as she lifted her head and sat on the arm of the sofa where her mother sat. Ms. Mears spoke, "Carol baby, this here is Mr. Dean. He's a private eye hired by Sofia's mom."

Dean saw Carol turn her head slightly towards her mother as she responded, "Why would Ms. Gates hire a private eye?"

Dean decided to enter the conversation, "Her daughter Sofia hasn't come home in over three days."

She looked at him with curiosity and frankly stated, "She's been out before without telling her mother and always returned. Maybe she's recovering from a party or with someone she doesn't want her mother to know about. I'm sure she'll be back before the night is over."

"I hope so but if you don't mind, I would like to know the last time you saw or talked to her?" asked Dean.

"Don't mind at all. Just the other day, we went to a party at my friend's house in the Bronx," she curtly replied.

"Does your friend have a name?" countered Dean.

Carol laughed at the question, "No he goes by friend, of course, he has a name, it's Jesus Ramos."

"Is he a student at Berkheart as well?" asked Dean.

She laughed harder now, "No, first, he's a guy so attending an all-girls school is a no/no and if he were a girl, his criminal record would automatically disqualify him from the registration process."

"Carol, don't insult your friend like that, he's a good kid," chastised Ms. Mears.

Sorry mom, I didn't mean it that way. Mr. Dean, I don't know if my mom told you but in order to apply for the Berkheart lottery, you need to hit off several criteria. The most basic one is your IQ must be at least a superior level to even have a chance of applying.

"Even if Jesus was female and I'm not trying to be insulting but his IQ would be average at best. However, if IQ tested for creativity then all bets would be off because he would have ranked first. What he lacked in academics he more than made up with his artistic skills. His sketches, drawings, and paintings are out of this world. He even had enough business savvy to understand that his art could translate into income."

"How so?" asked an intrigued Dean.

"He decided the best way for him to work on his art and get paid was to get into tattoos. He went out into the streets, listened and learned who was putting out the best tats in the neighborhood. When he found that artist, he approached and asked if he could apprentice with him. The artist agreed and Jesus absorbed his teachings like a sponge. With what he was taught, coupled with his creativity he worked his way up to being the head tattoo artist by the time he was seventeen."

Dean cut in and asked, "Impressive, may I ask how you met a male, Puerto Rican tattoo artist from the South Bronx going to an all-girls school in Manhattan?"

She smiled and added, "When Sofia and I became friends, she introduced me to many of the pretty rich girls wandering the school hallways. Each one I met wanted to hang out with Sofia the "trend-setter" from Jersey. One day as I walked towards Sofia's locker, I could see two girls talking with her. I heard one say something about a club they wanted her to join. I could also see the one talking about the club pointing to the back of her friend's neck. As I got closer, I could see a tattoo of a White Lily on the girl's neck but it didn't actually look like a tattoo but a painting with the quality and skill that if you put it on canvas, it would be hung in an art museum, it was that fucking amazing."

"Carol, language!" shouted her mother.

She laughed, "Sorry, mom. After seeing that piece, I knew that I wanted to be marked but it had to be from the artist that did the White Lily. When I finally got to Sofia and the girls, I asked the girl with the tattoo who did it. At first, the snobby bitch didn't respond but then Sofia urged her to tell me and she did. She told me that she got it up in Harlem at a place called, Hunter's, and the tattoo master was a Puerto Rican guy named, Jesus."

121

"And did you get the White Lily tattoo?" asked Dean.

Again, she smiled, "No, because I wasn't asked to join the club. But that didn't stop me from going up to Harlem and meeting Jesus. When I entered the shop, he was at the counter. He took one look at me and told me God had brought us together. He went on to say that, the reason I came to him was that I was searching for something that would convey who I was. I agreed with him and told him to mark me with something like his rendition of the White Lily which I told him should hang in the MOMA."

Dean responded, "How did he take to that comment?"

Carol laughed, "Typical man, his ego inflated like a Macy's Thanksgiving Day balloon. He told me that every piece he creates is of art museum quality. I laughed at him but in the back of mind I knew he was right and told him to hurry and mark me with his next masterpiece."

Dean cut in, "What did you decide to get?"

"Well, he didn't even bat an eye when I requested that the design be that of an open book with the opening line of my favorite book, Ralph Ellison's, 'Invisible Man.'"

Dean intrigued by her answer countered, "Why that particular book? Isn't that the story of an African American man whose color renders him invisible in society? And isn't the opening line, 'I am an invisible man.'"

Carol nodded her head, "Wow, I'm impressed, the majority of people not of color have no idea who Ralph Ellison was or of his great American novel. Your understanding of the book is also correct but think about this, do I or you, and forgive me for making the assumption that you are native, have to be African American to be rendered invisible in our society. I don't believe so, and for the opening line I removed the word 'man' and had it replaced with 'Person.'"

"Point well taken, and no need to assume, your observation skills are impressive. I am native and a proud member of the Tohono O'odham tribe," Dean stated in admiration and asked, "Do you think Jesus will talk to me?"

"I don't see why not. But he doesn't start at Hunter's until three in the afternoon. If you go by, just let him know that I sent you otherwise he'll smell cop all over you." She laughed.

He had to laugh too because if Chris heard her, he would have busted his chops for the rest of the day. As he got up to leave, he remembered something turned to Carol and asked, "When you rushed into the house, you said that something happened at school today but you didn't get to tell your mother what that was."

She nodded, "Oh, right, I forgot. This morning we had an impromptu assembly at the school. The principal informed the student body that a freshman had died the previous evening."

Her mother moved to her mouth as she commented, "Oh, what a horrible thing to happen, are you alright, honey." Carol responded, "I'm fine, mom but my heart breaks for family and the young girl. She was drunk and fell down the stairs of her home. The school took the opportunity to remind the student body of the dangers of drinking. They also offered counseling, if anyone wanted it."

Dean asked, "Did you know the girl that died?"

"No, I did not," replied Carol.

"Could she have been part of the White Lily Club?" Dean countered.

"Sorry, I wouldn't even know. Remember the girls in that club don't talk to anyone. The only reason I knew of the club was because I overheard the conversation between Sofia and the girls," replied Carol.

Dean thanked them both before exiting their home and walking to Chris's car.

Once inside the car, Chris asked Dean how it went inside. Dean gave him a complete rundown about the school, Jesus, the student's death, the conversation between Sofia and the girls regarding a club and the coincidence of his friend Detective Duncan and Carol's uncle coming up in the force together. Chris drove for a couple of minutes before telling Dean that he didn't believe in coincidences to which Dean nodded and agreed. Chris also added that it wasn't just the relationship with Duncan and the uncle but the fact that a female student from the school had just died.

He ended his conversation telling Dean that it just didn't seem right. Dean picked up further on Chris's conversation.

"In some Native cultures including my own, when a true warrior meets with other natives or non-natives and seeks information from them, images of animals would pass in their field of vision. If two of the same animal passed together by that individual the warrior is speaking with, it would tell the warrior the true nature of that individual," Dean explained to Chris.

"Wait, now you're fucking messing with me. That means as you talk to me now there may be a monkey, sitting in the backseat. Get the fuck outa here, the Shadow Wolf, shit I can get with but come on seeing things is another ballgame altogether, matter of fact we white man have a word for that, 'Bat-shit crazy,'" laughed Chris.

Dean laughed as well, "No, you prick, I'm dead serious. Since this may be a little much for you to comprehend, let's use you as an example. At our first meeting in the bar, I noticed that behind you were with a team of horses. The spirit world was telling me that the horse represents your soul or life force. To a warrior, the horse was a symbol of personal power that inspires others and motivates one's actions in life. That symbol has many good qualities such as faithfulness, freedom to run free, friendship and cooperation. But its most important quality and which will come in handy as we search for your niece, is guiding others to overcome obstacles."

Chris looked dumbfounded but recovered, "Shit, I'm being conceited, but some of those, actually, are me. OK, medicine man what fucking zoo animal roamed the Mears house while you were there?"

Dean smiled, "Nice, with that type of insight you might have some Indian blood in you."

Chris laughed, "I hope the fuck not."

"Asshole, when I spoke with Ms. Mears, a wolf appeared by her side. The wolf is part of a pack or family and is associated with intelligence, social and familial values. They are known to outwit enemies and have the skill to protect not only oneself but more importantly one's family."

"But the way, you first described her and not to sound insulting but it sounded like she was someone many would consider plain. OK, what about the daughter?" asked Chris.

"First, my description of Ms. Mears was not that she was plain but average. As for your question, kudos, White man it was a good one. When Carol rushed into the living room, several deer accompanied her. Their characteristics include gentleness, the ability to listen, grace and appreciation for the beauty of balance, understanding of what's necessary for survival, power of gratitude and giving and the ability to sacrifice for the higher good," replied Dean.

"Just what the world needed another fucking do-gooder. Alright, what's next now that we have a lead on the next fucking Picasso tattoo artist," asked Chris.

"Easy, we drive to Harlem and pay a visit to the artist but before we get there let me call Duncan and get some information on Carol and her family as well as the school," responded Dean.

Dean tried several times to get through to Duncan's phone but only got the voicemail. He decided not to leave a message and would try him again later.

124

Chapter 20

Abraham walked towards his office on Lexington and 68th street. It wasn't a fancy address or building but it was near the school and the Dakota apartments which suited his purpose.

Just before entering the building's lobby, his phone vibrated. He kept his ringer off because he felt it unnecessary for others around him to know that he was either needed or summoned and frankly, he craved the anonymity of it. He stepped into the lobby and away from the foot traffic and answered his phone.

"What the fuck is going on?" snapped the caller.

"Whoa, calm down and tell me what the hell are you talking about? If it's about the Ambassador's concerns, I've handled that already," he snapped back.

"I know about that fucking asshole and I don't give two shits about him. I just got a call from one of my confidential informants who told me that there's a private dick nosing around asking about some missing girl from the school," answered an angered caller.

"So who gives a shit? There are close to five hundred girls in that fucking school. What's got your panties in such a twist?" Abraham countered.

"That same CI said that the girl's mother hired the dick to help locate her daughter. And although you're right it's just one student out of five hundred the reason I got my panties in a twist is that same dick is now heading to Hunter's place to ask about that missing girl," answered the caller.

"Again, so fucking what, I'm pretty sure it has nothing to do with him or our place," responded Abraham but in the back of his mind, he was hoping it wasn't a club girl because that would mean he would have to permanently silence Hunter.

The caller must have read his mind because they answered Abraham's thought, "Good but why don't we make sure it's not a club girl or has anything to do with Hunter. My thinking is that it has nothing to do with either, because he would have been on the phone to you ASAP, right?"

"Without question, he knows the importance of keeping me abreast of the girls and anything that may affect them. Plus, let's not forget Hailey is my backup. She would have definitely notified me of any problems or issues with the girls. Listen, just sit tight and let me call and tell him to get out of the shop. I'll meet him at his apartment and have a talk with him. Once I'm done I'll call you and give you the rundown," Abraham answered with a tone that carried calmness but in reality, masked a nagging feeling of dread.

"Fine, but get back to me as soon as you get any information and remember Abraham the importance of keeping our thing from prying eyes and ears," the caller reminded Abraham eerily.

"No fucking need to remind me of anything. I told you I will handle it that should be enough for you," he replied and hung up the phone. He took the elevator up to his office and dialed Hunter's number.

Hunter picked up on the second ring. He was glad it was Abraham because he wanted to give him the good news that he was able to take care of Megan without incident, "Hey, boss what's shaking."

"Might be you right before I fucking cut your heart out if you don't answer me correctly," Abraham replied menacingly.

Although Abraham was not physically in front of Hunter, he still trembled at his bosses' intimidating voice, "What's wrong. I did exactly what you told me to do. Hailey and I had no issues or problems with carrying out your orders. Actually, Hailey called me this morning and as you predicted the school had an assembly to inform students and the faculty of a student's death. She also told me that no one suspected a thing, so I thought we were good," he stated confidently.

"Well, according to my sources, there is a private investigator heading to your shop as we speak," said Abraham.

"What the fuck for?" replied Hunter.

"He wants to question you about a girl from the school who's gone missing. Apparently, she may have been to your shop. Do you know or remembered the girl, her name is Sofia?" asked Abraham.

Shit, shit, how the fuck did he find out about her, Hunter thought to himself. Does he know that she was with me? Or that I had Hailey kill her and dump her body in the ocean. No, no, he can't know, if he did, he wouldn't be calling me. Instead, he would be dumping my body next to the girl. Oh, fuck, Jesus knew her and introduced her to me. But calm down Hunter no one at the party including Jesus saw you leave with her. Plus, everyone was either high or toasted so even if they saw us talking, it would've been a blur or faded memory. Good, I'll just play it off. I can't lie and say I've never heard of her especially if she got marked by my own employee but I can tell Abraham that I may know her just not by name but as a customer with a tattoo.

"The name doesn't ring a bell but if she got tatted at my place then we may have crossed paths. It's my business practice to see each tattoo my employees completed and ask the customer if they were satisfied with their piece. Other than that being a possibility, I don't know her from Adam. You want me to get outta here and lay low?" asked Hunter.

"I was thinking about it but now that there may be a possibility you've seen or met the girl it might be best to stay and answer the guy's questions. As long as you're telling me the truth and it may have been in passing that you met her, we're safe. I want you to wait 15 minutes after the guy leaves before you call me. Got it?" asked Abraham.

"Don't fucking worry, I got this. Call you later," replied Hunter.

Chris pulled up to the curb in front of Hunter's on a 125th and Saint Nicholas Avenue in Harlem. He turned to Dean, "This time I want to walk in with you. This Jesus may know Sofia and his boss might have seen them together at some point. I want to flip my creds to see their reactions. Sometimes seeing the badge can scare an individual who may be hiding something."

"There are some tells that can help identify whether they are not truthful, like excessive blinking, profuse sweating or my favorite repeating questions asked of them. So if you don't mind, let me run the interview and introduce you as a consulting private investigator."

Dean nodded his head in agreement, "If you didn't suggest it that was the way, I wanted to play this. They need to know if there was foul play and I'm not saying there was but notice has to be given that prison is on the table."

"Fuck prison, if my niece has been harmed in any way and one of these assholes is in on it, the only time they are getting is to beg for mercy just before I put a bullet behind their ear. Oh and on a lighter note, do me a favor if you see an animal next to them, let me know with a sound that represents them, you know like if it's a cow, work in the sound mooo into the conversation," laughed Chris.

"Fuck you. Oh, shit did I say I saw horses around you that time in the bar. What I meant to say was that you were surrounded by donkeys, you ass," cracked up Dean as they both entered Hunter's.

Hunter's was not at all, like Dean was picturing it. He expected it to be an apartment-sized cramped space cluttered with tattoo magazines, worn-out sofas, and chairs that could have come from the local Salvation Army. He thought there would be customers sitting smoking cigarettes, nursing beers looking more like dirty bikers then high school-age kids. The bikers he imagined would be getting tattoos declaring their love for mom on one arm and a dagger through an eye of a skull dripping blood on the opposite arm. To both their surprise, what they saw was more akin to a waiting room at some uptown plastic surgeon's office complete with a receptionist and coffee and tea counter.

Dean looked over at Chris and shrugged his shoulders with a sound of surprise in his voice commented, "It goes to show you never assume anything. I won't speak for you but leather couches, recliners, coffee, tea, current magazines, Money, Forbes, and even the Economist, shit, I would never have guessed this in a million years. Did we come to the right place or is this some place, someone like you would come for that 'special operation' you were saving for all your life," laughed Dean.

"Fuck you, Tonto," Chris laughed and continued, "You have to be bringing in some real cash to run something this fancy. Either his clients have some serious money or it's a front," Chris countered.

They walked up to the front desk where a young woman with a nametag, that identified her as Crystal. She looked at both of them with a tired smile, "How can I help you guys?"

"Afternoon Crystal, I'm Special Agent Gates and this here is my partner, Dean," responded Chris at the same time flipping his credentials' to show her.

As with most people, her first reaction should have been shock but Crystal looked bored with life and her current job, which worried Chris. If the badge didn't elicit a fear response, he would have to get tough with her. He was hoping to avoid that before even speaking with Hunter. She looked him over again and simply stated, "OK bigshots, let's try this again. How can I help you?"

Chris now got the, I don't give a fuck who you are vibe, from her but tried to be nice, "We would like to speak with the owner, please," he asked.

"Do you have an appointment?" she countered.

Dean could see Chris straightened up and change his facial expression to one that expressed annoyance when he countered, "Crystal, do you think a federal agent would need an appointment? Just the presence of a government official should tip you off that it must be important. But if you want to get an attitude and act like an asshole then there is going to be a serious problem, do I make myself clear?"

She looked like a deer in headlights.

"Crystal," she stuttered and blinked several times before answering, "Sorry, I wasn't trying to be funny or give you a hard time. You know what let me just go back and get him."

Chris gave her a contrite smile, "Yes, why don't you do that."

Dean whispered, "You have to admit that was funny. Did you do that on purpose to get that response?"

Chris cupped his hand over his mouth and whispered, "Yep, couldn't resist. It took everything I had not to crack up."

Crystal came back five minutes later with her boss in tow, "Hello, gentleman, my name is Hunter and I am the owner. How can I be of service to you and the FBI?" asked Hunter.

Chris introduced himself, flipped opened his credentials' introduced Dean and answered, "We are conducting an investigation into the disappearance of a young girl. *He placed a photo of Sofia on the receptionist's counter separating him from Hunter.* The investigation has yielded information identifying your establishment as a place she may have visited recently. Her name is Sofia Elizabeth Romano, aged seventeen. Witnesses have informed us that a tattoo artist by the name of Jesus may have worked on her. Do you remember ever seeing her?" asked Chris.

Both men saw it and Hunter thought it was well hidden but the picture of Sofia caused him to blink repeatedly only for a couple of seconds but what gave him away was the color in face changed a shade paler, two small but important tells usually exhibited by individuals trying to keep something hidden.

"Offhand, I do not; however, if she got inked from my place, there would be a chance we've met," replied Hunter.

"Why would you say there may be a chance you've met her if she was inked here?" asked Chris.

Hunter explained, "When a costumer's tac is completed, sorry you look confused by that word. It's another word we use in the business for tattoo, as in tac it on. Each finished design must be shown to me as part of our quality control. After seeing it, I ask the customer if it was satisfactory or not."

"Have you gotten any clients that were not happy with the work done here?" asked Chris.

"To be honest, no, but it goes to the quality of work done by my artists. I employ only the best in the business," responded a smug Hunter, "so if she was inked here, there was a good chance that I asked her that question. However, that's where my involvement with the client ends unless there is a problem. Since we don't get bad reviews, she must have been another satisfied client. If you don't mind asking, did your witness say who put the irons to her?"

"Irons, what does that even mean?" asked Chris.

"Sorry, using tattoo slang again. Irons are what we affectionately call in the business a tattoo machine," replied Hunter.

"As a matter of fact, they did. The witness stated that she was worked on by a tattoo artist by the name of Jesus," Chris countered.

"That doesn't surprise me, he's our best and most sort after custom artist. Seems like you're in luck today, he's in the back now putting together a sleeve," answered Hunter.

This time Dean chimed in, "Don't tell me, more tattoo slang."

Hunter sheepishly replied, "Again, I'm sorry but let me just say there might be more used during this conversation. As for what sleeve means, it is slang for a full arm tattoo that runs all the way around the arm to the shoulder."

Dean cut in, "We just might have to ask you for a tattooist dictionary at this rate."

Hunter laughed, "It can get cumbersome for those not in the know. If you want to meet Jesus, I could take you to the back. It'll give you an opportunity to see how the magic is done. He's probably pounding skin as we speak," he stopped and pointed at Dean, "Here's where that dictionary would come in handy, pounding is just another word for working. Once we get to his room, you'll have to wear scrubs and masks. My place is not like the parlor you fellows were perhaps expecting. I'm very strict on keeping the work area sterile and away from any possible contaminants," Hunter explained.

As they walked by the receptionist's desk, they noticed a waiting area just before a long hallway with several glass doors on either side. As you passed each door, one could see what looked like dentist chairs occupied with a client and a tattoo artist alongside them working their machines.

Dean counted eight rooms; four on either side and all were with clients and artists. He also remembered seeing three other customers either filling out what looked like consent forms and paging through binders containing pictures of people with tattoos.

"It looks like your booked up solid today and you still have people waiting in the wings. Is it this busy all the time?" asked Dean.

"So much so that I had to hire ten artists just to keep up with the demand, sadly it's become a trend. Tattoos are no longer taboo like when I got my first tattoo or started carving," he laughed, "if you haven't caught on when I talk, I will always revert back to the slang used in the profession like carving which another word for tattooing."

"If you don't mind me asking, what would a sleeve run someone in your place?" asked Dean.

"It could vary from as low as $550 to close to $5,000 depending on what's it based on and who's doing the carving. Take the young girl Jesus is working on now. Her father is a well-known hedge fund manager, of course, he doesn't know she's in here but her mother signed the parental consent form. Now she's what we call in the business a 'wannabe' activist."

Chris looked confused, "I don't understand."

Hunter smiled with a devilish tinge, "She considers herself a liberal like her mother and feels that the field in which her father makes his millions is corrupt and harmful to those in poverty. She's not stupid because she knows to go against her father might jeopardize her inheritance. So she decides to get back at him by protesting in a much quieter way. What better way than to put your views on your body where you could hide it until it was time to reveal it to the world? Her choice of protest was the intricate poem by Dante Alighieri, the Divine Comedy. She just wanted his first stanza, Inferno, which described the nine circles of hell."

Chris shook his head, "That seems like a lot of work."

Hunter replied, "Naw, you just use a stencil. See the one being used by Jesus. It's from the famous painting, Dante's Inferno, by Michelangelo. He traces the outline in black. Once it stops bleeding, he'll put in the various colors."

"How long will it take to finish the job?" asked Chris.

"About six hours from start to finish," replied Hunter.

"And why did you have to get the mother to sign a consent?" countered Chris.

"The girl you see is only sixteen that's the reason we needed a parent's consent. In New York, no consent is needed for those that are eighteen and over. And just in case, your next question is how much for her tattoo, it's going to run her mom a cool $5,000."

"That's the price of used car. I'm glad you also cleared up the age issue because those girls in the waiting room don't look older than sixteen, seventeen. You're telling me that they all have signed consent forms?" asked Chris

"That's correct, Agent Gates, like I said it's a New York State law and I've already told you I'm a stickler for the rules," responded Hunter.

"OK, how about you look up Sofia and see if she's been a client. If she is, she should have a signed consent for the work being that she's only seventeen," countered Chris.

"Of course, I run a tight ship. Why would I want to jeopardize such a profitable business on giving tattoos to minors? Come on, let's go to my office and see if she's in the system," answered Hunter.

They followed him to the office where Hunter searched his database after several minutes he looked up from the computer. "Funny, are you sure she got a tattoo at my place. I don't have any records of a Sofia Romano. Could she have used a different name?" asked Hunter.

131

"She could have but if I know her, she wouldn't come to a place that required her mother's signature. Do you know if Jesus works outside of your place?" asked Chris.

"Not to my knowledge. Technically, he's not supposed to, he could face fines for working on minors in unsafe conditions. You'll have to talk with him but as far as I know, he's only worked at my place. Agent Gates, may I ask do you know this girl Sofia?" replied Hunter.

"Why would you want to know that?" replied a surprised Chris.

"It's just you made it sound like you personally knew this girl. I didn't mean anything by it," explained Hunter.

"No need to worry, and yes I personally know her. She's my niece and my sister's only child," replied Chris.

There it was again the blinking of the eye and his facial color change. Chris noticed out of the corner of his eye, Dean stared not directly at Hunter but around him.

"I'm sorry I wasn't any help. I truly hope you find your niece," whispered Hunter.

"No, don't worry; believe me you've helped enough. Why don't you go over and see if Jesus will give us some time to talk," Chris answered.

Hunter left them in his office and went to see about getting Jesus. Chris turned to Dean, "Alright, I know you saw something. What was it?" asked Chris.

"He was surrounded by coyotes which are known to be tricksters with intelligence and stealth intertwined with guile. They are sneaky, sly and dangerous in a cowardly way," responded Dean.

"So do you think he has something to do with my niece missing?" asked Chris.

"My gut says he does, but I can't at this point put my finger how or why. Let's definitely keep an eye out for him. Think, you could use your resources at the bureau to look into his finances. I don't think it was him that came up with the money to either buy or rent this spot. If we get the name of an investor, maybe, they would know something, it's worth a shot," asked Dean.

Chris nodded his head, "No sweat, I have a great cyber unit that could look up that information. What else you need?"

"How about having them also comb through his client database clients with similar tattoos? If you want more leverage on this guy, you could also see if there any minors without a signed consent form. If there are any, you could use that to sweat him," responded Dean.

"Shit, anything else, I could do for you, Captain. If I didn't know any better, I would think you were a detective," laughed Chris.

"Any dumb animal could ask questions like you're doing. It's the grunt work that you seem to shy away from like research, getting files, even reading reports. Shit, I'm surprised no one's caught on to your lazy ass sooner. You know come to think of it, maybe the coyotes weren't around Hunter but with you, all the while," chortled Dean.

"Kiss my ass, Chief Strong Bow, just let me know what animal comes in with Jesus," replied Chris.

"FYI, these visions of the spirit world come and go without notice. It can happen when I'm talking to someone or if someone has malicious thoughts about me. But my experience has been, they come to me the majority of times when an individual is trying to hide something from me," countered Dean.

Chris wanted to make a wisecrack but the door to Hunter's office opened and in walked Hunter with Jesus. Hunter introduced them to Jesus as FBI agents and told Jesus that they wanted to ask him a couple of questions about a missing girl. Jesus nodded his head and agreed to meet with them. Chris asked Hunter to leave them alone for the interview.

Chris began, "Thanks for taking some time away from your work to talk with us."

"Listen, I was raised correctly. My parents taught my siblings and me from jump, unless you have something to hide the police were our friends. Don't look at me like I'm crazy. I understand it's not the norm for a young Latino to say that but I had great role models. So be my guest and ask me anything you like," smiled Jesus.

"You don't know how refreshing it's to hear that. My compliments to your parents, your receptionist could learn a thing or two from you," replied Chris.

"Ah, I see you've encountered Ms. Ice Queen," cracked up Jesus. "She's like that with everyone except Hunter. I think she has a thing for him. Unfortunately, she's not his type, too old and clean," he smiled.

"Old, she can't be over twenty-four and by clean you mean she takes showers and smells nice?" asked Chris

Jesus slapped his legs and gave out a hearty laugh, "Good one, showers and smelling nice. No, by clean I mean she doesn't have any tattoos. Hunter likes his girls real young and marked but it seems Crystal hasn't got the message."

Dean stepped into the conversation, "Are you sure Hunter's tastes in girls doesn't run into minors?"

Jesus got serious, "Hey, I didn't say minors. What I was saying is that he likes young adults. I've only seen him with young women between eighteen and twenty."

Chris put up his hands in a stop motion, "OK, thank you for clarifying the ages. Can we get back to the reason we are here?"

Chris could see Jesus ease up a bit, "Yeah, that's cool."

"OK, I know Hunter told you that we were investigating the disappearance of a young girl." *Chris took out Sofia's photo and handed it to him. He was about to also state her name and age but Jesus cut into the conversation.*

"Hey, that's Sofia, is she the one that's missing?" asked Jesus.

"As far as we know, she hasn't returned home and it's been three days now. Can you tell me how you know her?" asked Chris.

"Sure a couple of months ago, she came to one of my house parties with a bunch of girls from Berkheart," replied Jesus.

"Really and how do you know girls from Berkheart?" asked Chris.

"Hunter has some kind of in with the students there. It's an all-girl high school whose students come from money. You know rich girls always looking to piss off their daddies. And you know how they do it, tattoos. It drives their parents mad. I don't know how Hunter started that relationship but the girls in that school know to come here for that piss off your daddy tat," laughed Jesus.

"And how do they know about your parties?" asked Chris.

"I throw a monthly house party and invite everyone I've ever inked. The only rule to be let in the party is for the person to bring someone with a tattoo or interested in being marked for the first time," answered Jesus.

"I got to hand it to you, great marketing and brand build-up," replied Chris.

"Thanks, it's been working, I usually get about seven to ten jobs for that month," responded Jesus.

"You bring in that much business to Hunter. Do you get a cut of the advertising?" asked Chris.

"Naw, that's on my own dime. He knows and is good with it. Plus he does his own recruiting of clients. Don't get me wrong, I love working for Hunter but it gets boring sometimes. His place has good foot traffic so a lot of advertising isn't needed. That's why he just concentrates on recruiting from the school. The problem for me is that all those girls he brings in want the same fucking design. It dulls my skillset to pump out cookie-cutter work. So I've made an arrangement with him, continue to work here but in my free time do freelance work at my home studio," replied Jesus.

"Funny, Hunter told us that he would not allow you to work outside his place claimed it could get him in trouble," responded Chris.

"Nope, he probably thought I would lie to you about freelancing but like I said there's no reason to lie to you," countered Jesus.

"Why would he think you would lie?" asked Chris.

"First off, it's underground so I don't ask for I.D. and I only take cash," smiled Jesus.

"To be honest, I don't give a shit. Our only concern is finding Sofia. What can you tell me about when you met and being at your last party," asked Chris.

"I think we met at last month's party. I do remember that we hit it off when I approached her in the party," he responded.

Dean jumped in the conversation and asked, "How did she know about your party?"

"A young girl by the name of Carol, she came to me with a request to do a tattoo of her favorite book. I believe it was the Invisible Man by Ralph Ellison. I especially remember her because at that point no one has ever asked for a book to be inked on him or her. It was actually a cool request. Of course, I did it and added a quote from the book. Don't mean to brag but it was a fucking masterpiece," exclaimed Jesus.

"Modest much," laughed Dean.

"Nah, just being real, after getting that piece, she must have shown it all around her neighborhood cause she became a regular and would always bring in kids for me to work on like Sofia. The next month, your niece didn't come with Carol. I believe she came with some of Hailey's friends. That day when we were alone, she told me she was interested in being inked but didn't want anyone to know. No offense but your niece was beautiful and I figured she was probably popular so I offered her my deal."

"What was the deal?" asked Chris.

"She wouldn't have to pay for the pieced as long as I could use her as a walking billboard but she didn't go for it," stated Jesus.

Before Chris could ask Jesus to explain the billboard comment, Dean cut in, "Who's this Hailey and do you know which friends she came to the party with?"

"Offhand, I don't remember who was around Hailey at the time but she's the most popular girl in that school. She's also Hunter's school contact. Her friends are like a sexy girl gang. They are always up her ass like she's a frigging Kardashian," Jesus cracked up on his own joke.

"Would this Hailey know Sofia or who she may hang out with?" countered Chris.

"Hailey knows everyone but I don't think Sofia was in her clique," replied Jesus.

"Alright, that's still great information. It gives us another person of interest to follow-up on. Tell me more about this walking billboard Sofia didn't want?" asked Chris.

"I make a deal with the individual who wants one of my custom pieces. If they allow me to show my masterpiece during parties or at special events then the work is free. If they opt-out of the advertising then I charge them at a discounted rate so that I don't lose the business. Sofia didn't want to advertise her piece so I gave her a great discount instead," Jesus explained.

Chris asked, "Did she give a reason for passing on the advertisement?"

"As a matter of fact, she did. She told me that it was something personal. I didn't push it but she went further and told me that she wanted it to be a tribute to her father who she says was murdered," Jesus explained.

"What did she finally decide to get?" asked Dean.

"She wanted me to do a bird in motion above her hip in red and black. She said it represented her flying towards the heavens where her father was waiting for her. She said that red and black where both their favorite colors," he responded.

Dean remembered something and asked, "You said earlier that the girls from the school always ask for the same stencil or tattoo. Do you remember the tattoo they always get?"

"Sure, it's a white lily and every one of those girls gets it done on the nape of their neck. Hailey once told me they place there so their hair covered it and their parents don't see it. Don't get me wrong, I call it a stencil because it's the same design but each one is done freestyle without an actual pattern but again it's just a white lily. Those girls are another reason I work outside the shop," explained Jesus.

"What's the reason?" asked Dean.

"They cover my work, forgive me for being conceited, but my work is just too good to be hidden," answered Jesus.

"Has Hunter or any of the girls tell you the reason they all have the same tattoo?" asked Chris.

"The only thing Hunter says to me about the girls is when they are scheduled to come in and the girls don't say much, actually they never seem to be excited or thrilled. It seems as though it's being forced on them. But then again, those rich white girls are moodier than a two-year who hadn't napped."

"That was a good one," laughed Dean.

Jesus pondered for a moment as though trying to remember something, "You know what, I do remember a girl who just recently got the tattoo. She was the only girl that I could remember who was happy about being marked with the lily. She told me that the Lily is only given to a select few. It meant that you belonged to an exclusive private club of rich girls. She said that you have to be asked to join. When she described it to me, it sounded like that fucking Bones and something boys club at Yale," laughed Jesus.

Fuck, don't say, Hailey, please don't say her name. Hunter was eavesdropping in the security room. When he started working for Abraham and was offered this new place to do tattooing, he knew that it wasn't on the up and up. So he installed cameras and microphones in every room and had it hooked up to the room he was currently inside. No one but him knew of the room. He thought of it as an insurance policy if anything should go south. It was equipped with computers that recorded all calls and video shot during the day. If nothing of value was heard or seen on the tapes, he would erase them and start it over the next day. However, if he ever came into something, he could use then it would be saved for a rainy or get of jail for free chip. What he was hearing was not good. They have him lying about the knowledge of Jesus's freelancing and that he's been to his parties and now they connected him the girls from Berkheart and now they had Hailey's name. They are going to want to talk to him again about the club and Hailey. Shit, Shit what the fuck is he going to do? He has to tell Abraham then make sure Hailey doesn't go to school in the morning. If he shuts down the business or runs away, they'll get suspicious. He thinks maybe kill Hailey, but they already know about him and her, so it still comes back to him. Damn, Hailey always told him to leave the girl recruitment to her, man if he could go back in time, he would change it all and not talked Sofia into coming to the marina. Well, he's the asshole because there is no such thing as time travel, so he has to do something, quick.

He needs more time to think, so he picks up the phone and calls Crystal at the front desk. He tells her that if the FBI asks to see him again, she is to tell them that he had to head out of the office but they could call him on his personal phone. He gave her permission to give his personal number out.

Dean asked, "I know you said you didn't remember the girls or their names but do you how we could maybe talk to this Hailey girl?"

"I don't know her last name or phone number. She's a regular at the shop but you could ask Hunter, I'm sure he won't mind giving you her contact information. And if by any chance he doesn't have her information, she's a student at the school. Just drive there in the morning or after school and ask around," he commented.

Dean and Chris got up and shook Jesus's hand advised him that if they had any further questions, they would contact him. They walked out of the office with him and headed to the receptionist so that she could let Hunter know they were done. She told them that he had to run out for a meeting but gave her the permission to give his personal cell phone number in case they needed him. They thanked her and headed out the door and towards Chris's car.

"Unicorn representing purity in his work and the innocence and dreams of his artistry," replied Dean.

"Kiss my ass, no fucking way Indians had visions with a unicorn. It's not even a fucking animal, they aren't real, fuck that you've been yanking my chain all along," cracked up Chris.

Dean was enjoying Chris's playful rant, "As crazy as it sounds, it's true and remember it's a vision we're not fucking picking zoo animals. In our culture, the unicorn is magical which is contained in its horn. In Jesus's case, the magic is in his hands."

"I like the kid too, did you happen to see some of the pictures hung up behind him. Carol was right when she said it was museum quality," replied Chris before continuing.

"Oh and don't think I'm not going on the internet to check out that unicorn shit. Alright, what's next, should we call Hunter and the get information on this Hailey girl?" asked Chris

"No, I have a feeling, he's spooked and needs time to regroup. I'm not sure how or why but he knows something about Sofia. Since School's already out, see if your people can get in touch with the principal at Berkheart Academy, no, wait let me ask Duncan about it. I was calling him about some background on him and Carol's family; I'll just add the school and Hailey to that list. Hopefully, he could get us an address so we could drive over and talk to her," instructed Dean.

"That's actually a better idea, it'll free up my people to just concentrate on those forensic and financial requests we made earlier," responded Chris.

Chapter 21

Duncan was driving down Lexington Ave when he heard his phone vibrating on the console. He quickly took his eyes off the street to scan the name on the screen and saw that it was the captain. He slowed down and double-parked making sure to put on his hazards. It must be important, the captain only called when someone was giving her grief or she needed something.

"What's up, Cap?" he asked.

"Where the fuck have you been?" snapped the captain.

"Whoa, what the fuck crawled up your ass. I've been working the armed robbery cases on Lexington," countered Duncan.

"The bug up my ass is your fucking Apache friend. He's called the desk sergeant this morning looking for you. It seems he's left several messages on your phone and you have yet to call him back," she replied.

"I already know that and he said to call him when I had the chance and I haven't so far today. There was no urgency in his message, so I was going to call him once I got back to the station," countered Duncan defensively.

"Well, it seems to me if someone is calling the desk sergeant after leaving you several messages without a response, it usually fucking means the guy needs to talk. Why don't you get off your ass and call him ASAP and after you talk to him call me back," shouted the captain.

Duncan was about to say something but the captain didn't give him a chance.

"And just so we're on the same page, let me repeat myself, call him now then call me, got it?" she stated in a gruff and unyielding manner.

"Let's get something straight Captain, watch how the fuck you talk to me. I can give two shits about your rank. As for Tonto, he's just working a missing girl case which doesn't involve me so don't get your fucking panties in twist. When I have a minute, I'll call him, then you, but in the meantime, 'Fuck you,'" Duncan hung up the phone before the captain could respond.

Duncan was about to call Dean when a taxi behind him start to blow its horn. He quickly got out of the car and jogged towards the taxi with his badge raised up in his hand. When he reached the open window of the taxi, he shoved the badge in the driver's face, "You got some set of balls blowing your horn at an NYPD detective, fuck face!" shouted Duncan.

The taxi driver paled and looked as though he was trying to sink back into his seat, "Sorry, detective, please forgive me. If I knew you were NYPD, I would have changed lanes," the driver stated practically in tears.

Fucking immigrants, thought Duncan, *always doing shit before thinking them through,* "Next time, asshole, use your fucking brain. Now get the fuck out of here before I change my mind and beat the shit out of you," shouted Duncan.

The taxi driver gave Duncan just enough time to step away from the car as he sped out of there. Duncan smiled at the rush he got when he scared the shit out of someone. He walked back to the car dialing Dean's phone number.

Dean picked it up on the third ring, "Hey, why the fuck you tracking me down like some spurned divorce bitch looking for her alimony check," laughed Duncan.

Dean laughed along with Duncan, "Spoken like a deadbeat ex-husband running from an ex-wife. Listen you remember when I told you I was working a missing person case for the New York SAC?"

"Yeah, what about it?" asked Duncan.

"I forgot to mention that it was his niece that was missing," replied Dean.

"Ah, shit that fucking blows. I thought you were going back to follow up with the girl's mother?" stated Duncan.

"That's right, I did and you are not going to believe this. His niece's name is Sofia and she went to a school in your district, Berkheart Academy, know it?" asked Dean.

"Of course, but it's not just a high school. It's the Yale/Harvard/Princeton of all-girl private high schools. Many of their graduates become future politicians and successful business executives. You have to know someone or have lots and lots of money to get into that exclusive school," responded Duncan.

"That's what the mother said," countered Dean.

"How did she get into the school? This FBI uncle has money or does the sister's husband," asked Duncan.

"Neither, it was the husband's life insurance policy. He was murdered two years ago. The sister used that money for her daughter's education," answered Dean.

"Shit, that sucks. It must be hard on the girl to see all those rich girls and know the only reason she can attend the school with them is because her father was killed," replied Duncan.

"Damn, you say it like that and it does sound fucked up. There's more, I learned that Sofia befriended a girl at the school. I just came back from interviewing that girl with her mother and it turns out that we live in a small world," explained Dean.

"What the fuck is that supposed to even mean?" laughed Duncan.

"It turns out the mother actually knows you," added Dean.

"Get the fuck out of here, what's her name?" asked Duncan.

"Her name is Emily Mears, ring a bell?" replied Dean.

"Hell, yeah, her husband, Frankie, salt of the earth, was a good man and father. I was frigging sorry he got the big C. I think from the time he was diagnosed to his death was about a month. Tommy let me know about it. I think he said Frankie got the diagnosis in late May. The only blessing was that he got to see his little girl graduate from middle school in June before he passed away," Duncan somberly added.

"I know it was heartbreaking to hear. She told me that you knew her brother, Tommy," added Dean.

"She had to have said more than that, Tommy came up the detective ranks with me. Emily and Tommy were originally from the Lower East Side of Manhattan. Frankie was the one who moved Emily to Jersey when he got hired out by the Port of Elizabeth as a dockworker. Tommy stood in the City and went to the academy that's where we met and became friends. He really didn't want to stay on the streets. His ambition was to move into management. Eventually, that's what he did, becoming my captain. That's who She-Ra took over for two years ago," laughed Duncan, "his niece Carol was a frigging Brainiac that's part of the reason she got into Berkheart lottery," responded Duncan.

"Yes, Emily told me her high IQ was what made her eligible for the school's lottery," countered Dean.

"I know this call isn't about the life and times of Duncan, right?" chortled Duncan.

Dean laughed, "No, I thought it was just funny how small the world is. I really called for a favor."

Duncan laughed, "Shit, I think I prefer the telling of my life story but I'll settle for favor. What is it that you need?"

"Although I might find that story interesting, what I need is a contact at the school. Emily's daughter had mentioned that Sofia had gotten a tattoo done by the same artist that did hers. I was able to locate him and the shop. I just came back from there. The artist's name is Jesus and he told me that he believed another girl who according to him is the most popular girl in Berkheart might know more about Sofia and her circle of friends. If I could talk to someone from the school, maybe I could find a couple of students who may have seen Sofia."

"Yeah, no problem but it'll have to wait till I get back to the station house," replied Duncan

"Of course, that's why I kept calling. I was hoping to catch you before you went home for the day," countered Dean.

"Home, you're kidding right, I live and breathe this shit. Oh, almost forgot to ask, what was the popular girl's name that artist gave you?" asked Duncan.

"Unfortunately, he didn't have a last name but he did say her first name was Hailey. That's the other reason to speak to a school representative. They could help me find out this Hailey's last name and known address," replied Dean.

Chapter 22

Sofia could not believe what Hailey just told her. She was still reeling from the fact that Hunter wanted her dead. This was beyond her comprehension. Here stood a young girl, much like herself, who saved her life but admitting to murdering her own sister. Sofia's mind was spinning as though she had windmills in her head. She couldn't decide at that moment whether to run, lash out at Hailey or cry, beg and plead for her not to harm her. That indecision thought lasted only seconds before she understood what had to be done. Hailey wanted her to be her little sister, so she decided to play along just long enough to bring Hailey's guard down. At that point, Sofia would have to hit her with her food tray. Once Hailey was down, she would make a run for the front door.

"Sorry, Hailey, did you just say that you killed your little sister?" asked a stunned Sofia.

Hailey nodded her head, "I did but you know I don't want you to judge me for that. It was necessary. It's like that saying; 'Only the strongest survive' she would have killed me if I didn't get her first."

"But that was your little sister, didn't you love her?" asked Sofia carefully.

Hailey's smile faded and was replaced with an eerie sneer that sent shivers down Sofia's spine, "Of course, I loved her. So much so that killing her was my gift to her. Because of me, she would be free from the future pain she would have endured if she lived."

Sofia knew that she was in deep shit if she didn't get away from this crazy bitch. However, she knew in order for her to have a chance at surviving this ordeal she had to keep Hailey talking, "I'm sorry, Hailey, I don't understand. How does murder become the victim's gift?"

"Well, let's start with my mother. I knew killing her would eventually happen. In the back of my mind, once that was done, I would have to take care of my little sister. I was too young for that, plus the only way I was going to survive was probably selling my body. The money would keep me in a single room occupancy place or motel. If my sister were alive, she unfortunately, have to help with rent. Truth be told, I really didn't want that. So when she decided to kill me, it made my choice all the more easier. Now she didn't have to do things, little girls should never be asked to do. That to me is the ultimate love and sacrifice," Hailey whispered.

"But isn't the job of stopping a child's pain supposed to be a parent, especially a mother?" countered Sofia and seeing Hailey's eyes flare up she immediately regretted the question.

Then just as quickly as it had flared Hailey's eyes moistened before she answered, "Mila and I were born into a cesspool of life, to a sewer of a mother and worthless piece of shit sperm donors."

Sofia sat there dumbfounded and could not come up with a reply or question. Hailey took the silence as a gesture for her to continue, "Diamond, some fucking name for a mother, huh, well, a jewel she wasn't. A fucking heroin addict who blamed us for her drug addiction and the reason men didn't stay with her. According to her, those men didn't want to raise drug-addicted retarded children."

Sofia stared in disbelief and felt guilty about growing up in a loving family but she knew not to mention that so she sat still and let Hailey tell her story.

"Mila and I saw things that little girls should never see or be around. I see that look of disbelief in your eyes but trust me living in that hellish environment especially being raised by a drug fiend for a mother taught us how to survive. Listen to this, when I was eleven and Mila was eight, I asked my mother how she paid the rent without a job. You wanna know what she told us?" asked Hailey.

Sofia surprised to be asked a question, could only come up with the most obvious one, "No what?"

Hailey laughed with feeling, "A quick fucking backhand across my mouth with an admonishment to mind my fucking business."

Sofia put her hand to her mouth, "Oh god, that's terrible, I sorry to hear that."

Hailey smiled, "Hey, it was what it was but not all was lost. She did give me some motherly advice that day."

Again, Sofia could not help herself and asked, "What did she say?"

"She told us that the secret to getting money without having a nine to five was to simply open your legs to any man willing to pay. She promised us that if we did that, we would never go hungry or homeless."

Sofia felt sick to her stomach, the pain Hailey and her sister must have endured was heartbreaking. Sofia felt terrible but realized that she still didn't understand how killing her sister in the end helped Hailey, "I'm sorry but you still haven't explained how killing Mila saved her."

"It's coming. You see, that great sound fucking advice given to us by my mother lifted a veil from my eyes. I now understood why so many men paraded through our apartment, ending up in her bedroom. It also explained the constant moaning and moving of furniture noise that came from her room daily. Although I understood, Mila did not and I didn't make the effort to explain it to her. She thought the world of our mother and since we didn't have much, I didn't want to take that away. Eventually, her love for her mother regardless of our situation grew stronger. As for me, it turned into hatred and animosity," explained Hailey.

Sofia raised her hand as though in school, "Why not call child protective services?"

Hailey grunted, "Really, what would you do if you worked in the system and walked into our situation?"

Sofia felt a stab of naiveté, "I would have removed the both of you from your mother."

"Bingo, but you are only half right. They would have taken us away from my mother but then separated me from my sister. Most foster families are looking for younger kids so I would have been nixed out. At least with my mother, I could watch over my sister," explained Hailey.

"What happened then?" asked Sofia.

"It all changed the day my mother told us that we needed to contribute. I was fourteen and Mila was eleven. She explained to us that drugs had done a toll on her looks and body. She wasn't that attractive blonde white girl anymore so it was getting harder and harder to turn tricks. However, she had two young pretty virgins that looked exactly like her. In her mind, she figured we could bring in twice the money she used to."

Sofia who didn't think she could be horrified anymore was dead wrong, "Did she actually ask you to prostitute for her?"

Hailey laughed, "Yep, you're just like my little sister, cute and naïve, prostitute was not her exact wording, more like, Hailey you and your sister have to start earning your keep around here. I can't support us like I used to."

Sofia could see Hailey gaze off into the somewhere as she continued.

"Mila, bless her heart, asked without hesitation, what she needed to do. That sick piece of shit looked her dead in the eyes and said: "let some of my male friends play with your private parts for a little while"."

Sofia could not help but get emotional and felt the tears swelling in her eyes, "What was Mila's reaction to hearing that?"

"I told you she loved and adored our mother and agreed to do it. We were all in the kitchen as this 'discussion' was taking place. I yelled and told my mother that there was no fucking way would I let my baby sister be raped for her fucking drug habit," replied Hailey.

"What did she say after you yelled?" asked Sofia.

"She punched me in the face so hard that I fell back against the kitchen counter knocking over a block holding knifes," replied Hailey.

Sofia was mortified, "Where was Mila when you got hit?"

"Next to my mom crying, she pleaded for me to stop fighting and just do what our mother asked. At that moment, I knew she would die for my mother if she asked her to," stated a somber Hailey.

As sick as it made Sofia feel hearing this, she needed to hear the ending, "Did your mother strike you again?"

"Not at first, she came closer to me and ordered me to wash up and get dressed. She told me that she had some special clothes in the room for me to wear," explained Hailey.

Sofia looked at Hailey in confusion, "Special clothes?"

Hailey smiled and nodded her head, "She bought me a catholic school skirt, blouse, and knee-high socks. The 'client' wanted me to look the part of a catholic schoolgirl. When she said that I gave her my 'you're fucking crazy look' and told her to go and fuck herself. I did that knowing that she would come at me again. But that time I was ready for her ass because I palmed a knife that had fallen next to me after I hit the counter. As soon as I cursed, she attacked. That's when I pushed off the counter, knocked her arms away from me, grabbed her hair yanked her head back exposing her neck and swiped the kitchen knife across her throat," explained Hailey in a nonchalant manner.

Sofia felt the color drain from her face rendering her speechless.

So Hailey continued with her story, "It happened so fast. My mother was dead before she hit the floor. I dropped the knife and turned to make sure my sister was all right. We both were in shock but her demeanor immediately changed to anger. She let out a bloody yell, grabbed another knife from the counter and charged at me. Although I was in shock, I was aware enough to know if I didn't do anything, I would also be laying on the floor dead. So with both my hands, I caught her wrists in front of me and was able with my momentum force the blade to turn back toward her. Since I was stronger and bigger the force I generated, help push the knife deep into her chest. The hilt of the knife stuck out from her chest. My sister didn't have any time to react, only look at the hilt of the knife when she fell to the floor dead."

Sofia still in disbelief managed to ask, "Oh my god. Did you go to jail for it?"

Hailey let out an eerie chuckle, "Nope, it gets fucking better. Instead of becoming a fucking prostitute, I became the recruiter for a pimp. What fucking irony, huh?"

Sofia now looked confused, "How, didn't you or someone that heard the commotion call the police?"

Hailey smiled, "Didn't have to because that special someone my mother said was coming to break me in was a fucking cop. He and his partner walked into the crime scene minutes after it happened. They had keys to my mother's apartment."

Sofia didn't know if she could take any more of this but like viewing an accident could not help but be intrigued, "Did you know them?"

"No, my mother never mentioned them and I've never seen them until that day," responded Hailey.

"Did they arrest you or take you down to the station?" asked Sofia.

"Nope, they did something even better. They gave me options to either get the needle for two counts of first-degree murder or work for them, not as a prostitute but a recruiter of prostitutes. To me, it was a no brainer, first I didn't have to sell my ass and two but most importantly I got to live."

"This is unbelievable but Hunter isn't a cop, right?" asked Sofia.

Sofia could see what looked like sympathy from Hailey when she spoke, "Prick, asshole and coward, yes but cop no. He's part of the program and unfortunately for you meeting him was like the famous cliché, you were at the wrong place at the wrong time, sorry."

Hailey was about to tell Sofia more but was interrupted by the phone ringing in her pants. Since she had a tray of food in her arms, she started to back out of the room, "Listen, I have to answer this call. Once I'm finished, I'll bring back your food warmed up," Hailey stated as she backed out of the room and closed the door locking Sofia once again in the room.

Chapter 23

"What the fuck is going on! You said some private dick, not the damn FBI was coming," shouted Abraham. He had just dialed his boss's phone.

"Relax, Abraham, take a deep breath and tell me exactly what you're talking about," his boss calmly asked.

"Hunter just called all frantic about two FBI agents that came to his shop to ask about some missing girl, named Sofia. He said he didn't know who she was but one of his tattooists, Jesus, did and he told the FBI that she was at his last house party."

"Who gives a shit if she was at his party? It doesn't have anything to do with us," replied his boss.

"True but Jesus also told that FBI that this Sofia girl also hung out with girls from Berkheart," explained Abraham.

"OK, I can understand how you might get a little nervous but this Sofia is not one of our girls. There is nothing that links her to us and once they find her it'll all blow over," responded his boss.

"And I would be good with that but Jesus mentioned to the FBI that one of the girls was Hailey," whispered Abraham.

"Goddammit, Abraham, that should have been the first thing you told me. Now it's serious but still manageable just have Hailey to lay low until the shit blows over. Plus, I'm not worried about her, its Hunter that scares me. He'll talk if it would save his ass, trust me."

Abraham countered, "I agree."

"It's time to clean house, let's start with Hunter and since it's your fucking screw-up," his boss could not finish his sentence because Abraham cut him off.

"How the fuck is this screw-up my fault, I didn't meet the fucking missing girl or have anything to with her," shouted Abraham.

"I put you in charge of the Berkheart operation, remember. You recruited Hunter, set his business up and after Hailey recruits a new girl, she brings them to those Dakota parties you run as part of your operation. So if you ask me that makes you qualified as someone responsible for cleaning this shit up," his boss stated smugly.

"If you want to point fucking fingers, you just said it was you that recruited me, so it's your screw-up as well," Abraham stated menacingly.

"Touché, well played, Abraham, but let's not forget who you're addressing. I won't have a problem with just cutting your fucking tongue out and shoving it up your ass, to remind you about respect, got me?" his boss stated in an eerily calm voice that actually sent shivers down Abraham's back.

"Yeah, I got you. Sorry about that it's just fucked up that the shits hitting the fan faster than I ever expected," replied a subdued Abraham.

"Come on, you're smart, cunning and my personal favorite, ruthless. I have every confidence that you'll come up with a plan to get us out of this potential disaster," replied his boss.

"Thanks, boss. I know you said Hunter should be the first to go but let's kill two birds with one stone," suggested Abraham.

"I'm listening," countered his boss.

"How about take out Hailey and have Hunter take the fall?" asked Abraham.

"Won't he give you a hard time about being the patsy?" asked his boss.

"The pussy that he is, he'll argue but I'll explain that we'll make Hailey's death look like an accident," laughed Abraham.

"OK, I'm curious, go on," replied his boss.

"We get Hailey to Hunter's apartment where I will be waiting. The moment she enters the apartment, I grab her and choke her with a belt that belongs to Hunter. After she's dead, we strip her naked and place her in his bed and have him straddle her. I'll make sure he holds the belt after I'm done, so his prints could be on it. We mess up the bed to look as though they were having sex. Hunter calls 911 and tells the operator that Hailey lost conscience accidentally while they were playing an asphyxia sex game," explained Abraham.

"Interesting why that specific game?" asked his boss.

"It's been in the news lately so it won't seem farfetched and, in those cases, the deaths were ruled accidental. He might get away and if not, the most he'll do is a couple of years. I'll make him understand that it might be time because of his felony conviction. If he balks, I can offer him a bullet to the head instead," explained Abraham.

"Like I said smart, cunning and ruthless but did you consider that he may turn on us," countered his boss.

"I thought about that, what if we offer him a million dollars, new identity, and location. If he has to do any time, add 500,000 to each year he does. I'm thinking no more than two to three years max making him at a minimum another million. Trust me, money always wins out," explained Abraham.

"I like it, go ahead put it in motion and call me once it's done," replied his boss.

Abraham looked down at his phone and shook his head. Why he thought did he have to hitch his ride to this asshole. Now he had to make sure the plan worked or he'll be the one with a bullet in the brain. He picked up his phone and entered Hunter's phone number.

Hunter picked up on the second ring, "Oh, hey Abraham, I thought you were Hailey. I've been trying for the last fifteen minutes to get in touch with her but the calls go straight to voicemail."

"Don't worry about her right now. You need to meet me at your apartment so we could strategize on how to manage this before it gets out of hand and Hunter don't get any ideas about flying the coup, understand?" commented Abraham.

"Come on really, Abraham. Why would I call you for help, if I was planning to run? Maybe you should be worried about Hailey instead," Hunter responded.

"I know that was just a friendly reminder and you are one hundred percent correct about Hailey but we'll talk more in your apartment," laughed Abraham.

Abraham tried Hailey's phone but it went straight to voicemail. He left her message to meet him at Hunter's place and if she had any questions, just call him back.

Hailey wasn't able to answer Abraham's call because she was at the local movie theatre watching the latest John Woo movie. She loved action movies, the shooting, car chases and flat out thrill of shit happening at a fast pace. Her phone vibrated again, she looked at the number and saw that it was Abraham. She wasn't happy that he called three times in the last ten minutes. Fuck that she thought it was her time to relax he'll have to wait until the movie was over.

She enjoyed the movie so much that she forgot that she had to call Abraham back even after arriving at her place. Hailey after settling in went to the kitchen and put together some food on a tray for Sofia. She walked down the hall, entered Sofia's room, and spent about twenty minutes before being interrupted by her phone vibrating. Hailey excused herself from Sofia and left the room with the tray before locking the door. Her initial move was to ignore Abraham's call again but upon seeing the phone number displayed on the screen, she relented because this caller you didn't fuck with unless you were tired of living.

"There are a couple of federal agents looking for you," responded the caller without a greeting.

"Why the fuck would feds being looking for me?" she countered.

"They want to ask you questions about that girl you took swimming for Hunter. You did take her to the beach, right?" asked the caller in a menacing voice.

She could feel the hairs on her neck stand on end; it always did when talking to this person "Of course, when I say I'll do something, it gets done. You of all people should fucking know that. How about some credit, remember I told you about it," she blurted out with arrogance.

"You want credit go to a fucking bank. Maybe you should remember that I saved your fucking scrawny ass from the getting the needle for killing both your fucking whore mother and baby sister," shouted the caller.

Hailey just stood in her living room with the phone to her ear and tears in her eyes as she squeezed the phone, "I've told you a fucking million times it was self-defense. They would have killed me if I didn't protect myself. You should do yourself a favor and don't fucking ever bring that shit up again. Oh, I swear to god, I will..."

She didn't finish her last line because the caller interrupted her in a calm manner, "Please, Hailey, let's not make any threats you won't be able to deliver on. You already know that I could easily walk up to you and snap your neck like a twig without breaking a sweat. So let's just focus on stopping the feds from getting to us."

Hailey felt powerless and shamed for she knew the caller was right about killing her without conscience. She thought it was time to focus at the time at hand and think about escaping her hell at a better opportunity.

Hailey absently nodded as though the caller could see her, "Fine, how you plan to stop them from coming to us?"

"We take care of our liabilities, the first being Hunter, which, will be your job. I don't care how you do it just get it done. Afterward, make sure you get to the safe house and wait for me," the caller explained.

"What about Abraham, wouldn't he get suspicious if Hunter can't be found?" replied Hailey.

"Let me worry about that, just deal with Hunter," and with that the caller hung up.

Nice, she thought to herself, she finally gets to put down that piece of shit, Hunter and she knew exactly how to do it. That scumbag has been trying to get her to sleep with him since they met. Fucking moron didn't know how much she hated him.

151

She knew the only way for him to come to her apartment was to make it an enticing invitation that hinted at the possibility of sex. Hunter didn't think Hailey hated him she always felt he thought she was just playing hard to get. So as soon as he sees her wearing the low-cut form-fitting black dress from the last party. The one she remembered him drooling along the side of his mouth like some fucking horny teenager, getting him to the bedroom would be a cakewalk. This was the way it had to be because she knew in order for her to survive this situation, others had to die. In the end, her savior was her boss because they decided she was valuable and Hunter and Abraham were not but she also understood that her position could change in a heartbeat if her boss found Sofia staying in the safe house. Hailey walked over to the kitchen and made her phone call.

Chapter 24

"Jesus, Hailey, where the fuck you been. I've been calling you for over an hour now," asked Hunter more scared than angry.

"Relax, Hunter, I was enjoying my alone time. I just came out of the movies. What's so important you have to call for an hour straight?" she replied.

"A couple of federal agents came around the shop today looking for that girl. I told them that I never met her but fucking Jesus had to say something," a pissed off Hunter stated.

"OK, what did Jesus tell them?" asked Hailey.

"That she attended one of his house parties," replied Hunter.

"So what, a lot of girls attend his parties," replied a calm Hailey.

"Yeah, but he also told them that he did a custom piece on her," explained Hunter.

"Again, he does custom pieces all the time, no big deal," responded Hailey.

"Jesus Christ, Hailey stop sounding so fucking calm," shouted Hunter.

"It's just you haven't given me something to worry about that's all," soothed Hailey.

"Well, he fucking gave your name to the FBI as someone who knew girls at the school," he replied.

"Still not a problem, I'll just tell them I don't remember talking to her," laughed Hailey.

Hunter snorted, "Well, since you were fucking having me time and I couldn't get in touch with you, I fucking panicked and called Abraham."

"Let me guess, the ape told you that we all needed to meet and put together a strategy," chortled Hailey.

"Shit, how the fuck did you know that. I mean not in those words exactly but close enough. He wants to meet at my place in twenty minutes. So get your shit together and meet me there. I'm leaving the shop now," Hunter commanded.

"Slow it down, Cowboy and listen to me. Was I right just now about what Abraham would say?" asked Hailey.

"Yep, but so what, he's giving us an order and I intend to obey it," snapped Hunter.

"I didn't say disobey. Just not rush to the apartment. Listen, I just got out of the subway and had to stop a friend's apartment to check on her cat while she was on vacation. If I had to go to my apartment then go to your place, it'll take forever. So if you want me to go to your apartment and don't want to deal with Abraham alone then come pick me up at my apartment," she calmly suggested.

"Get the fuck outta here. I'll lose my parking space. You know how hard it is to find a spot; it'll be over an hour before that happens so no fucking way. You'll just have to use your metro card," demanded Hunter.

"You are such a fucking prick, Hunter. Alright, how about this, what if I make it worth your while?" Hailey breathlessly stated. She could hear his breathing get heavier and slower. Fucking men were so easy to manipulate it made her sick.

"I'm listening but it has to be something that I can't resist and wouldn't mind driving in fucking circles for an hour," replied an excited Hunter.

"I promise you that I'll give you something you've been wanting since you met me, just park the car and come up to the apartment," whispered Hailey.

Hunter could feel his body temperature rising as well as everything else. He could picture Hailey wearing nothing as she opened the apartment door. "Fuck, I'll be there in ten minutes but it better be worth it, Hailey."

"Shut the fuck up and get here," responded Hailey.

Hunter needed to call Abraham and let him know about the change of plans which would probably give him a coronary but Hunter didn't think Hailey would give him another shot if he didn't do what she asked.

"Hey, finally got in touch with Hailey. She's in a friend's house but was on her way home. She wants me to pick her up there," Hunter explained to Abraham.

"So why the fuck you calling me for, go and bring her back to your place," replied Abraham before hanging up on Hunter.

Hunter thought that was easy. Maybe Hailey was right about not panicking. His mind immediately calmed. He started to feel good because here was a chance at getting that fine young piece of ass, he wanted for some time now. It always seemed to him that Hailey would look at him with disgust and disdain. Maybe she really isn't so calm about the situation. This could be her way of having him put in a good word with Abraham. He laughed; she'll be fucking pissed once she realizes she gave it up to him for nothing. Shit, it's not his fault if she wasn't smart enough to see the writing on the wall.

Hunter pulled up to Hailey's apartment. Ironically, he found a parking space across the street. He whistled and remembered that it had started out as a fucked-up day maybe the parking and Hailey's freebie were signs of his fortune changing for the better. He laughed heartier climbing the stairs and entering the entryway where he rang her buzzer.

Hailey heard the bell, walked over to the intercom, and decided to fuck some more with Hunter, "Who is it?"

"Cut the shit, Hailey, or you take the fucking train," shouted Hunter.

"Damn, asshole, I just fucking with you. But if you really want me to go on my own then I'll have to take this black cocktail dress and stilettos off," she responded.

Now he felt his pulse going a hundred miles a minute, if she wore that black mini dress, he'll burst before entering the threshold, "Sorry about that it's my nerves again," he replied sheepishly.

"No worries, I think I could calm them down for you. Come on up," she stated breathlessly and buzzed him in.

He walked the length of the first-floor hallway located her apartment door and knocked. Hailey opened the door. She was dressed in a low-cut form-fitting black cocktail dress with spaghetti straps, no bra and standing on a pair of red six-inch stilettos.

The only thought that came to Hunter's mind was slipping those straps down to let the dress fall from her shoulders. He almost lost it but quickly recovered as she took his hand and led him into the apartment closing the door behind them.

As he watched her walk slowly in front of him, he thought she walked with a model's movement as though on a catwalk. He followed behind her like a lost puppy. They slowly and it seemed purposely walked through her living room, kitchen and just outside what he assumed was her bedroom door.

He could not take his eyes off her tight ass and spectacular calves that flexed with each step she took. His vision was so focused on her body that he didn't notice the entire floor surface of the apartment was covered in plastic sheeting. He was still staring at her ass, when Hailey stopped in front of her bedroom door. She turned around and faced him. She lifted his chin so that his eyes went from her ass to her eyes.

"This is how I want this night to go and if you have a problem with it then we can forget it and head over to your place. Agree?" she whispered.

Hunter nodded. "Good, now I'm going to let you take me on my bed and do with me what you like but it's a one-time deal. You will not say a word to anyone about this night, especially Abraham, we clear?" she asked.

Hunter nodded a second time.

"Excellent. Now my bedroom lights are turned off but that's for a reason. Since this is only a one-time thing, I wanted to do something extra for you that will make your head spin more than this dress and stilettos did," She whispered in his ear with such sensuous delight that she could see him literally squirming.

How fucking pathetic men are, Hailey thought as she led him into her bedroom. She closed the door and as she reached for the light switch she whispered, "I'm about to take you to heaven, baby."

Hunter was already reaching to unzip his pants when light flooded the room. It was so sudden and bright that Hunter had to take a couple of seconds for his eyes to adjust to the room. When his eyes finally adjusted, he took in the room and almost passed out. To his horror, he saw Sofia alive and spread eagle on Hailey's bed. Each appendage tied to a bedpost. His horror morphed immediately into blind fury as he realized that he was betrayed.

"You fucking bitch, you are dead," Hunter yelled and turned to grab Hailey by her throat but she was not behind him. He didn't have time to look elsewhere because something swept across his stomach making it feel like it was on fire.

"Aghhh," was his only response as he immediately fell backwards onto the floor holding his stomach on the way down.

"Jesus Christ, Hailey, what the fuck did you do?" moaned Hunter as he sat on the floor looking down at his hand as they tried to keep his innards from falling out of his stomach that was when he noticed that he was sitting on plastic which encapsulated the entire room.

Realizing now that he had been setup and was about to die, Hunter started sobbing uncontrollably, "How could you do this to me, oh god, it hurts. Please, Hailey, call an ambulance, I'm bleeding the fuck out. Ohhh, god, I don't wanna die," Hunter continued to look down at his innards wrapped around his hands. Hunter stopped sobbing for a moment when he heard the plastic on the floor being disturbed next to him. He managed to look up and see Hailey looking down on him smiling and holding a 45-caliber automatic with a silencer attached.

"Please don't do this, Hailey," pleaded Hunter.

"Why shouldn't I, you and Abraham were going to kill me either at your apartment or somewhere else," whispered Hailey.

"You have to believe me, Hailey; I was going to warn you in the ride over. I swear," sobbed Hunter.

She laughed at him, "You are such a fucking coward can't even die like a man." She then lifted her leg and with her red six-inch heel, she sensuously pushed Hunter's shoulder so that he could fall onto his back.

Hunter made no resistance. He knew there was nothing he could do. In his mind, this was it. So like the piece of shit that he was he decided to go out leering at Hailey. Hunter took one last look up at the smiling face of Hailey and watched helplessly as she pointed the gun at his face. He wasn't sure but thought he heard Hailey laughing just before the room went dark.

Hailey stepped away from Hunters body and walked towards Sofia who was still tied to the bedposts. Hailey knew from Sofia's vantage point that she probably saw Hunter's stomach being sliced open with the switchblade but not the kill shot into his eye. Hailey reached out with her knife and cut off the ropes holding Sofia's arms and legs to the bed.

"I suggest you keep your eyes on me. There's no need to see his body and I'm sorry I had to use you like this. You have to realize that he came here to kill me," Hailey explained.

Sofia still in shock asked, "Why let him see me? You could have done all this without me."

Hailey nodded in agreement, "Yes, that is true but I wanted him to die knowing that I didn't kill you. It was my 'fuck you' to him."

"Does that mean you can take me to the police now?" asked Sofia with a degree of hope.

"I'm sorry but you'll have to go back into the room. It's still not safe. Hunter's boss, Abraham, is still out there. He was the one that ordered my death. I have to know work on taking him out or we'll never be safe. I promise you that after he's taken care of things will get better," replied Hailey.

Sofia felt that speck of hope quickly diminish when she heard the phrase; things will be better instead of, you'll be home soon.

Hailey gently placed her hand on Sofia's shoulder, "Come on I have to lock you in your room again but it'll be only for a short time. Oh and I didn't forget your dinner. Let me clean this mess up first," and with that she guided Sofia back towards the locked room and placed her in it.

Hailey walked back into her bedroom and stood alongside Hunter's body. She knew she had to get rid of the body. Her boss would be pissed that she used this apartment, which was their "safe house" to commit the murder instead of her apartment.

What her boss didn't know was that this was where she kept Sofia locked up. No one knew of the safe house, not even Abraham so she felt good that they wouldn't have found out about Sofia being alive. Her boss would initially be pissed off. However, would get over it. She did do as her boss asked and took out Hunter. She stood there besides the body trying to figure how to get rid of it. It took about a minute, because she remembered watching some cable show about mobsters. In it, they talked about a hit man who used to kill his target in an apartment, then take the body into the bathtub and dismember it placing the body parts suitcases. He would then take the suitcases to the city dump for disposal. Fuckin genius but she didn't have the time. It would be too much work. She decided to just drag the body and stuff it in the closet. They would be getting the fuck out of the city anyway and the apartment was registered under a false name that could never be traced back to her or her boss.

Meanwhile, Sofia was back in the locked room thinking about what just happened. She felt as though she was in some horror novel. She wanted to get up and walk out of the movie theatre but she couldn't because it actually happened.

In her heart, she was conflicted on how she felt about Hailey. On the one hand, she was grateful that she saved her twice from Hunter. However, she was scared to death of her because it seemed that killing for her was second nature. Then she thought about her brutal childhood but that should never be used as justification for her ruthless. Sofia's head hurt like hell. She's being held captive by a murderer who likens her to her little sister. Deep in the back of her mind Sofia knew that in the end she needed to get away from Hailey it was the only way for her to survive and make it home. And to think this all started because she took up Jesus' offer to attend his party. Sofia steeled herself again on the task and began to concentrate on how she was going to escape.

Chapter 25

Abraham parked his car just outside Hunter's apartment. It dawned on him as he drove over that it was more beneficial to him if Hunter picked up Hailey and brought her back to his apartment, this way someone could later attest that they saw them together. This way it could bolster the murder–suicide scenario that would be playing out.

It was now up to him to make sure the scenario looked legitimate enough to have the police declare it closed. As he explained to Hunter, he would choke Hailey using one of Hunter's belts. Hunter would also be naked so that his DNA would be on Hailey. Abraham had to make sure he stayed atop her until he could reach for his gun. What Hunter wouldn't know or be told was that under his clothes, that Abraham would be holding, was a concealed gun. The moment Hunter rises from Hailey's body and steps away from her body, Abraham will walk to the side of him and shoot him in the temple.

Once both loose ends were tied up, he would call his boss and suggest that they dismantle the club and get the hell out of Dodge. Abraham knew his boss would be pissed at having to close up shop but it was the only way if they wanted to stay out of prison. Abraham also was fearful that he would be in his boss's crosshairs because he was ultimately in charge of the operation. However, he would argue that it was Hunter to blame for not knowing how to keep his dick in his pants.

Abraham walked towards the front entrance of Hunter's building and entered the lobby. He decided not to take the elevator since it would be quicker just to climb the three flights of stairs. Since the apartment belonged to the business and was given to Hunter as part of his salary, Abraham had a master key. He used it now to gain entrance into the apartment. The apartment was dark and quiet. He tried to turn on the hallway lamp but it didn't work. He ran his hand along the wall until he hit the light switch for the living room but that also didn't work. It wasn't a feeling of dread when that second light didn't go on more like when the hairs on the back of your neck stand on end anticipating something was about to happen. His instincts proved to be accurate when he turned towards his window and saw the silhouette of someone standing by it.

He immediately drew his weapon and was about to fire when the lamp on the table alongside the window turned on.

"Jesus Christ, I almost fucking shot you. Why are you here? I already told you I had it under control," he shouted. Nothing really scared Abraham especially after doing time at the state penitentiary but the person standing by his window made him think of his mortality.

"Who gives a shit, what you told me. What you should be doing is apologizing for making me come out here to deal with you and your shit for brains crew," remarked the person by the window.

"Listen, I'm sorry you had to come here but I told you that I was going to deal with both Hunter and Hailey," pleaded Abraham.

"OK, now that I'm here tell me how you plan to deal with them," countered the person by the window.

"It's going to be a murder–suicide but it won't work with you in Hunter's apartment," Abraham snapped.

Chuckling, the person by the window simply stated, "Sorry, Abraham your brilliant plan doesn't have a chance of happening."

Abraham hoped the person couldn't see him start to perspire profusely, "Why the fuck not. Just give me fifteen minutes. They should be here in less than five."

"That's just it, Abraham," stated the person by the window as a hand rose from the side of the recliner holding a snub-nosed 38 revolver. "Hunter's already dead."

Abraham's color drained from his face, "You killed him?"

"Nah, I left that to Hailey," the person replied.

"Why the fuck would she do that?" asked Abraham.

"Easy, once I told her that you felt she was a liability and sent Hunter to silence her she was gung-ho," laughed the person by the window.

In that moment, Abraham realized that he and Hunter would be the patsy for the boss. That realization made him immediately reach for his gun but it was too late, he felt three quick rabbit punches to his chest that sent him down to the floor. He tried to get his bearings and rise up but felt his head explode like a brick had struck him then he felt nothing.

Chapter 26

As they exited Hunter's tattoo parlor, Dean suggested they get something to eat. Chris told him about one of his favorite spots in Harlem, Mana's. It was on 125th and Lenox Avenue and had some of the best-fried chicken in New York. They arrived in less than fifteen minutes without any heavy traffic to delay them. They both chose the fried chicken and cornbread and sat in the upstairs seating section since it had the least amount of people providing them some privacy to discuss the case. It also gave Chris an opportunity to contact his team and catch up on his earlier requests for information.

"My guys spoke with the principle of the academy. She said that there is no student at the academy with the name of Hailey. They did, however, discover twelve fucking Madison's and twenty-one girls, named Mackenzie, but not one fucking Hailey," laughed Chris as he continued, "but not all is lost Tonto there is some light at the end of the tunnel. They did find out that over the last two years she's heard of a group of girls that formed some type of club but it's so secretive that even her sources couldn't get any information as to what type of club it was."

"Come on, you mean to tell me especially with all those girls no one has talked about it?" smiled Dean.

"I'm surprised by that sexist stereotype comment. What are you saying all girls do is talk and gossip?" laughed Chris.

"Pretty much, don't forget I have a sister and mother and they talk nonstop don't know the word or meaning of quiet," countered Dean.

Chris smiled, "Can't argue that point but my crews were talking more about adults and administrators at the school. The Principal did indicate that rumors were that the club was so exclusive that you have to be asked to join by a current member. What's even better was that although she didn't have a student by that name, the other day a student stopped in her office to complain about a girl not from the school, by the name of Hailey."

"Now you are talking so there is a girl, named Hailey. What was the girl's complaint about?" asked Dean.

"The student said that this Hailey kept pressuring her to attend some exclusive uptown executive party in the evening after school curfew," responded Chris.

"Doesn't sound too promising, I mean parties and missing curfew, that's in a normal day of a teenager," was Dean's response.

"My thoughts exactly, and my guys also didn't put much into it. However, what piqued their interest was the other reason the girl complained was this Hailey girl told her that in order to get into the party she would have to be tattooed," explained Chris excitedly.

"Well, I stand to be corrected. All along, I've been under the impression that the FBI sat on their ass until the locals found something. Then you people would ride into town on your white stallions and take the credit. It does my heart good to know that your citizen's tax money is actually being used and not wasted on donuts and coffee," laughed Dean.

"Fuck you and that made up tribe you supposedly belong to. You want to hear more or you going to keep fucking around," laughed Chris.

"Hell yeah, what's this girl's name and can we talk to her?" asked Dean.

"Her name is Katherine and the team already interviewed her and some other girls that she identified as being part of that club the principle heard about," replied Chris.

"Alright, you got my full undivided attention," Dean responded.

"You are not going to believe this shit and I still don't know how this ties into my missing niece," replied Chris then continued, "but it seems that this girl, Hailey, was well known around the school. Although many of the students indicated that she was always on school grounds, they couldn't actually say with certainty whether she was a student or not."

"Were you able to get a description of this Hailey?" asked Dean.

"Even better, some of the girls had cellphone photos of Hailey. I'm sure she was unaware that she was being photographed," replied Chris.

"Probably, too busy talking to see someone taking her picture, nice job, you happen to have the photos?" responded Dean.

"Sure, give me a second while I pull them up," Chris replied as he opened an email message on his phone containing two photos. The first was one of Hailey alone and the second with her and two other students. He looked at the photos for a minute before turning the phone over to Dean to see.

"Wow, she's a looker and young can't be more than nineteen but can definitely pass for a sixteen-year-old. Did you get to identify the two girls she's with?" Dean asked.

"That one on her right is a girl, named Megan. The only reason one of the students showed us this particular photo is because this girl Megan tragically died the night before," replied Chris.

"Damn, that's horrible. Her parents must be devastated. Not to sound cold but that lead is done and the other girl?" asked Dean.

"The blond girl with her back to the camera is Stacey. Follow Hailey's hand and finger. You can see that she is pointing to the back of Stacey's neck which you see is a tattoo of a White Lily," stated Chris.

"Jesus wasn't full of hot air, that is a beautifully detailed piece but I could also see how doing many of those becomes mundane, no creativity at all but that also means that Hunter lied to us," countered Dean.

Chris nodded his head and added, "Bingo, which also means that asshole may have met or even spoken to my niece."

"Sorry, my friend but I have to agree with that assessment. Kudos to your team, they must have looked at thousands of photos to get these nuggets," Dean expressed in awe.

Chris smiled at not only the fact that Dean called him a friend but at his compliment of his team, "I'm not going to lie to you, they bitched and moaned about having to sit through these young girls' phones searching for pictures but they couldn't have done it without Katherine who was there to help."

"Did they get an address or location as to where our mystery girl, Hailey, lives?" asked Dean

"Unfortunately, we did not and before you ask or tell me to get Hunter for further questioning, I sent a couple of agents over to the studio to pick him up. We'll let him sweat in lockup maybe he'll be more forthcoming," Chris replied and continued, "On the financial side, no big surprises, the asshole doesn't own the shop. It actually belongs to a REIT or Real Estate Investment Trust which I just learned is a company that owns or finances income-producing real estate," replied Chris pausing a bit.

"Agree, he didn't have the brains or money to rent such a classy place. Did we get the name of the REIT Company?" asked Dean.

"Shit, can't a fucking guy catch his breath before asking a question to which I already had an answer to," laughed Chris then continued, "Yes, of course, I got the name of the company. It's owned by a big-time investment bank, Wiley and Pearson. The purchase is legal and is used as an income-producing vehicle. Hunter was hired as the managing director of the building. We've also uncovered a payment to Hunter by Wiley and Pearson in the amount of twenty-five thousand dollars for the use of his name on the business. Nice gig, if you had the right connections and it seems our Mr. Hunter did," replied Chris.

"Did you find any connections between Hailey and Hunter?" asked Dean.

"Not at the moment," sighed Chris.

"Maybe he paid her to try and get the academy girls to come in for tattoos? If so, that's how she probably came into contact with Sofia," responded Dean.

"But he told us that he doesn't recall seeing Sofia and at that point we only had Jesus telling us that maybe this Hailey may have seen Sofia at one of his parties. But we have no clear-cut connection between Hailey and Hunter. The thing we now have is that Hunter may know more then he's saying but it's still circumstantial," replied Chris.

"I still think we're getting closer. We just need to break Hunter down. He's soft and if pushed, could give up valuable information maybe another lead we could follow. Don't you guys water board for fun," laughed Dean.

"Fucking prick, go tell your ancestors to go back and see if they could renegotiate for New York but this time tell them to use money instead of beans," cracked Chris as his phone rang.

Dean had to laugh at that one but noticed Chris's demeanor change as he listened to the person on the other end of the line. After listening, Chris gave the caller instructions then looked directly at Dean, "My boys got to Hunter's apartment. The door was opened a bit so they entered fearing that he may have had an accident and may have needed medical attention. Seems like good old Hunter didn't need medical attention at all because he wasn't there. However, someone was there, dead, a male body on the living room floor."

Dean looked at Chris with curiosity, "Now why would there be a male dead body in Hunter's apartment. Do we know his identity and how he died?"

"The man was murdered, three shots to the chest in a nice pattern with the coup de grace in the forehead. The coroner thinks it was a small-caliber gun like a 38 special. We got lucky because the man did have an ID on him, Abraham Jeramiah Rogers. Ring a bell?" asked Chris.

"Nope, but I bet our boy, Hunter knows why. His aura was represented by a snake remember and although they are not known to be killers or violent, they still are like common criminals, sly and sneaky committing petty crimes like lifting a wallet or purse," stated Dean.

"Your fucking mystic mumble-jumble might actually work because you're spot on. Hunter is a petty criminal with multiple petty thief convictions plus a couple of assault and battery charges, all women of course. As for our mystery girl, Hailey, she was arrested for shoplifting but here's some fucked up information, her mother and little sister were found murdered in their apartment while Hailey was on one of her shoplifting runs. Maybe Hunter knew her from criminal acquaintances or even from girls at the school," stated Chris.

Dean shook his head, "That is some heavy shit to be carrying around for a teenager. But I'm more inclined to think the school is the link somehow. He knows girls at the school so he's around it. She probably saw the students and teachers as surrogate sisters and mothers. It may have been her way of healing or even satisfying the need to be with someone."

"So now you're some fucking, bleeding heart social worker trying to assess a teenager with a fucked-up life," replied Chris.

Dean smiled, "No I'm just trying to figure out how they all play into helping us locate Sofia. This Hailey girl is going to be our link to your niece. I don't know how or why but trust me she is the one who is going to give us that information that will help in our search."

Dean stopped for a moment put his fingers to his head then looked at Chris, "You know what; you may be on to something."

Chris laughed, "Really mind telling me what that something is."

Dean laughed, "You said maybe they knew each other through acquaintances like in the criminal system."

"Yeah, so what are you thinking?" asked Chris.

"I got a hunch. You think you could have your team scour both Hunter and Hailey's rap sheets. See who the arresting officers were for each of their arrests. And if that's not too much, do the same for that body found at Hunters?" asked Dean

"Of course, no problem but if you got something else, you're thinking about, let me know, maybe I could help with that as well?" Chris offered.

"I know you could definitely help me but I haven't thought this idea out entirely yet. I take it your heading to the crime scene at Hunters, right?" asked Dean.

"Yep, I want to walk the crime scene and see if there may be some clue as to who this Hailey person is. Who knows, I might get lucky and come across her address or better yet a phone number for Hailey? What about you, you wanna come up with me?" Chris asked.

"Actually, no, I need to head back to Jersey City. I realized that there was so much information that I forgot to ask about in the first interview with Ms. Mears that I'm going to head back to ask," replied Dean.

"Does she know that you are coming back today?" asked Chris.

"Yes, she's the one who told me to come back later in the evening," replied Dean.

"You want me to have a couple of my agents take over to Jersey?" asked Chris.

"Nah, they have an app now that text for livery service, maybe you heard of it, Uber," laughed Dean.

"Well, asshole, did you know about Lyft which is cheaper than Uber. Oh, it's an app as well," countered Chris who saw Dean smile, "Call me when you're done so that I could bring you up to speed on whatever I may have found in the apartment."

Dean was about to exit the car when he remembered something, "Hey, Chris, maybe this could help us with Hunter. I remembered a case I had back in Arizona. A native girl went missing. No one knew what happened to her or where she could be. The only information the police had at the time was from her school principal who reported her missing. He told the police that she was supposed to meet him after school to discuss college applications and their deadlines and it was not like her not to show up for a meeting regarding anything to do with school. Since she didn't cancel or call that she would be late, he decided to report it to the police."

Chris jumped in, "Why didn't he try the parents first? Maybe, she just forgot or had to do something with them."

Dean smiled, "Wow, you actually sound like a detective."

Dean saw Chris giving him the middle finger and laughed, "I thought the same thing. Now add the fact that the principal reported the same day and not the usual twenty-four hours. That made me suspicious about the principle. I thought he may have known more but I couldn't interview him because he hired an attorney right away."

"That move right there would have been a big ass red flag, so what happened?" asked Chris.

"I decided to go to the school where the principle was to meet the young girl. When I arrived, I noticed a new SUV parked out in front of the school. I learned that it belonged to the principal. Now I know you yank my chain about being Indian but there are people in the states who think we don't have electricity or even televisions."

Dean heard Chris almost choke on his own laughter, "Don't tell me you do, it'll ruin my image of kids on horseback flinging tomahawks in Custer targets."

Dean couldn't help himself on that one and laughed harder than Chris, "Shit, are you always fucking on?"

Chris smiled, "Always, I'll also be here all week, no two-drink minimum."

"Prick, now as I was saying. I remembered watching T.V. at home when a commercial came on from a car dealership selling SUVs. The commercial bragged about all of their new SUVs having a navigational system installed free. Their pitch for having the new SUV with this system was that it was that the avid outdoorsman who wanted an undiscovered secluded fishing or camp spot but didn't want to write down the location didn't have to with the new system. The system would track and plot the location into its system so that all the owner had to do was press the code name attached to the logistics recorded into its mainframe. It even displayed an area map that would plot the area's longitude and latitude," explained Dean.

"Does this long-ass story have a point and if it does, could you tell me it today," Chris joked.

"It does and here it is. In that case, I was able to convince the police to get a search warrant for the navigation company to provide a printout of the area map of the principle's car movements for the day prior and after the girl went missing," explained Dean.

"And what did you learn from the map?" asked Chris.

"It showed that the principal had gone to a location deep into the desert the day the girl went missing. Although I wasn't able to interview the principal, the police let me read his statement where he told them that he went straight home when the girl did not show up for her meeting. That contradicted the information pulled from the map in his vehicle. I convinced the police to take me to the spot in the desert identified on the map. When we arrived, it was immediately apparent that the spot was actually a shallow grave with the girl's body in it," answered Dean.

"You want to do the same with Hunter's car?" asked Chris.

"Yes, I'm sure he has the latest model, whatever and it probably contains the newest version of the same system. There may be a good chance Hailey's address or location is on it," Dean triumphantly announced.

"You've got to be shitting me, Red. You fucking hype yourself up some badass offshoot of your dad's Shadow Wolf unit, talk about visions of circus animals following you, brag about being in touch with the spirit world and now you tell me the way you solved your last missing person case with new fucking technology and not with your ancestors assistance," cackled Chris.

Dean started laughing heartily, "Listen that was all true and on point but it doesn't come together unless you incorporate adaptability and using your strengths with the resources provided to you at any given time. The resources provided to the 21st century Tohono O'odham Indian just happened to be satellite imaging uploaded into the navigation system of new vehicles. Isn't there a saying something like, 'go with the times?'"

"Indian, my ass, you're probably one-sixteenth Cherokee and the only thing that may get you some credit is that black long hair, which by the way makes you look like some fucking tall woman from the backside," Chided Chris as he smiled.

"Ass wipe, just call me if you hear anything interesting, and let's meet up tonight at the same restaurant we met at in the city," Dean responded and he could see Chris nod his head in confirmation.

Chapter 27

Hailey waited for the phone call, she knew would be coming and wasn't disappointed when her phone vibrated. She put it on that mode so that Sofia wouldn't wake up.

"We good?" was her question to the voice on the other side even before they spoke.

"Really, you thought Abraham would be a problem for me. How about asking the more important question, like what can Hailey do for me and how fast can she get it done," was the response to her question.

Hailey shuddered and knew she couldn't piss this person off. They held all the cards. She could have been easily dead or incarcerated if not for their quick action, "Sorry, my nerves are still raw after whacking that fucking pervert, Hunter. Let me start over, hey, boss, did what you asked. Do you need me to do anything else?"

"See, that wasn't so hard, was it?" asked the caller.

"Not at all, I'll make sure not to do that again," Hailey, answered sheepishly.

"OK, let's get back to the problem at hand. It seems that those fucking feds got a stick up their ass for this Sofia girl. Which is making me a bit concerned. You really fucked me on this," the caller spoke with a trace of anger boarding on yelling when Hailey interrupted.

"I told you, I had nothing to do with her. It was fucking Hunter. He was thinking with his dick. As soon as she told him, she couldn't sleep with him because she was still a virgin, the asshole thought, she would go for being a recruit for the club. I'm the one who tried to talk some sense to him. I swear to you, it was Hunter's fault. Remember, I cleaned the fucking mess up. You should be proud of my quick thinking," she hated begging but the person on the other end of the line was no fucking joke.

"OK, Hailey, I'll give you the praise you desperately seek and tell you that you get to live another day because of your quick thinking but, Hailey, make no mistake, if I find out that the girl is still breathing, you won't be," expressed the caller.

Hailey didn't like hearing that last comment. It was as though the caller knew that Sofia was still alive. If that was true, she would not get out of this alive. However, there was no way she was going to keep living a solitary life. She was desperate and in need of a family and Sofia was the closest thing to that. Hailey had to figure something out and fast because the caller would be coming to the safe house soon. She came back to reality when she heard the caller start to shout louder into the phone.

"Hailey, are you fucking listening to me!" shouted the caller.

"Yeah, there's no reason to yell. I'm telling you again not to worry. That girl is doing a Little Mermaid," she laughed.

"What the fuck does doing a little mermaid mean?" the caller asked.

"Means she's under the sea get it like the song from Disney's movie, 'the Little Mermaid,'" she chuckled.

Although the caller wanted to reach through the phone and choke the bitch, they couldn't because she just eased the tension and it was actually a good line, "Alright, I'll have to give you that one. Listen, I'm heading back to my place to change and pack an overnight bag. Once I'm done, I'll head up there to pick you up. We need to be away from this mess for a couple of days. I have another safe house upstate we could use till everything dies down."

"Will you call me before you leave your place so that I could be ready?" Hailey asked.

"Yeah, go ahead and start sanitizing the place. I'll come in and double-check everything and make sure nothing is left behind," replied the caller.

Hailey hung up the phone and now realized that the only way to keep her new family intact was to kill the caller. That was easier said than done. She needed a foolproof plan. This adversary would be like no other she's faced, the asshole was street savvy and tough as nails. She had to make sure her plan was airtight because the caller was one paranoid individual that had the ability to smell a trap a mile away.

One way may be to leave Sofia in the apartment, meet the caller in the street with her stuff and head upstate where she would kill the caller then head back to the city and live happily ever after with Sofia. She laughed to herself because the caller wanted to come into the apartment and would not be waiting outside for her. Shit, she thought why things didn't ever come easy for her. There was no choice the caller had to die in the apartment. She just needed to figure out how to do that without attracting attention. She walked across the living room towards the first bedroom in the apartment. In New York, the room was classified as a bedroom but anywhere else in the United States, it would be called a broom closet. She opened the door and there still sitting on the inflatable mattress tucked on the floor in the corner sat Sofia.

"How's my little sister doing?" asked Hailey.

Although Sofia knew Hailey was crazy, she was tired and fed up and her short and loud response expressed this, "How the fuck you think I'm doing. I was kidnapped and witnessed a murder. Oh, and for the record, you are not my fucking sister."

Hailey's smile turned inward as she strolled up to Sofia and with speed of an attacking cobra and struck Sofia with an open hand with such force that it sent her backward onto the mattress. She looked up at Hailey with murderous intentions but stopped short of retaliating.

Hailey gave her a large smile, "Listen, Sofia, the first thing you'll have to learn about living with me are the rules. The first and most important one is to show me respect. You are never to talk to me in that manner. If you do, punishment will be administered not with restricting food or entertainment but simply the palm of my hand. Next is show gratitude to me for taking care of you and not sticking you in the gut and throwing you overboard the night Hunter told me to, are we clear?"

Hailey saw Sofia give her a simple nod of acknowledgment.

"Good, now we have a slight problem that needs to be addressed. The call I just received was from my boss, who will be making an unfriendly visit."

Sofia asked in a whisper, "Why would it be an unfriendly visit?"

"I suspect that the caller knows that I lied about killing and dumping your body in the ocean. Think about it if I'm the caller and I walked in and saw that my orders were not carried out. I would put two bullets in my chest and one to my forehead for good measure. Then I would introduce you to either Smith or Wesson then sanitize the apartment. Now can you see our dilemma? I don't know about you but I'm in no mood to die today," laughed Hailey.

Sofia nodded, "Alright, I'm listening what is it we need to do so that it doesn't go down that way."

Hailey smiled jubilantly, "That's my girl, just what I wanted to hear. Well, my thinking is that it can't be fancy, just practical. I asked the caller to call me once they were near the apartment that way, I could be ready."

Sofia cut in, "OK, then what?"

"They have a key to get into the apartment. I'll be in the kitchen with my gun out and ready to rock when they open the door. I'll call out and say that I'm in the kitchen getting something to drink and ask if they wanted something. My hope is that they'll walk into the living room and sit on the couch. If that's the case, the couch faces the window where the television is also located. The news will be on, as a distraction. Since the kitchen is behind the couch, I could walk up behind them where I'll put one round behind their ear."

"You said yourself that this person is paranoid. I don't think they would give their back to someone they know is a killer," replied Sofia.

"You were paying attention. Yes, you are correct they might just come straight to the kitchen instead. If they decide to enter the kitchen first, I'll be prepared. My gun will be out with the safety off. As soon as they turn into the kitchen, a bullet will be traveling into their face but I don't think it'll be that easy, so you'll have to help me," explained Hailey.

Sofia raised both her eyebrows, "Me, how am I going to help you against such a killer, especially when I'm not armed?"

"Easy, I'm going to give you a knife. All I need you to do is to wait in the hallway ready to attack. If I am killed, they will think it is over. They won't expect you; remember you're supposed to be dead. I hope that the surprise attack will be enough for you to kill them. So, what's the verdict, you in or what?" Hailey asked.

"Shit yea, if it means staying alive and seeing my family again, I'll do anything," Sofia stated with determined confidence.

"Good, because it might just come to that," replied Hailey.

The caller knew Hailey wouldn't confess to having the girl. She had what many called a superior complex. That fucking girl thought her shit didn't stink and professed to be always right. She thought she could outsmart everyone; the young, old, male, female because of her good looks and brains.

That all may be true but in this instance, little miss know it all was not aware that the caller had installed several cameras situated along the pier leading up to the yacht's slip in the marina where Hunter took Sofia. The cameras were installed as an insurance policy for the caller. Many of the Dakota patrons liked to conduct their pedophilia away from the masses and continually used their yacht for their disgusting exploits. If any of those patrons decided not to pay for their services or suddenly grew a conscience and tried to close down the club, the caller would simply play a snippet of their deeds and remind them of their obligation and commitment to the club and its owner.

The caller had one such camera that recorded Hailey coming off the yacht with her arm under the girl's shoulders as if the girl was drunk and needed assistance. The yacht never went out into the ocean as Hailey indicated. The caller tried on several occasions to give Hailey the opportunity to come clean about the girl but she was so convinced that she successfully fooled everyone that she felt no need to admit to it. The caller still hadn't figured out why Hailey wanted the girl alive but that didn't matter. They had no choice now both Hailey and the girl must die or the caller risked being detected by law enforcement and that was not acceptable. The decision was not easy but both parties would be laid to rest tonight.

Chapter 28

Antonio walked towards Hoboken's Fiore's Deli located on Fourth and Adams streets. He was thinking about the Ham and Mozzarella sandwiches that he was going to pick up for him, Chris and Elizabeth when his cell phone chimed. He palmed it from his pocket and saw Joey's number come up.

"What's up, Joey?" asked Antonio.

"Thomas Handley," was all he said.

"Who the fuck is Thomas Handley?" asked Antonio.

"According to the dead donut man, he approached him about purchasing photos of eighth-grade girls he may have had," responded Joey.

"How did this Thomas prick know to approach your donut man?" asked Antonio.

"Come on, Boss, how we know which suckers wanna play the rackets," laughed Joey.

"Sorry, you're right. Anyone interested in playing the numbers, buying product or borrowing money usually knows of someone who ran the games, women, and drugs. Which meant that he probably was part of some sick pedophile underground network or group," replied Antonio.

"Yeah, something like that, I didn't have the time to ask the how, when, where and why questions on the particulars of whether there was a network of group but I got enough information that could maybe help us," responded Joey.

"Alright, don't keep me in suspense, what information did you get?" asked Antonio.

"This asshole, Thomas is from money and works as the vice president of a downtown investment bank. He's into young girls around fourteen or fifteen and would buy pictures of girls getting ready to go into high school. The donut guy had heard through the grapevine that our bigshot was able to purchase some photos but after he learned the girls in the photos came from the 'ghetto' his words not mine, Mr. bigshot stopped buying," explained Joey.

"What the fuck does that mean?" asked Antonio.

"Apparently, Mr. bigshot only wanted to have pictures and mess with girls that came from money," replied Joey.

"Sick and fucking picky, did you get any information as to where this Mr. bigshot got the ghetto girl pictures?" asked Antonio.

"Nope, he didn't have any information on that front," replied Joey.

"Okay, but how does this help us with finding Sofia?" asked Antonio.

"If this asshole didn't know who sold Mr. bigshot the photos, maybe he knew where he was targeting the girls with money," explained Joey.

"OK, did you find out the area the sick fuck was targeting?" asked Antonio.

"Even fucking better than an area, the guy named the school where this guy was supposedly scoping out his victims," replied Joey.

"Alright, don't keep me fucking waiting, what's the name?" asked an apprehensive Antonio.

"Sorry, Boss its Berkheart Academy, Sofia's school. Tell me how you want to play this?" asked a subdued Joey.

"Fuck, that's not something I wanted to hear," shouted Antonio stopping everyone in Fiore's from speaking or moving.

"Let me call Chris and see how he wants it done. Stay put for a minute. I'll call you back," replied Antonio. He immediately noticed the change in the atmosphere and waved his hands at the patrons and staff signaling them to go on with their business as he walked to the back of Fiores where a couple of tables were set up for original Hobokenites. He sat at the back of the store away from prying eyes and ears, pulled out his phone and dialed Chris's phone.

"What's up Antonio?" answered Chris.

"Some fucking shitty news is what I got," replied a somber Antonio.

"Shit, that's not what I want to hear," answered a weary Chris.

"Our mutual friend found out about a scumbag preying on teenage girls. He thinks this asshole may be able to give us information that could help us with Sofia," explained Antonio.

Chris didn't let him finish, "Thank god, I thought you were going to say they found our girl dead."

"I would not have been able to talk to you if that happened but this information is upsetting to me and will be to you as well. The guy's been preying on the girls from Berkheart," Antonio explained.

"I'll kill that fucking piece shit. Who is this guy?" asked an angry Chris.

"Easy, Chris, if anyone's getting whacked, it'll be on me, not you. The guy's a player on Wall Street, a vice president of an investment bank," replied Antonio.

The phone was silent for a moment, "Then you and your crew get everything you can from him then make sure that he doesn't ever hurt another girl, you understand," replied Chris.

"Loud and clear my brother. I figured that would be the route you wanted to take, I just wanted to make sure, talk to you later," answered Antonio.

"Wait, where's Joey now," asked Chris.

"He just finished up. Why, you need him for something?" asked Antonio.

"Yea, Dean just took an Uber to Ms. Mears's house in Jersey City. You think you could have Joey head there and wait for Dean to come out," Chris wasn't finished when Antonio interrupted.

"You need him to pick Dean up afterward and bring him somewhere else?" asked Antonio.

"Actually, no, what I want Joey to do is to tail Dean. He's supposed to call me after his follow-up with Ms. Mears. He said he had some questions he forgot to ask her. So I'm thinking he might find out something useful and try and go about it alone," responded Chris.

"You think he doesn't trust us? That's why he took an Uber instead of you taking him?" asked Antonio.

"No, if he didn't trust us, he wouldn't tell me where he was going. I think he doesn't want me or you to be there if or when he finds Sofia because she may not be alive," replied Chris.

"Told you, he was a fucking stand-up guy, no problem, I'll call Joey now, watch you back, brother," stated a concerned Antonio.

"Don't worry about me just you be careful," laughed Chris.

Chapter 29

The caller was still thinking about the conversation with Hailey when they opened the front door to the apartment and smelled fresh flowers. It was the only luxury allowed in the apartment and it was intended to transport the caller away from the harsh gritty hectic city life. The flowers made the apartment a more tranquil and serene oasis of calmness which allowed the caller to transcend into a relaxed state.

As that metamorphosis took place, the next order of pleasure was that cold beer and pastrami on rye sandwich that needed fixing so that they could then head over to the living room drop into the couch and watch some television. This rest and food break was essential to bring them the energy and strength necessary to eliminate a formidable foe like Hailey. She was one fucking tough-ass dirty street fighter, always coiled tight and ready to spring. Shit, many hard men tried to manhandle the "pretty teenager" only to succumb to her viciousness. She fought them as though she had Special Forces training and had participated in the first battle for Fallujah in Iraq. Her eyes carried that thousand-yard stare associated with combat soldiers. The caller knew that temperament and toughness of a mean mad dog not afraid of violence was what kept Hailey alive up until this point. It sincerely bummed the caller out that she had to be put down like a rabid dog. She had been such a vital part of the operation but their survival was paramount even if it meant Hailey's death.

Mario, the owner of Fiore's Deli, just placed Antonio's order on the table. Antonio was about to thank him when his phone starting vibrating. He looked at the number and saw Joey's name scroll across the screen.

"Hey, Joey, everything good with our boy?" asked Antonio.

"Yeah, just wanted to update you on his location, I didn't know if you wanted me to give you the play by play," replied Joey.

"I guess we'll do that since my brother wasn't too specific. What's going on with him now?" asked Antonio.

"I just got to Jersey City in time to see him emerge from that Mears house. He got into an Uber," explained Joey.

"How the fuck did you know that it was an Uber," laughed Antonio.

"Prick, the car had a visor with Uber spelled out across it," laughed Joey.

"OK, where is he now?" asked Antonio.

"He was dropped off in front of a nice apartment building in Harlem off of 126th Lenox Avenue. I was going to follow him into the building but had to turn back so I didn't get to see who in the building he went to see," explained Joey.

"Why did you turn back? He doesn't know you," responded Antonio.

"I know that but five minutes after entering and as I approached the lobby, I noticed a woman opposite me going towards the same lobby. She looked like she lived there and would have called the cops if I entered at the same time especially since I would be considered a stranger. So I just kept walking past the lobby walked around the corner and sat back in the car where I'm at now," explained Joey.

"Good move but I'm sure Chris would want to know who Dean is meeting with. Go back and get me the address and take a photo of the mailbox with the names of the residents. I'll send it to Chris and we could both look over the names to see if we know anyone," instructed Antonio.

"Alright, give me five minutes and I'll get it to you," stated Joey as he hung up the phone.

The caller finished making the sandwich, placed it on a plate lifted it with one hand and grabbed a beer with the other one. They walked slowly into the dark living room but suddenly stopped at its threshold because the hairs on their neck stood on edge, they felt a familiar, strong presence inside that room. After what felt like hours but in reality were mere seconds, the caller spoke into the living room, "What gave me away?"

"You wouldn't believe it if I told you. It was a combination of coincidence, luck, and chance that lead me to you," replied Dean

"How about I put down my tray, turn on the light? I would love to hear how exactly," asked the caller.

"Come on, Duncan, really, you think I'm that dumb to let you free your hands. Just use your elbow to turn up the light switch," said a smiling Dean.

Duncan moved slowly over to the wall and using his left elbow pushed up the light switch revealing Dean sitting on the recliner facing his couch. He also noticed Dean holding a 9mm with an attached silencer.

"Why don't you have a seat on the couch so we could talk," Dean stated.

"Sure, but with that silencer pointed at me, it's looking like after we're done talking the only one leaving this apartment alive is you, right?" asked Duncan in a nonchalant manner.

"Pretty much no need to lie to a killer especially one with your voraciousness and skill," replied Dean.

"I guess, it doesn't make any sense to beg for mercy," answered Duncan.

"Naw, plus we both know that signifies weakness and you're far from that," replied Dean.

"You're right but I also have pride and getting shot with my hands full of food and drink doesn't really elude to someone being skillful or tough," smiled Duncan.

"And fresh flowers throughout a single man's apartment does?" smiled Dean.

"Touché, nicely played, would you like to know my theory as to why you haven't told your federal friends about me or shot me yet," stated Duncan

"You may and please don't leave anything out," answered Dean but just then his phone began to ring.

"You going to answer that?" asked Duncan.

"Nope, I don't want anyone knowing I'm here with you. I would rather call the individual back when my attention could be more focused on them instead of on you," Dean simply stated.

Duncan nodded his head in understanding because he would have played it the same way.

"Well, let's start off with right now you're trying to come to grips with the knowledge that you were working with a killer right next to you without the slightest suspicion from you," explained Duncan.

Dean nodded, "Go on."

"But what you're really interested in is how could a decorated homicide detective in the greatest city in the world turn out to be a cold-blooded killer, am I on point so far," replied Duncan.

"Yep," responded Dean as he moved his gun hand slightly to signal Duncan to continue.

"Before I continue, I'm curious; you first said that it was a combination of coincidence, luck, and chance that lead you here. What exactly did you mean by that statement?" asked Duncan.

"As I'm sure you know I've been searching for a missing girl by the name of Sofia. In my investigation, we came across a girl she had come in last contact with named Carol who attended the same school, Berkheart. We went to this Carol's home and spoke with her and her mother, Ms. Mears," explained Dean.

"So, somehow, your interviews with Emily or as you know her as, Ms. Mears led you to me," a stunned Duncan replied.

Dean laughed, "Yes but let me finish. It is actually fascinating the way it all played out. In Carol's initial interview, we learned that her daughter went to the rich and exclusive woman's boarding school, Berkheart and that she got in by winning a lottery for those parents who could not afford the tuition. Now I said to myself, what were the fucking odds of winning such a lottery? I decided to do some research and find out. After the interview, I called an accountant friend of mine for the odds of such a game. He crunched the numbers and came up with a one and one hundred thirty million, one has to be fucking lucky for that to happen," laughed Dean.

Duncan snapped out it and joked, "What now you don't believe in luck."

"Nope, I'm of the sense, one makes their own luck or at least buys it," chuckled Dean then continued, "Further into that interview, Carol proudly mentioned that her brother Tommy was a captain in the NYPD and stationed in the 19th precinct. I remembered that you were stationed there. I asked her if she knew of you. Bingo, she said that she not only knew you but was a close friend as well," explained Dean.

"So far it is still just coincidence which still doesn't explain how you knew it was me. By the way, you think I could put this shit down my arms are tired," asked Duncan

"You're right that didn't yet do it for me and no keep your arms where they are, you curl more weight than that. I only knew it was you after she volunteered more information without me having to ask another question," stated Dean.

Duncan chuckled, "She did always have a problem with running her mouth."

"She told me that you and her brother came up in the academy together and were promoted to first-grade detectives at the same time. Here's something interesting, you could have been promoted to management but chose to stay with the boys in the Homicide Unit. She said her brother wanted the promotion and took it. That was what made me start to suspect you," smiled Dean.

"Come on, how the fuck does me not wanting a promotion automatically make you suspicious of me," replied Duncan.

"I worked with a lot of cops and for the most part, the only thing they look forward to, is their retirement. Usually, they want to retire with the highest amount of earnings possible. In order to do that, one needs to get as much rank as possible since the retirement board averages one's last three years of service. The higher the position the more money your pension will be. Your partner followed the pattern but you didn't. I thought that meant you were either already rich or had money earning on the street giving you straight-up cash, and I thought it was the latter because of your wardrobe and ride."

"That was good analysis but unfortunately flawed. You didn't take into account that many of us in the trenches hate management enough not to be part of it. That's the reason I declined the promotion," responded Duncan.

"I can see that happening with other detectives and I wanted to give you the benefit of the doubt. That's why I went back to Emily for some follow-up questions. That second interview sealed it for me."

Duncan cut in, "How so?"

"Well first thing, you are right about her not knowing how to keep her mouth shut. Second, she really thinks of you as family. All I had to do was ask about you and she gave me everything including the most revealing piece, not only did her brother come up with you but her husband's cousin, Danny got on the force. Her brother got Danny to be assigned as your fucking partner," stated Dean.

"Fucking best partner and friend anyone could have hands down," responded Duncan.

"Really if he was that much of a friend, why'd you fucking kill him," replied a disgusted Dean.

"Shit, you figured that out, congratulations, Chief getting closer. That was maybe the hardest thing I had to do but essential in order for me to survive," explained Duncan.

"Survive what, your reputation, from working with you its spot on. What the hell changed for you to kill a man you trusted with your life," asked Dean.

"I got a tip from a friend from Internal Affairs that they were going to start investigating the both of us. Someone in the community dropped a dime on our illegal extracurricular activities. Once IA had that information, they had to open a case on us. It would have been ugly if they found us out. That same IA contact told me that IA was going to pick up Danny for questioning. It would only be a matter of time before he turned and testified against me for immunity. I couldn't let that happen. We were running multiple hustles including hooking girls from Berkheart, fleecing the local drug dealers and offering protection to the local stores," explained Duncan.

"You mean peddling minors to fat-rich men, you sick fuck," responded Dean.

"Don't get fucking sanctimonious on my ass. I know you killed without conscience. And those rich teenage girls from Berkheart were fucking old men long before my crew came around. The only difference is with me running them, they got to earn money for something they gave for free," countered Duncan.

"Who the fuck said it was any of your business whether they were fucking for free or not. Maybe you didn't realize it but they had a choice on who they wanted to fuck. Your way took away their choice and made them prostitutes," responded Dean.

"I decided it was my business. If this shit was going down in my sector, it meant it was open for us to exploit and we did. Danny had no problem with any of our hustles as long it paid well and he stayed in the shadows. Shit, he's the one that wanted his cousin's daughter, Carol to go to Berkheart as payback for his cousin getting him hooked up with force. He thought since we dealt so much with their students, faculty, and donors, Carol would have an in with them."

Dean interrupted Duncan, "Speaking of Berkheart that little hustle with the lottery put the final nail in your guilty coffin. Emily confessed to me that you and Danny talked to a couple of donors that gave money to Berkheart about the lottery. She didn't have to tell me that you guys blackmailed them into taking Carol. The piece I can't figure is how you got hooked up with the students at Berkheart in the first place."

"That's easy. Danny and I were successful because we didn't run the hustles alone. We had ears, eyes, and bodies everywhere. You have to understand that the money coming to us was from rich, powerful and connected people. All I had to do, to keep it running, was to grease every palm that could help or hurt it. That included the entire crew of doormen at the Dakota, who keep an eye on who came into the building and who called us if there was a problem. A lot of money went to our brothers in blue that we used for protection or information. Everyone knows your local politicians needed compensation, money and ass. But in all honesty, and I tell you all this because I know you're not letting me walk out of here alive you should be killing the parents of the girls working for us. You see, Mr. High and fucking mighty, the parents of our girls were the first ones on line, looking for a fucking payment, once they learned their daughters were selling ass. We paid them as well for their secrecy or like they called it discretion," laughed Duncan.

"That's fucking disgusting but please continue with your explanation on how all this came to be," responded Dean as he again flicked his gun hand to prod Duncan on.

"I have to say your fucking case, this missing girl turned out to be some kick in the balls," laughed Duncan.

"How's that?" asked Dean.

"I've been running that school ring for over three fucking years with no problem. Don't get me wrong we had to deal with local politicians beating the girls, maybe a cop or two getting freebies without my permission, even had to entertain an investigative journalist just to keep this shit quiet. And here comes some friggin Indian searching for a missing girl and with all the fucking illicit prostitution in the five boroughs, she happens to be seen with my girls. What a cluster fuck this turned out to be. Shit, it was a good fucking run though, sorry, had to vent," smiled Duncan.

"Sometimes one's luck runs out, it just happens to be your turn at the 'I'm fucked table,'" laughed Dean.

Duncan nodded his head in agreement, "I know you didn't come here to hear me, bitch. You want to know how I was able to get that academy angle, right."

"Bingo, give that contestant the prize," replied Dean.

"I've already mentioned the various people that we had to pay off but the most important one has been a New York City Parole Officer. He's fucking more bent then the letter S. I had caught wind of the asshole when he recruited some of his parolees to rob stores in my sector. At the time, he didn't know that the stores were under my protection. One day, we had gone to a liquor store over on 96ᵗʰ and Lexington. When we entered, this assholes parolee was shaken down the owner. You should have seen the owner happy as shit that we were there. He ratted the guy out within seconds of our being there," Duncan laughed, "the kid almost shit his pants. We took him out back, first beat the living shit out of him then got him to tell us about his parole officer. After that day, we owned the asshole and used him to help recruit our workforce. Anytime someone was placed on his book, we knew about it," Duncan had to stop explaining as Dean chimed in.

"What does that mean, in his book?" asked Dean.

"Sorry, it just means the roster of parolees he has to manage. We in law enforcement refer to it as a book," answered Duncan as he saw Dean waved his gun to go on, "Well, he had contacted me about a white-collar ex-con that had recently been put on his books. This ex-con knew everything there was to know about the financial markets. Prior to being locked up, he was one of the top financial advisors in the city. So, I thought since I was making money hand over foot, it was time to play the stock market. My guy gave me his address and I went to his home and explained to him that he now worked for me. In case you want to know why he would even think about doing it, we told him we could have his probation to be revoked," explained Duncan.

"What was he in for, insider trading?" asked Dean and then added, "Go ahead and place the plate and drink directly in front of you on the floor, slowly," Dean stated.

"Thank you and by the way, nice fucking move removing the coffee table. I guess, you figured I would have probably kicked it at you before rushing you," laughed Duncan as he continued, "Not insider trading, the firm he pledged allegiance to turned out to be part of a Ponzi scheme. The owners left him as the patsy and he took a hard ass fall. I did a background check on him and found out that he had a checkered past as well. Matter of fact, his father was murdered. Cops had eyes on him for the job but couldn't prove it. My thought has always been once a criminal always a criminal so I approached him and made him an offer he couldn't refuse."

"What a fucking sucker. So he believed you could violate his probation, which would automatically send him back to prison," laughed Dean.

"Wouldn't you if it was your word against a highly decorated homicide detective?" smiled Duncan.

"My bad, I made the statement even before realizing that you were in the driver's seat with that hook. What was this guy's name?" asked Dean.

"Abraham like in the bible," replied Duncan.

Dean put his hand out in stop motion, "Wait. I heard that name before, was that the body that was found at that kid Hunter's apartment with four 38 slugs in him today."

Duncan nodded his head in affirmation, "The one and only."

Dean continued, "what did you use to cap him with that 38-throwaway wrapped around your ankle," Dean stated pointing his gun hand towards Duncan's right ankle.

"I had to put him down. The idiot and his moron assistant panicked when you and the feds starting asking questions about the girls from the school. Then you were going to actually talk to some of the girls and they both shitted a brick. It was sooner or later before the asshole gave me up," replied Duncan.

"Did they actually know about the girls being run out of the school?" asked Dean.

Duncan laughed, "The school prostitution ring actually was being overseen by Abraham, and Hunter was his office manager."

"I still don't get how it all started," asked Dean.

"Innocently, believe it or not, Danny and I have the school in our sector. One day, we were collecting protection money from one of the cafes across the street from the school. Girls from the school would go there for lunch. One particular day, we were standing next to an older man. This guy smelled and looked like money dressed in an Armani suit with shoes to match. The girl came into the café with her knee-high socks and short school skirt and a tight-fitting blouse tucked into it. The guy maybe didn't realize he was talking out loud when he said he would pay anything to fuck that young girl," explained Duncan.

"And from that, you came up with fucking pedophile prostitution," gasped Dean.

"Listen I was about money and getting as much as I could. Here was a situation that presented itself to me. I took the next step and whispered to the guy, if you got the money, she's yours," stated Duncan.

"Did the guy look at you like the sick fuck you are and beeline it out of the café?" asked Dean.

"Quite the opposite, his only question was how much? And there it was Berkheart was open for business," answered Duncan who saw that Dean was still confused; "I also had administrators from Berkheart on the payroll like the Director of Funding. The guy was dipping into the school fund and Danny found out about it. So we paid him a visit and asked that he provide a little kickback to us when he took for himself. I was able to use his influence to allow a young girl that worked for me, hang around the school and the students. I used the young girl to recruit the girls that wanted to earn extra money by sleeping with old fucks."

"That's when you decided to look at your other hustles to help with the ring, right," stated Dean.

"You want me to finish or you going to fucking interrupt every five minutes," chuckled Duncan then continued, "Yep, nowadays these fucking kids do so much shit to their bodies like get tattoos and piercings. I went back to my man at parole and asked him to hook me up with a tattoo artist with a good street rep. That's where Hunter comes in. He was on the books for drug possession. We couldn't recruit the girls because they already had money and usually had no problem getting whatever they wanted. What I needed was a young girl like them to blend in and talk about how she was doing something outrageous and getting paid for it. These fucking rich girls love to think that rebel shit is cool so what better than to have a fellow student doing shit under the nose of the school and parents. I didn't know of any girls in the school except Carol but I knew she wouldn't go for it."

"You are one sick fucking person," Dean stated, "and it's a shame that young girls would degrade themselves like that, these kids nowadays have some serious mental problems."

"You would be surprised how easy it was to recruit these girls," was all Duncan could add.

"Which reminds me the girl that recruits for you, and was seen by the other girls I've interviewed is Hailey right," replied Dean.

Duncan nodded his head approvingly, "That girl had to grow up fast, if not, she would have been giving free ass to the dealers and junkies that surrounded her mother."

"Is that how you came to know her, you were one of those dealers?" asked Dean.

"Fuck you. I got more class than that to be fucking around with a meth ho but listen you have to hear this girl's story. It's fucking unbelievable, matter of fact if I wasn't there, I sure wouldn't have. She lived with her mother and younger sister over on 103rd and 1st Avenue in what we called in the neighborhood as the 'white boy projects.' This particular set of housing projects consisted of the trashy white poor New Yorkers. In other New York City housing projects, blacks and Hispanics were the population and the drugs available was either Heroin or Crack, not in her projects. Meth ruled in those apartments and her mother was hooked on it. So much she sold her body on an hourly basis to anyone who would buy her a ten-dollar rock," explained Duncan.

"She did that with this Hailey and the sister in the apartment?" asked Dean.

"Of course, they saw and heard everything. Now, it was just dumb luck that I got to the apartment when I did. Usually, Danny and I will not respond to a domestic disturbance call but we just left a Chinese restaurant we loved right next door. We were also bored so we decided to take the call. When we got to the apartment door, it was unlocked so we entered on the premise someone may have been hurt. The apartment showed signs that a struggle had taken place, papers, and books on the floor, selves that held the books hanging from the walls. The couch overturned with blood covering it and splattered against the wall. It was serious; we drew our weapons and began to clear each room. When we entered the kitchen, Hailey was standing there in a daze with blood all over her body," explained Duncan.

"Who did she stab, one of her mother's johns?" asked Dean.

Duncan smiled, "They would have definitely deserved it. No, she slit her mother's throat."

Duncan saw Dean's face pale, "Why the fuck would she do that?"

"She wanted Hailey and her baby sister to start contributing to the family," replied Duncan.

"You mean she killed her mother because she was asked to work and chip in. That doesn't make sense," stated Dean.

"It does if by working meant she meant giving up your ass to strangers," explained Duncan.

"Fuck, that is some sick shit, did the younger sister witness the killing?" asked Dean.

"Yes, but she wouldn't have been a good witness," responded Duncan.

"Why, she would have been too traumatized?" countered Dean.

"Nope, dead, Hailey stabbed her to death," a nonplussed Duncan replied.

"Holy shit, why the fuck did she do that?" asked an exasperated Dean.

"According to Hailey, they were all in the kitchen with her mother. Her mother took the opportunity to tell them that a man would be coming to the house shortly to sample her at first she thought it was us, cops and I tried to tell her we were not there for her but she didn't believe us. Hailey did not take kindly to that and flat out told her mother no. Her mother was not taking no for an answer and grabbed Hailey by her hair. Luckily, for her, she had been holding a knife as she was preparing a meal for her and her sister. Once balanced and in control, she was able to stand and face her mother. It was at that point that she grabbed her mother's hair and pulled her head back as she slit her throat," explained Dean.

"Jesus Christ, those poor girls," was all Dean could say.

"I told you she had a fucked-up life but it gets worse. Her sister had seen the whole thing. Hailey told me up to that point her sister was a meek shy girl. The moment the knife left her mother's throat and she saw her fall to the floor dead something snapped insider of her. She exploded in a rage and attacked Hailey. Hailey was trying to hold her back because she didn't want to hurt her sister but she saw her grab another knife from the kitchen counter. She said to her disbelief her sister lunged at her with the knife intending to kill her. Hailey was bigger and stronger so she was able to redirect the knife from her towards her sister. The momentum easily took the knife directly into her sister's chest instantly killing her," explained Duncan.

Stunned Dean could not speak for a moment, "That may be the saddest thing I've ever heard. Neither child had a fucking chance. But it still doesn't explain how Hailey goes from a double murder to a recruiter for a pimp."

"Ouch, do I look black or Puerto Rican to you? I'm no pimp. What I was doing was providing entertainment to powerful men nothing more nothing less," smiled Duncan.

"Not only are you one sick fuck but a racist bastard as well," simmered Dean.

Duncan was enjoying the fact that he was pissing Dean off. Shit, he thought it's the only thing he had left before Dean killed him, plus it also gave him an opportunity to brag about his operation.

"Naw, not a racist, if anything, I would call myself an entrepreneur. Now prior to entering that apartment Danny and I were already running girls at Berkheart. It was a small operation at the time. After a couple of months, we started hearing that a couple of Wall Street brokers whose daughters were attending the school without their kids' knowledge were taking a couple of juniors and seniors to diner and hotels. Those men thought no one knew about those trysts but teenage girls can't keep their mouths shut and the streets picked up on it, and like I told you we had eyes and ears everywhere. We met with those girls and told them they should be making money for their hard work and all we wanted was a cut. They were smart enough to know we would be providing protection and safe location for their affairs," explained Duncan.

"You make it sound so simple, child prostitution and enslavement," seethed Dean.

"Damn, take it easy, no one ever got hurt and all were satisfied with the arrangements. Over time, we realized that this was a cash cow so like all business models, expansion was the next step. The only problem was once these girls graduated the men, we targeted lost interest since they wanted minors not adults. We needed a plan to keep them interested and the money flowing. Seeing Hailey beaten, bruised and bloody but looking defiant and tough, it was evident she could be the one to help grow our operation," explained Duncan.

"How so?" asked Dean.

"Well, she was fucking gorgeous and more importantly, young. That made it easier to plant her into the school. She also had that charisma most popular kid flocked to. She started recruiting immediately and was so successful that we had girls begging to be part of our club. We decided to brand our product with lily tattoos as a way of induction and control. That's where Hunter and Jesus came in with Abraham running the whole operation. It was one fucking moneymaker until now. I guess its poetic justice that a young girl not part of the club would be the one to bring it down." Duncan gave a hearty laugh.

Chris was in his office downtown when his cell phone chimed. He saw it was a friend of the family, "Hey, Joey, what's up?"

"Same old shit, Handsome, Antonio give you the rundown on where I'm at?" asked Joey.

"Yea, just waiting on you with the names, I'll check them in our database see if he's seeing someone know to us. Go ahead and read me the names, go slow though, I can't type for shit," laughed Chris.

Joey laughed as well, "Fucking technology thank god, my kids know something about this shit. OK, I'm in the lobby vestibule standing in front of the mailboxes and the first I see is last name, Abbott first initial C. Next is Bowman first initial F."

Chris smiled to himself, "At least, it's in alphabetic order, but nothing so far."

"Next up is Coleman first initial R., next up is Duncan first initial M."

Joey was going to the next name when Chris stopped him.

"That, Duncan, has to be Dean's friend from NYPD. He probably wants his help with something. Listen Joey go ahead and head up there and introduce

yourself and tell Dean you're going to tag along with him until I catch up with him," explained Chris.

"He won't be pissed that you're having him followed?" asked Joey.

"Naw, I'm sure he expects it and make sure you make nice with Detective Duncan, just in case you need him in the future," laughed Chris.

"Fuck you, Handsome, already know a pig no need to have another one in my business," chortled Joey after hanging up. He was about to ring Duncan's bell but didn't have to as a man came out from the elevator and opened the front door allowing Joey to step into the lobby. The mailbox associated with Duncan listed his apartment as 3A. When he entered the lobby, Joey could see the first door by the entrance to the stairwell was 1A. That meant Duncan's apartment was on the third floor by the entrance to the stairwell. Since Joey always prided himself on his looks and body, he would take the stairs instead of the elevator.

"I'm sure, Hunter, Jesus and Hailey are on the run any idea where I can find them?" asked Dean.

"Jesus, you don't have to worry about he wasn't involved in the operation. Abraham used him for what he was a tattooist. As for Hunter, no need to look, I had Hailey take care of that punk ass. But Hailey's a different story, Dean, what would make you think that I'd give her up?" smiled Duncan.

"Oh come on, that's easy. You're the type of person who needs to win at everything. Take now, for instance, you are good as dead but, in your mind, since I don't know where Hailey is and you do. In your book, you now will die knowing that I'm fucked making you the clear winner of this standoff," explained Dean.

Duncan laughed, "Shit is that's exactly what I'm doing, trying to go down winning. You got me Dean and your right once I'm dead, Hailey's in the wind and you and anyone else is fucked."

"On that point your right, she'll be gone. However, you're wrong about winning," Dean, explained as he saw Duncan raise an eyebrow.

"What do you mean, I'm wrong about winning?" interjected Duncan.

"Well, if she got away from me, then she not only beat me but you as well. She'll be debt-free from you, plus she probably has some of your money hidden for a rainy day like today," explained Dean.

Duncan hit his leg and laughed, "Damn that is a good point. Listen, I could live with being bested by a fucking Indian probably descendent from Geronimo. People would talk about me going out like a man. But if I let Hailey live and take my money with her, my name would bring laughter and not respect."

Dean just stared at Duncan as he rationalized aloud and thought to himself, what a fucking sick egotistical bastard this guy is but he let him continue.

"You should have been a shrink, that mental shit you just pulled was golden. I liked it so much that I'm going to hand Hailey over to you. She's holed up at my safe apartment in Riverdale." He gave Dean the address and added, "No one knows the address but her so she should be alone," responded Duncan when he stopped for a second before speaking, "How did you get the captain to give you my address?"

Dean was impressed with Duncan's quick deduction, "What makes you think she gave me your address?" replied Dean.

Duncan smiled, "The only person that knows my actual home address is the captain. I used a fake address in my personal files. The sergeant in human resources loved fifteen-year-old brunettes. Hailey doesn't even have this address."

"Your instinct about her wanting to be the first female chief was on point. All I had to do was tell her that my case was about to break but I needed your help to get it done. She wanted to know if it would make the press. I told her I believed it would and with that, she gladly told me. So, in reality, the only winner out this mess will be her when she's promoted," Dean could see that he struck a nerve because Duncan was no longer smiling.

"That fucking conniving bitch, I knew she couldn't be trusted. I'm going fuckin kill her," yelled Duncan as he reached down towards his ankle holster.

"NO," yelled Dean as he pumped two rounds into Duncan's chest. Dean sat there glad he had the gun cocked and ready to fire. He was taken aback by Duncan's violent reaction towards his captain for just providing his address. Dean got up was about to go wipe his fingerprints from everything he touched in the apartment when he realized that he was wearing gloves. He removed the silencer from his gun. He put the gun in his shoulder holster and the silencer in his cross-body chest bag. The bag held his gun as well as his native weapon of choice (the tomahawk) and a first aid kit with extra ammunition. His sister always busted his chops about the bag telling him women used such a bag to carry children. Dean always felt good when thinking about his baby sister but now was not the time. He had to focus his energy on Hailey because her presence was in the air and he knew a bloody battle was afoot. He walked over to the light switch by the front door and turned off the lights. He took one last look at the apartment before slowly opening the front door and stepping into the hallway. He slowly closed the door and turned towards the elevator where he abruptly stopped.

"You must be Duncan's Captain," Dean asked trying to shake off his immediate surprise at seeing Duncan's captain standing ten feet from him pointing a gun at him.

"And why can't I be the girlfriend?" smiled the captain.

"He told me that only one that knew the address was you. Plus you knew I was coming here since I asked you for his address," replied Dean.

"Guilty, listen while I have you here, you didn't go in there and derail my chances to become chief of police, did you?" asked the captain, "Cause I was close to making a case against him that would have made it a lot easier and faster to that top spot."

She looked at Dean and knew her ticket to the top ended with Duncan's death at the hands of Dean. The only way to save it was to kill Dean and spin it to her advantage. He killed a decorated cop and she stopped a cop killer. She smiled at the cleverness and irony.

Joey made it to the third-floor landing and was about to open the door to the hallway when he heard voices talking. If he heard it right, it sounded like Dean was talking to a woman. He put his hand on the handle and began to push down on it to open the door.

Dean saw her devilish smile immediately knew he was a dead man. He wasn't disappointed as he instantly saw flames explode in front of his eyes and felt his chest cave in with the force of an anvil being thrown from a rooftop.

As the door slid open slowly Joey recognized the woman as the one that came into the building behind Dean. She was pointing a gun at Dean. He stepped into the hallway allowing the door to begin to close. The woman didn't notice Joey yet, so he slowly reached into his jacket for his gun. Joey could see her hand moving like she was about to pull the trigger.

"No!" yelled Joey as the woman's gun flashed twice. After the second shot, the Captain heard a male's voice shouting behind. She quickly turned with her gun moving along with her. Joey was momentarily stunned when he saw Dean fall as he was shot but had the presence of mind to pull his weapon at the same time he yelled. He and the Captain's guns found their targets at the same time both firing seconds apart engulfing the hallway with fire, smoke, and cordite.

Chapter 30

Chris had been calling both Dean and Joey for the last ten minutes but neither was answering their phones. He decided to try Antonio who may have had luck in speaking with one of them.

"Hey, Antonio, you get in touch with either Dean or Joey in the last ten or fifteen minutes?" asked Chris.

"Nope, I told Joey to call you with anything. What's a matter you worried?" asked Antonio.

"Nah, just hate waiting for someone to get back to me," responded Chris.

"Head up there yourself and check it out," was Antonio's response.

Chris started laughing, "That's what I'm doing now. I'm driving uptown to an NYPD Detective's apartment by the name of Duncan. Dean knows him from a couple of cases he's worked with NYPD. I'll call you back once I get there."

It was the gurgling sound coming from his right side that stirred Dean from his sleep. He didn't remember falling asleep though. He concentrated a little harder then slowly opened his eyes and moved his head towards the sound. Shit, he could see the Captain sitting up alongside the wall by Duncan's apartment door. She had one of her hands covering her neck right below her chin. Blood was seeping through her fingers. She had been shot in the neck. He thought that was impossible because he didn't have a chance to draw his weapon. He craned his head away from the Captain towards the stairwell and elevator and could see the soles of someone else who was lying down on the hallway floor. He initially tried to sit-up by placing both palms on the floor in order to push himself up but he couldn't move his left arm. So he rolled to his right side and used his right arm to push himself into a sitting position. He looked at his arm and saw that he had been shot in his shoulder. Blood was seeping through his shirt and jacket. He quickly assessed the rest of his body and found that another bullet had deflected off the handle of his tomahawk situated in his chest cross bag. He knew if that handle was not there, he would have certainly died. Dean finally stood and walked over to the Captain. She couldn't speak but still tried to communicate with Dean. At first, he couldn't read her lips but as she slowed her lip movements, he understood the one word she was trying to convey, "Help."

He smiled down at her, reached into his bag and pulled out his tomahawk, "Sure I'll help you just like you helped him down there and tried to do with me," replied Dean. He then placed the dull end of the ax head on top of the hand covering her neck wound. He pushed down with enough pressure that gave her no choice but to drop her hand. He held her hand down as the open neck wound started pumping out blood. The Captain's eyes widened and began to tear as she realized that he was making sure that she bled to death.

Dean pushed against the Captain's chest with the tomahawk to make sure she was dead. Once satisfied, he slowly walked over to the body on the floor. He was about to kneel down to see if the man had any identification on him when his phone began to vibrate. Dean looked down at the screen and saw that it was Chris calling him. He decided that he could wait to call him back because he needed to see who this person was and get the hell away from the carnage before the police arrived.

Joey Gregorio was the name listed on his New Jersey driver's license. He still held onto a 38 special handgun and was dead as a doorknob. The Captain's bullet struck him just above the right cheekbone. Dean checked his jacket pockets and lifted a cellphone and keys to a Mazda. He silently thanked the man for coming to his aid and figured him to be a friend of Antonio's. He'll have to thank Antonio if he survived the next twenty minutes. Dean opened the door to the stairwell and as fast as he could ran down to the lobby.

In a matter of seconds, Dean deduced where Joey had parked his Mazda. If he was following someone and they entered a building, he would have parked across the street about forty feet from the entrance, preferably by a fire hydrant so that pulling out or backing out would not be a problem. So the first thing Dean looked for as he exited the building was a fire hydrant across the street. He spotted the fire hydrant immediately and right next to it was a black CX-5. He laughed to himself because as he hit the open-door button the horn sounded. He should have thought about using the keys instead of analyzing the area.

He pulled out and drove about ten minutes before finding a park. He quickly pulled in under several trees alongside the street. He immediately opened his bag and removed the first aid kit. The gauze pads and medical tape were already situated at the top so that access could be quick. Dean didn't have the time to clean out the shoulder wound so he just covered it with gauze and taped it up. He pulled out into the street and headed towards what he believed was going to be the climax to his search for Sofia.

Chapter 31

The address Dean had gotten from Duncan was about a twenty-minute drive. He needed to confront Hailey alone and not with either Chris or Antonio. In his mind, he wasn't sure if this Hailey knew where Sofia was or if she actually had her at the apartment but he couldn't chance Chris or Antonio jeopardizing the situation. However, he was not at one hundred percent sure about facing Hailey alone after hearing her history from Duncan. He knew she would be a worthy adversary. So he decided to hedge his bets. He would call Chris about ten minutes into the drive and explain Duncan's role in all this then give him the address to the safe house. If he is not able to neutralize Hailey by himself, it would fall onto Chris to get the job done. After driving for about ten minutes, Dean made the call to Chris using Joey's phone.

"Hey, Joey, did you get to introduce yourself to Detective Duncan and Dean?" asked Chris.

"Sorry, Chris, it's Dean, not Joey," stated a somber Dean.

"Dean, where in the hell have you been? I've been trying to get you the phone. And why are you calling me from Joey's phone," asked Chris.

"I'll tell you that in a minute, where are you right now?" asked Dean.

"Around the corner from Duncan's place, you could tell me more when I get there," replied Chris.

"Keep driving and meet me at the following address," advised Dean.

"Fuck, that's about twenty-five minutes from here. Why there instead of Duncan's place?" yelled Chris.

"I'll tell you as you drive to the address, make sure your phone is on speaker. I don't need you getting into an accident," calmly replied Dean.

The calming response had the desired effect. Dean could hear Chris taking deep breaths to calm himself down, "Sorry about the yelling, I'm tired and running on empty. Is Joey alright?" asked Chris.

"Sorry, Chris, but your friend was shot and killed outside Duncan's apartment," a somber Dean answered.

"Shit, what the hell happened?" asked a shocked Chris.

Dean told Chris about coming out of Duncan's apartment and being confronted then shot by Duncan's Captain. He added that when he woke up after being shot, he saw that the Captain was bleeding from a neck wound with Joey laid across from her on his back dead. He had been shot in the face. He told Chris they must have fired at the same time hitting each other. Dean told Chris that when he got to the Captain, she was barely breathing. She had her hand over the hole in her neck to stem the bleeding.

"So you left her alive in the hallway?" asked a confused Chris.

"Nope, before I got out of the building, I helped her gain entrance into another realm. It was the least I could do for what she did to me and Joey," Dean could hear Chris get choked up over the phone, "Hey, you alright?"

"Fuck no. Joey was not only a friend but family. I'm his kid's godfather. How the hell am I going to explain to him that his father's never coming back?"

Dean felt terrible, "I'm really sorry, Chris.

"It's not your fault. His kid is only seven years old and how the hell am I going to even look at his wife Annabelle without breaking down," a heartbroken Chris responded.

Although Dean didn't know Joey, he felt his heart hurting for his family, "Believe me if I had the opportunity to prevent it from happening, I would have done everything in my power to do so."

"I know, it's just something Antonio and I have to deal with, forget it for now. Did Duncan tell you why his captain might have wanted to kill the both of you?" asked a concerned Chris.

"Couldn't ask Duncan he wasn't with me," replied Dean.

"Now I'm confused, a minute ago you said you came out of Duncan's apartment. Did he stay in the apartment or he wasn't there and you decided to check it out on your own?" asked Chris.

"No, he was in his apartment dead," a nonplussed Dean replied.

"Did the captain kill him?" asked Chris.

"No, I killed him just before exiting his apartment," replied Dean.

Chris almost swerved off the road, "You fucking killed a cop, Dean. Are you fucking crazy?" It was too much Chris had to pull over in front of a fire hydrant.

"Just hear me out, Chris. Duncan was a dirty cop. When I confronted him on it, he went for his hideaway piece. I had to protect myself," stated Dean.

Chris took a deep breath, "Is that why you didn't want me at Duncan's apartment?"

"That, plus I'm going to need your help dealing with this Hailey girl," explained Dean.

195

Chris wouldn't tell Dean this but he felt he could trust him, "Go ahead I'm listening."

"Remember when I went back to talk to Ms. Mears?" asked Dean.

"Yep, you were pissed with yourself about the initial interview because you wanted to ask her more detailed questions about her brother being on the force but got sidetracked with the possible lead on the tattooist Jesus," replied Chris.

"That's right, but there was something else that I missed and that was to ask about Carol's father," replied Dean.

"Shit, you are right but don't feel bad you had a good solid lead to follow up that's why it was overlooked," responded Chris.

"Thanks for that but an integral part of a missing person case is finding out everything there is to know about the missing person's family and in this case, I fucked up by not asking about a parent," explained Dean.

"OK I get it but what earth-shattering news did the mother provide you that sent you to Duncan place?" asked Chris.

"Well, in that first interview she told me about her brother and Duncan going through the New York City Police Academy together then becoming detectives in the precinct that had both Berkheart and Hunter's place in it. We thought it was too much of a coincidence to have her brother, the school, the niece, Sofia, Jesus, and Hunter connected in some way. You had agreed that there was some connection and felt someone in the mix was either profiting or getting something valuable from one of these relationships," explained Dean.

"That's right but I didn't know how it may be connected because there was not enough information. Plus, like you, I don't believe in mere coincidences," replied Chris.

"You were half right someone did profit from all of the connections but it wasn't the brother," explained Dean.

"Let me guess, it was Duncan but where's the connection?" asked Chris.

"Yep, that it was. I learned that Carol's father's cousin, Danny was also a detective with the 19th precinct, you wanna guess who was his partner?" teased Dean.

"Fucking unbelievable, it was Duncan?" asked an excited Chris now that dots are being connected.

"I knew you didn't get that badge from the bottom of a Cracker Jack box," chuckled Dean, "He and Duncan were ambushed in a botched drug bust a couple of years back. The perp hit the Danny twice in the chest with a 357 magnum as soon as he stepped through the front door," stated Dean "but here's the sad part, she doesn't even blame the fucking guy, still sees him as a surrogate uncle to Carol."

"I still don't like where you are going with this because it sounds like you're saying both cops were dirty and you still haven't made the case, it's all circumstantial."

"It was but before Duncan went for his piece in the apartment we talked about what he ran on the streets with his partner," explained Dean.

"And the asshole just gave up that information?" asked Chris.

"Of course, he knew he was a dead man. His ego went into full bragging mode. It got to a point where all I needed to do was ask a question and he would answer it. One of the things I asked him was to tell me what really went down with his partner," replied Dean.

"And," was the only word Chris responded with.

"His partner was talking about wanting to start a family and wanting to slow down even considered a transfer to another division where he could maybe settle down and start a family. At the same time someone from the neighborhood they controlled dimed them out. Duncan got nervous and starting thinking that his partner would eventually go to internal affairs or IA would go to his partner. So he decided to kill two birds with one stone," explained Dean.

"Let me guess, Duncan let his partner walk into an ambush where the dealer shot him. Then the dealer was killed by Duncan, eliminating any potential witness for internal affairs and elevating Duncan to hero making it impossible for internal affairs to open a case," a deflated Chris stated.

"Yep, that's the way it went down," replied Dean.

"But how did he convince the dealer to kill a cop?" asked Chris.

"He told me that he gave the dealer a choice, kill his partner or see his wife and three toddlers get shot to death," replied Dean.

"Shit, that is one cold-blooded killer. I guess, I should thank you for snuffing that shit bird," responded Chris then asked, "But before you met up with him at his apartment, what made me start to suspect it might be Duncan?"

"The fact that Carol actually won the lottery at Berkheart, I called a friend whose job is to calculate the odds for winning various events for Vegas casinos. I asked him what would be the odds for winning the Berkheart lottery," replied Dean.

"OK, you got me on the edge of my seat. What was his answer and don't say the cliché, 'one in a fucking million,'" responded Chris.

"No, it was more like one in twenty-five thousand. In my follow-up with Ms. Mears, I told her about the odds of her winning that lottery. And to her credit, she didn't confess to cheating. She did, however, say that prior to her husband's death and her daughter being selected in the lottery, both her husband's cousin and Duncan met with school administrators. I think it was her way of saying it was fixed but she wouldn't come out and openly admit to it," explained Dean.

Dean in his mind could see Chris nodding his head, "Yeah, I would have come to the same conclusion, Duncan needed to be questioned."

At that moment, Chris's phone beeped with an incoming call, "Dean, this is the office let me get it hold on." Chris accepted the call and spoke with an agent downtown.

A couple of minutes passed before Chris came back on the line with Dean, "Just got confirmation on a different connection with your boy, Duncan."

"Why did your team uncover something that connects Duncan with Hailey?" asked Dean.

"No, not Hailey but Abraham and Hunter. It turns out that both Duncan and Danny were the arresting officers for both of them," responded Chris.

"Damn, it makes even more sense now. Listen I'm about five minutes out from the address. This Hailey is a tough son of a bitch that doesn't scare easily. When you get here, make sure you come in hot and if she's still standing put her down," Dean explained in a serious tone.

"Don't worry; if someone's standing and it's not you, I'm dropping them. But before you go let me ask you, did you leave any trace evidence, DNA or prints at the scene? *Chris didn't let Dean answer the question before he jumped in with a couple more questions.* How about cameras in and around the apartment and surrounding areas and did you think to see if there was any pointed at the building. What about witnesses?" Chris asked.

Chris could hear Dean laughing, "Now that's what I'm talking about. Instead of telling me to immediately halt and wait for officers to get here, your fucking first concern is to make sure I didn't leave any evidence that could point back to me."

Now Dean could hear Chris cracking up, "Shit, Dean, he's fucking lucky you did him a favor. Antonio and I would have had a heart to heart with the piece of shit; of course, it would have included a battery, cables, and tub of water."

Chris could hear Dean sighed heavily, "As you know Duncan told me a lot of things including Hailey's location."

"I know you said that's where you were going. Did he say why he easily gave her up?" asked Chris.

"Ego, Chris, he couldn't die letting someone best him especially a teenage girl. So by telling me, he's assured that she will lose either by being killed or imprisoned. But that wasn't why I want you to come to the address. He also told me that he was sure that Sofia was with Hailey probably against her will but still there alive."

"Shit, you should have fucking told me that first. I'll put my sirens on to clear the road faster," shouted Chris.

Dean again calmly replied, "That's why I didn't tell you first. I knew you would rush to get here at the same time. Please don't use the sirens, I don't want to alert the neighborhood and like I said come in hot. There's something else I need you to do."

"Damn, how the hell am I going to do something else when I'm fucking speeding to the address you gave me," replied Chris.

"Ask Antonio to put some of his men on this," suggested Dean.

That request piqued Chris's interest because to use Antonio's men meant something illegal and not meant for him, "Go ahead and tell me."

"Duncan also provided me with information about two individuals. Although they did not kidnap your niece, their involvement in illicit child pornography and exploitation made it possible for all the parties directly related to Sofia being held captive to thrive which provided the mindset and opportunity for her abduction," explained Dean.

"Alright, if it means it would help girls in the future that may be targeted by these scumbags, then give me the names and Antonio and I will take of it," a somber Chris replied.

"The first person he named was a big wig vice president of an investment bank linked to the academy. Duncan told me that this vice president had requested that he arrange for some young female teenagers to have sex with some Japanese businessmen in order to secure an international contract with Japan. That's how the White Lily Club was born out of that initial group of academy girls," explained Dean.

"Consider the piece of shit no longer among the living. Go on, give me the other shit face," replied Chris.

"This one is going to be priceless. The way in which Duncan ran his schemes was with the help of an employment recruiter but not just any recruiter. He used a parole officer that handled his district," Dean explained.

"Shit, there's another connection we couldn't explain. I have to admit that is some slick shit having an advance scout know each parolee's history and using it to his advantage. All this asshole needed to do was get a request from Duncan then look through his parolee book for the right match," an exasperated Chris replied.

"That's exactly it. This parole officer would call Duncan whenever someone new was added to his book that they could extort. His primary job was to target ex-cons that could do work Duncan needed and convince them to play for the team," Dean stated.

"Damn, Dean, there may be a slight problem this one," remarked Chris.

"And what would that be," replied Dean.

"Do we let him take the easy way out by fucking putting a bullet in his head or let him rot with those he fucked with on the inside," laughed Chris.

"Doesn't matter to me, let Antonio decide but make sure he's off the street for good," replied Dean and proceeded to give Chris the contact information on both subjects.

After hanging up with Dean, Chris dialed his brother, Antonio. He picked up on the first ring and before he could speak, Chris jumped right in, "Take these this name down and make sure he doesn't see the sunrise. Second, get to this address A fucking SAP. Sofia's there. Dean's about five minutes from reaching her but I'm 15 minutes out."

"Shit, Chris, I'm out the fucking door and consider those two extinct," shouted Antonio as he deftly ran out of his office and towards his car all the while dialing the number to one of his capos.

Chris made a second call this time to his Senior Special Agent, Johnson, "There is no time, Dean found Sofia and I'm on my way to meet him at the location," Chris was explaining before being interrupted by agent Johnson.

"Where, give me the address and I'll get aviation and SWAT on it?" replied a jubilant Johnson.

"Great ideas but no, Dean, and I will handle it from here. However, write this name down. I want you to arrest him and take him downtown," replied Chris.

"What do you want me to charge him with?"

"Think of something, he's a parole officer blackmailing his parolees to participate in illegal activities and if you need some motivation, he's involved with Sofia's disappearance?" a somber Chris added.

"Consider it taken care of and call me with news on Sofia, please," replied Johnson.

Chapter 32

Once Hailey left the room with her food tray, Sofia took the time to again look for a way to escape. It did not contain a window so she had to nix the idea of escaping through one. She again came back to the same conclusion in order for her to escape the room it would have to be through the door and the only way to do that was to confront Hailey. Was she ready to do that? Ready or not, she had to if she wanted to see her family again.

Sofia thought the best way to approach the pending confrontation with Hailey was too make use of the advantage of her warped thinking. She thought Sofia was her new little sister and in a sick, twisted and crazy way, it showed that she was capable of love. But for Sofia, it was that love that was her weakness and easily exploited. Her plan was to approach her as the younger sibling. She will defer to her older sister by acquiescing to her elder siblings' whims. To do this, she would loosely stand leaning forward and as she walked she would shuffle her feet. She will purposefully hang her head down and speak softly acknowledging and submitting to Hailey's authority. Her approach would be one of acceptance and to seal it would be to embrace Hailey. It will be at that point prior to embracing Hailey that Sofia will spring on the offensive and physically attack.

Unfortunately, she had no weapons only her fists. Sofia found that both funny and ironic. Her father taught her how to throw a punch and kick. Her uncles helped with her defense, Antonio would say a good defense was a good offense then preach about picking up anything you could get your hands on. Chris would actually teach her defensive techniques used by his agents. The irony was she never thought she would have to rely on any of it. In her heart, Sofia was not sure she would survive the confrontation but her mother instilled in her a never give up mentality. She knew that she would not hesitate and would make the attempt. She told herself that it was a win-win situation, if Hailey killed her, she got to see her father again and if she survived, she got to see her mother and uncles. Yes, she thought she had nothing to lose. She took a deep breath and prepared herself for battle.

Hailey approached the bedroom holding Sofia. She returned with a tray of food and refreshments. She knew that it really wasn't a bedroom but in New York, anything with four walls no matter the size constituted a bedroom, illegal of course. The room as it was would be considered a den or office space in any other state. It contained no furniture except for a chair and mattress that lay in the corner of the space.

Hailey felt Sofia now trusted her. She removed the gag and restraints from Sofia as she slept that first night which in her mind help develop the trust between them. Hailey wanted Sofia to feel like she was her family now and more specifically her new big sister. Hailey was confident with that the trust and bonding were taking place quicker and smoother since she took her restraints off, killed the man responsible for her captivity and providing hot food and refreshments. Yes, Hailey thought it was going along smoothly.

Hailey laughed inwardly, the meal she was bringing Sofia would feed a family of four. She took great pride in the fact that she took the time to cook chicken drumsticks with mash potatoes and gravy. Shit, she even baked the girl biscuits by hand just to impress her and that wasn't all. She also wanted to add something cute to go along with the hot meal. Hailey found a Coke in an old-fashioned bottle with the date the company was born stamped on it, 1886. Damn, she thought if it was her in the same spot, she would definitely agree to be someone's sister just for this collector's Coke bottle alone. God, she loved New York where else can you buy a collector's item at a corner store for a buck fifty.

She walked up to the bedroom door and since her hands were full with the tray, she had to use her foot to kick on the door and shout lightly for Sofia to open the door.

Sofia heard the door being kicked and Hailey asking her to open the door because her hands were full. She thought that if she was going to have an opportunity to get away from Hailey, it would have to be the moment she stepped into the room. Sofia opened the door and stepped back a couple of paces to enable Hailey to enter the bedroom.

Hailey slowly moved into the bedroom holding a tray with both hands. She gave Sofia a wide grin and lowered her head as if to signal Sofia to look at what she brought her. Sofia could see Hailey holding a tray with a plate of chicken drumsticks and mashed potatoes, biscuits, and gravy. She also noticed alongside the plate of food, an actual silver knife, fork and spoon with what looked like an old-fashioned bottle of soda.

In a matter of seconds, her concern about using her hands to attack Hailey dissipated. She saw a weapon on the tray that would be better than her fists. She determined in seconds that although the butter knife would be an ideal weapon, it would take too much time to grab plus it was obstructed by the soda bottle and plate. However, she felt that the soda bottle would be easier to grab and swing because it was situated towards the right side of her body, which was her dominant side. Another factor that came to mind was that the soda bottle stood upright and was close to the edge of the tray providing quick and easy access to it. It was settled quickly, the bottle was the choice, she quickly moved towards Hailey with her right arm and hand extending towards the soda bottle.

Hailey saw Sofia move towards her lifting her right arm and hand reaching for the soda bottle and was struck with a wave of anger. She could not believe that this ungrateful bitch was going to try to hit her. In her initial shock, Hailey was pissed that Sofia would even try such a thing but seconds later remembered that it was Sofia's independence and feistiness that made her want her to be part of her new family. Ironically, just like her mother and younger sister, it will also be the reason Sofia would have to be killed. Shit, she thought just when things were looking up. She gave Sofia many reasons to come be part of her family, now that she has made the choice not to be, it was time to send her to hell to be with her mother and sister.

Inwardly she laughed as she prepared herself for the upcoming strike, because no matter what Sofia did at this moment she would still be family just not a living member.

Sofia in one fluid motion grabbed the bottle pulled it back behind her head and swung it downward towards Hailey's head.

Sofia kept her eyes on Hailey as the bottle began its descent from ceiling to floor and could not believe what she saw. Hailey did not flinch nor did she seem surprised. Her outward appearance in those few seconds conveyed calmness and serene energy. It was as though this type of violence was nothing new to her. Sofia couldn't be too sure but it looked like Hailey smiled at her with pride while the bottle came down towards her head.

Hailey could not fault Sofia for choosing the bottle as her weapon of choice. It presented a close proximity weapon that would undoubtedly inflict immediate damage. That is if connected flush with the victim's temple and there lay Sofia's mistake because the blow needed to be flush anything else would make it a glancing blow which one could immediately recover from. No, if she were in Sofia's position, she would have chosen the knife. It was dull, but if the person propelled with enough speed and force, it could prove to be deadly. Since Sofia did not choose the knife, it was only fair that she take advantage and use it. As the bottle came towards her, Hailey lifted her right hand off the tray leaving her left to hold it and grabbed the knife now easily accessible with the bottle removed. Hailey then ducked towards her right and Sofia's left dropping the tray in the process and with the speed of a mongoose torqued her upper body back towards Sofia thrusting the knife with as much force as she could generate.

As the bottle arched downward towards Hailey's left ear. Sofia saw in a flash, Hailey grab the knife, drop the tray, dip away from her strike and spring towards her with the knife. Sofia instantaneously knew her blow would not inflict ultimate damage. She also realized that she was about to be stabbed in the stomach and there was nothing she could do to stop it. However, Sofia was neither scared nor worried about dying. The moment the knife connected, she felt content with the notion that although she would probably die slowly from a stomach wound, her family would be proud that she died fighting.

Hailey felt the knife enter Sofia's abdomen and heard the grunt that seeped out of Sofia's lips as the knife thudded into her abdomen. It was heartbreaking but necessary. She was a survivor and this situation was no different than any other she faced but it still made her sick.

Hailey looked at Sofia in her moisten eyes and saw a calmness before she fell to her knees and toppled backward onto the floor. Hailey stood over Sofia as she clutched her midsection. Blood seeped through her fingers. Hailey's attention returned to Sofia's face that now had a wide smile with blood flowing from the corners of it.

"Why the fuck did you have to try that? All you had to do was what I asked and everything would have been fine. We could have been a happy family. You made me do this. I don't understand why you choose to die needlessly," Hailey shouted.

Coughing up blood, Sofia answered with a calmness that scared the shit out of Hailey, "You are not and never will be family. I would rather die than be around you."

"Damnit, listen to me, it still doesn't have to end this way. It's just a gut wound. Those injuries take about thirty minutes before bleeding out," explained Hailey.

"You know, Hailey, it's not normal for a teenage girl to know shit like that," Sofia coughed a couple of times then resumed, "I'm really sorry you lived a hard life."

Unperturbed Hailey soldiered on, "Fuck you; I don't need your fucking pity. You want to live let me wrap that wound up and take you to an underground doctor we use. Once you had time to recover, we could talk about mending our relationship."

"You truly are fucking out of your mind. There is no relationship to mend, you kidnapped me and are holding me against my will. If you really cared about me, you would let me die in peace," whispered Sofia as she could feel herself getting weaker.

"So fucking melodramatic, you remind me of my little sister more and more. If you want to die, then it will have to be by yourself. There will be no one coming to claim your body except the rats, your choice," Hailey stated calmly.

"So fucking be it, I'd rather die with the shitty rats than to be anywhere around your fucking crazy-ass," shouted Sofia.

Hailey had enough with this insolent girl now acting like a child. She knelt down to slap some sense into Sofia when she distinctly heard the apartment door open and close. Damn, she thought now she had to explain this fuck up to Duncan. She knew he would be pissed but Sofia was already dying she'll simply point that out. If he's still pissed, she'll put a bullet between Sofia's eyes that she surmised would make him a happy camper.

Chapter 33

Dean felt bad not giving Chris the chance to get to the apartment simultaneously but what choice did he have, the odds of families reuniting with their missing child were slim. If you add getting back a child still alive, it was slimmer. No, he believed he made the right choice. If Sofia was in that apartment, it was his job to determine whether she was dead or alive. It would mean he could better prepare Chris for whatever presented itself in that apartment. The hard part knew Dean was in order to get Sofia back he had to go through Hailey.

Dean continued to drive just above the speed limit so as not to attract the police. He was steering the car with his left hand while he used his right hand to go into his bag that lay on the passenger side seat. He retrieved a small vessel that looked like a tube of Chapstick but instead of lip balm, it contained a stick of black paint.

Dean took his hands off the steering wheel for a moment, took the cap off the paint stick held it with one hand directly under one eye and smeared a line under it. He stole a glance at the review mirror to make sure its placement was correct. Satisfied, he did the same thing to his other eye. If someone looked at him, they would think he was about to play a sport because the same black pattern under a player's eyes is used to shield them from the glaring sun. In his case, it was used as a statement to the warrior he would be confronting. That statement told his adversary that his vision would not fall below the black line for it will be totally focused on the task at hand, attack without impunity. He reached into his bag a second time to retrieve a red paint stick. He smeared three lines above his forehead and down alongside both cheeks. The red paint signified the blood that would flow from him and his adversary. These markings many called war paint but to the warrior that displayed them, it represented their readiness for battle.

Dean thought about what Chris and Antonio would say if they saw him with his war paint. He smiled knowing they would have busted his balls and ridiculed him. They would probably call him a rodeo clown. But that's where the joking would end, especially when they saw the tomahawk sticking out of his bag and the seriousness and violence radiating from his eyes.

As he neared the apartment, Dean started to think about his plan of attack. His main concern was how to confront Hailey once inside the apartment. She would not think twice about hearing the door open because the only other key holder was Duncan. The problem lay once inside the apartment, what would be his next step. He envisioned one of two scenarios happening, Hailey being in the vicinity of the door when he entered. If that happened, he was sure that she would immediately commence with an attack so he must be ready to go on the offensive before she did. But the scenario, he preferred, would be for Hailey to be in one of the other rooms. It gave him an opportunity to orient himself with the layout of the apartment but more importantly as in tribal tradition, it provided him the chance to acknowledge his foe. Tribal tradition dictated that warriors from the attacking band acknowledge in the form of chants its presence as a show respect prior to engaging in battle.

Dean parked the car across the street from the apartment. He put his bag on his lap closed his eyes and began to chant in a cadence that enabled him to drift into a trance. This chant was done for warriors about to go into battle. It sharpened one's focus and attention to the violence that would play out shortly. Once done, Dean opened his bag and extracted his tomahawk and what looked like a shield the size of an iPad only thicker.

He swiftly walked across the street and entered the lobby of the building where the apartment was located. He fished out a key ring with two keys on it, one for the lobby door and the second for the apartment. The apartment was on the first floor situated to the back of the hallway. Dean walked up next to the front door and stood beside it. He did not want to stand in front of the door because it had a peephole. He placed his ear against the door and heard low muffled shouting. Dean thought this was good news because it meant that Hailey was not by the door. He quietly pushed the key into the lock and turned the knob slowly. Unfortunately, the door was like the building, old, which meant it moaned and creaked as he pushed it open. He entered the apartment and took stock of the layout. Since the apartment was in a 19th-century tenement building, it laid out in the typical railroad formation found during that period. It started with the living room followed by the kitchen and ended with the bedrooms all lined up as though on a railroad track.

It was just past the kitchen and in one of the bedrooms, he heard Hailey shout out, "It's about fucking time you prick. I thought…" she could not finish her sentence as she stepped into the kitchen and looked straight at Dean with neither confusion nor fear but curiosity.

"Who in the fuck are you, Chief? Wait; don't tell me you're just lost. The Indian Museum is downtown."

Hailey cracked up with that one but had one better, "Sorry, that was not nice of me but if someone would have told me we were dressing up for Thanksgiving, I would have put on my Pocahontas costume," this time she almost fell over from laughter.

Dean saw her move towards him with each joke and she gave the appearance of someone in complete control and added a friendly smile like someone enjoying the moment. But it was her essence that he felt most, tension mixed with the cloudiness of violent anger. He prepared himself accordingly.

"Duncan is not coming to save you, Hailey. It's just you and me," Dean stated calmly.

"Who the fuck gives a shit if Duncan's not coming and I don't need any fucking body to save me. Trust me I've done fine all by myself," Hailey shouted with the veins around her neck and forehead bulging.

"Forgive me, Hailey, it was not my intention to imply you needed saving. I just wanted you to know that Duncan will no longer be present in your world. As for you, doing fine for yourself, I believe that is an understatement. The fact that your mother used you as payment for drugs at twelve years old and then tried getting your younger sister to join you but you refused, is a testament of your strength and love. You and not your mother chose to liberate your sister from that humiliation and trauma. You, Hailey, are a true war…"

Dean could not finish the word because Hailey quickly reached down into her boot and came up with a switchblade. In a split second, she went from acquiring it to flipping it open. She then lunged towards and swung the blade at Dean's neck, "Fuck you, you bastard. How dare you speak about my family? You have no fucking right to bring up my life and family. I'm going to cut you to fucking pieces and feed you to the dogs."

Dean purposely spoke of Hailey's family as he knew it would enrage her and make her come to him. He knew his life depended on her rage. Rage, as tribal elders taught him, brought an individual blurred focus instead of clear vision one needed to attack and/or defend oneself. It disrupted the attention of a warrior, which was imperative in battle. Reminding Hailey of her family, Dean clouded her focus and caused her to attack without preparation. She should have taken hold of her surroundings before engaging in an attack it would have allowed her to see that Dean was armed and protected with a shield.

Her rage blinded her as she thrust her knife hand forward at Dean. She did not see him raise his hand holding the tomahawk above her head. When she finally saw the tomahawk coming down towards her head, she changed the direction of the knife towards the weapon but that move was quickly deflected by Dean's shield.

Hailey was just as fast with her countermove and was in the process of bringing back her arm for another strike but suddenly felt as though someone had hit her head with a brick. Falling to the floor Hailey was able to open one eye and saw that Dean had struck her with the flat solid part of the tomahawk. He stood above her with his legs spread apart. She quickly recovered by twisting her body so that her back was on the floor giving her the opportunity to strike back by whipping her right leg up between Dean's legs.

The vicious kick caught Dean cleanly in his balls sending a rapid response of electrical pain throughout his body. He dropped his shield and fell to one knee enabling Hailey to spring up on her legs and throw a straight right cross snapping back Dean's head back. The energy of the kick and punch put him on his ass and he instantly felt the momentum shift to Hailey. It scared the shit out of him. However, what saved his life was instead of advancing on Dean with more punches and kicks Hailey opted to dislodge the knife from Dean's shield. She desperately wanted to kill him and that Dean would later attribute it back to her rage. It was a deadly mistake on her part.

Dean shook the cobwebs from his brain in enough time to see Hailey reach towards his shield and begin to violently pull at the knife embedded in it. He saw her retrieve it, turn back and lunge at him with murderous intent. In her haste to get the knife, Dean regained his balance. He was able to move at her with his tomahawk blade side facing Hailey. He raised it above his head as she lunged at him. He brought it arching downward towards her head. She realized that he was already in motion with his ax coming towards her but it was too late she already was lunging with knife. Dean moved back enough to stop the knife from puncturing his heart but not quickly enough for it to connect into his thigh. The unexpected movement backward by Dean meant Hailey's arm moved downward towards his leg with her head tilting upward. As her head faced tilted towards the ceiling, she saw a light reflect onto the tomahawk's blade that was now barreling at her face. In that instant, Hailey knew it was over right before it sliced through her forehead and eye socket slashing blood and parts of her brain onto Dean and the walls. She died instantly.

Dean felt sick to his stomach when he heard the sickening thud the blade made as it connected to Hailey's forehead and the sight of her blood and brain matter spewing onto him seconds later was nauseating.

Dean looked down at Hailey's crumbled body then at the knife sticking out of his thigh. He decided to leave it in place until the paramedics arrived. His first priority was to find Sofia. He walked to the back of the apartment and as his mind cleared from the carnage that was behind him he heard someone sobbing. He continued towards the sounds until he reached the bedroom.

"I'm sorry, mom, so sorry," sobbed Sofia. She was still propped up against the wall perpendicular to the bedroom door. She tried unsuccessfully to stem the bleeding, coming from her stomach wound, with her hand. She was too weak though to put enough pressure on it to stop the blood from flowing through her fingers.

In a distance, she heard Hailey yelling at someone. Then it sounded like a scuffle was taking place but she had no idea who Hailey could be fighting. She wasn't sure but it sounded like a man. Then she heard nothing. She started to sob again, "Please god I want to see my mom again." She felt her body slowly shutting down. Sofia knew she was dying and it broke her heart that she would be the cause of more pain for her mother.

Sofia stopped sobbing for a minute because she heard what sounded like chanting. She thought to herself why would Hailey be chanting. She didn't care what Hailey was chanting, she just wanted her back in the room so she could beg her to stop the bleeding long enough for her to at least call her mom and say goodbye. The chanting stopped at the doorway. Sofia had her head down but could feel a presence in the room; although it was difficult, she raised her head high enough to see a figure standing in the doorway. She had to blink twice to notice that it was not Hailey. It was a man covered in red and black face paint. His right eye was swollen shut, blood poured from his mouth and a knife was sticking out of his thigh. She was frightened for a moment but something about him exuded peace and trustworthiness.

"Sofia, my name is Dean. I've been sent by your mother to bring you home," whispered Dean. He saw pain and anguish in her face but there was an abundance of resolve that he found reassuring.

She spoke in a low whisper, "Will I see her again?"

Her soft pleading voice pained him to his core and the answer might deflate what little optimism she may have but his mother always told him, honesty was the best policy, "That's up to you, Sofia. I will not lie to you; the way you're bleeding, you may not make it out of here alive."

She smiled even wider, "That's something you don't see."

Dean looked confused, "What's that?"

Sofia licked her bloody lips, "Honesty, it's quite refreshing, now tell me how I could help myself live?"

"Stay awake until the ambulance gets here it's a slight chance but the best one you have," was his response. Dean could see that she wanted to live but with the amount of blood she already lost, it might be too late. To her credit, she smiled and nodded her head as her way of saying she understood. Dean sat beside her, placed his hand over her stomach wound, and pressed hard to stem the bleeding. He was going to start chanting to keep her awake when he heard shouting from the front door.

"Dean! Dean! Where are you?" shouted Chris as he entered the apartment with his gun out leading him as he walked.

Chris slowly passed by the kitchen and almost threw up. He saw a young woman sitting on the floor back against a counter with her head split in two. The visual was as if a watermelon cut in the middle but not completely severed. Now he was worried about Dean.

"Dean! Talk to me!" shouted Chris as he approached the bedroom.

"In the bedroom," shouted Dean.

Chris holstered his gun and walked through the doorway. His eyes immediately went to Sofia, "Sofia!" he yelled running and dropping to her side opposite Dean. Chris grabbed her away from Dean and placed her across his lap.

He held her with one arm and stroked her face with his hand as he cried, "Hey, pumpkin, it's Uncle Chris, you're gonna be alright."

Sofia opened her eyes, "I'm sorry, Uncle Chris, this is my fault."

Chris put his finger across her lips, "Shhh, you need to save your strength so we can bring you home, baby."

Dean saw Chris's tears falling onto Sofia's face. It killed him to see this grown man and federal agent breaking before him. He got up and stepped towards the doorway waiting for the EMT to arrive. He had contacted them as he walked from the kitchen to the bedroom.

He was about to leave the bedroom when he heard someone yelling at the front door.

"Dean, Chris, where the fuck are you?" shouted Antonio as he ran towards the apartment Chris had told him about. He ran into the apartment and immediately saw Dean standing in the back of the apartment. He was taken aback as he neared the bloody Dean with a knife sticking out of his thigh, "Shit what the fuck happened to you?" But didn't give Dean an opportunity to speak as he brushed past him when he saw a pair of shoes on legs spread out on the floor. Those were the same shoes he bought his niece several weeks back.

"NO! No! No, Sofia," yelled Antonio as he ran into the room and saw his niece being held by his brother. No words needed to be said between the brothers as Antonio dropped down to the spot Dean just vacated and was handed Sofia by a crying Chris.

Dean looked down at Antonio and Chris both holding Sofia and sobbing. He saw Sofia smile and look at each of her uncles then looked up at him with a look of clarity. In that moment, he knew she could see and feel the spirit world that was now surrounding her. His eyes moistened further and the tears came down freely not of sadness but pure joy because she now understood that she had nothing to fear from the other side if she decided she could no longer hold on.

Chapter 34

"Damn, you found him already? OK, give me some information on this piece of shit," asked Mario "the Fridge" Scalito of his son who was researching Thomas Handley, Vice President at Wiley & Pearson Investment firm. Mario was another member of Antonio's crew and just like Joey a close family friend. Antonio was also Mario's son's godfather.

Anthony "Brains" Scalito, 19 and son of Mario replied, "Come on pop, you sit there and insult me as though this was some fucking brain surgery I was doing." Laughed Brains.

"Alright, don't be sensitive like your fucking godfather. Go ahead give me this assholes info so we could see what kind of jackoff we're dealing with," responded Mario.

"He comes from family money mostly from his father and grandfather who owned their own investment banks. It seems, little Tommy grew up in the Hamptons and attended private schools all his life. This fucking guy is the definition of Vanilla, private schools, Ivy League Universities, Harvard by the way. Daddy's little apprentice moved up the corporate ladder and made Vice President of the banks Domestic Investments Unit. Listen to this pop, he gets promoted to the Vice President of International Investment Unit after securing one of the most lucrative deals with the Japanese banking minister. It was that deal that allowed his bank to open independent American banks on the Japanese mainland," explained Brains.

"Shit, this is beginning to sound like an operation for the rich. It's run like some fucking well-tuned violin. The operation would still be making money if it wasn't for Sofia getting snatched. You see my boy that's why both your godfather and I want you to get out of life and go legit. This is the shit you got to deal with in our line of business. After we get Sofia back, you should really think about getting a good legit job after college," explained Mario.

"You and my godfather must have talked before asking for me to do the research on this guy," laughed Brains continuing, "He said the same thing but went a little further. He told me not to waste the opportunity he gave me when he called in his chip with the Dean at Stevens School of Technology to not only admit me into the school but give me a full ride."

"What did you tell him?" asked Mario.

"I told him, once we get Sofia back, I'll go back to school to get my degree in computers and forget working for the family," responded Brains.

"Bravo, I knew you would choose wisely. Now enough of this sentimental shit; does this prick, you're watching, have a family?" asked Mario.

"Married for the last twenty years, three girls ranging from 6 to 17, all in private school," remarked Brains.

"Fucking ironic isn't, the prick has girls two and has no problem raping teenage girls. The motherfucker would have killed himself if it were one of his girls. Hmmm, maybe, instead of killing the sick son of a bitch, we snatch his girls and put them on the streets and then make him collect the money they earn," thought Mario aloud.

"Come on pop, we're not angels but we would never do that, may I suggest that you just make him suffer before he dies. He will never know the pain he caused all those girls and their families but he shouldn't be given the opportunity to die quickly," suggested Brains.

"I ask myself, how in the hell did I get blessed to have an intelligent kid like you. Then I always remember the looks and brains came from your mother. The only credit I can claim is your toughness," laughed Mario before continuing, "Do me a favor and print out all the contact information including addresses for both his work and home. When you are finished with that, get the fuck out of here and remember that I love you." Mario gave his son a playful smack in the face.

"OK, pops, you gonna call my godfather?" asked Brains as he got up ready to leave.

"I've been trying for the last twenty minutes but he doesn't answer his phone. I even tried Chris but it's the same thing with him," responded Mario.

"So you gonna wait on them before making a move against this asshole?" countered Brains.

"Naw, I've been given my orders to take care of this and I will," smiled Mario and ushered his son on his way. Once his son left the house, he picked up his phone and called the family enforcer, Frankie "Knuckles" Giglearie.

"What's up, Mario?" asked Frankie after picking up his phone.

"That fuck has three daughters of his own, and two are teenagers," explained Mario. Frankie as all the members of Antonio's crew were tasked with helping find Sofia and were privy to all information collected and disseminated.

214

"How do you think Mr. Vice President would feel if we took his teenage daughters and had the crew put them out in the street?" asked Frankie.

Frankie could hear Mario laughing.

"I thought the same thing but Brains talked me out of it. Accused Antonio and I of having some type of morals," chuckled Mario.

"Bless that kid, he's always been naïve, glad to hear that he still is, gives me hope that he'll skip the family business," laughed Frankie.

"From God's lips to my ears, listen we're going to snatch the prick at a hotel he visits. Our people found out that although he initially was just funding and using the service for his clients, it seems he now dabbles in teenagers. I also found out that tonight is his young pussy night. I intend to pick the prick up and bring him to Jersey," replied Mario.

"Where did you decide to bring him?" asked Frankie.

"Fiore's basement, we'll set up shop in the basement. Once we're done with him, I figure we could chop him up and dump him somewhere upstate," Mario replied.

"Wait, you mean Fiore's Deli on Willow Street?" asked Frankie.

"Yep, the one and only, Jackie got tired of the crowds coming in for his famous Mozzarella. You remember him telling us one day that he made that cheese for families in the neighborhood. Once the Bergen Record wrote a story about him and that fucking cheese, everyone wanted to try it. Usually, storeowners would kill for that type of advertisement and business generated from it but Jackie just wanted to make enough money to support his family and live on. He told me he would sell it to the crew as long as we never sold it to a family or company that didn't have roots in Hoboken. So now Antonio is in the fucking deli business," chuckled Mario.

"Shit I knew you and the old-timers were gaining weight. The lot of you were fucking eating like you owned a deli," Frankie cracked up then continued, "I'll be there just make sure it's a clean snatch job. Who's putting together the team to grab the parole officer?" responded Frankie.

"Fuck you, you wish you had this body. As for the parole officer, Chris told me he had two of trusted agents taking care of that job," replied Mario.

Chapter 35

Tracy lay in the bed staring at Thomas Handley as he got out of bed and began to pull up his underwear. *Man, what I wouldn't do to stick a fucking nail file in his eye. No, maybe I'll call his fucking wife and tell her that this fucking pig has been fucking me for the last two years since I was fourteen? Ha with her fucking luck, the wife would blame her. I got to always remind her that no one gives a shit about her or the girls anyway especially the law. Doesn't Amber have to dress like some fucking high school cheerleader for that old ass judge? You can bet he's not going pass judgment on this prick. Maybe, the state trooper getting fucking freebies from fifteen-year-old Kristen could pull him over. Ha, like he's going to spend any time with the same people he's arrested. Nope, Hailey truly fucked us all on a promise and a dream, fucking bitch, that's who needs to pay the fucking price.*

"Fuck you looking like at, bitch, you better remember who the fuck I am," shouted Thomas.

"Jesus, baby, you don't have to shout, I was just admiring your body," Tracy tried to sound seductive.

"Bullshit, you have that 'I hope you fucking die' stare. Maybe this is a good time to remind you that if you ever go to the police, it will be me, a successful businessman they will believe. If that's not enough for you to keep your fucking mouth shut, remember you don't want to embarrass your Senator daddy and his standing in the community. That would be such a scandal," laughed Thomas.

She was about to give him some other lie just to shut him up when the door to the hotel room was suddenly kicked in. The sudden and violent moment paralyzed both she and Thomas enough for two large muscled men to run into the room, where one of the men punched Thomas hard enough to knock him out.

At that moment, she regained her senses and pleaded, "Please sir, don't hurt me. I'll do whatever you want me too."

The man that just delivered the vicious blow to the temple of Thomas smiled and, in a calming, and ironically soothing voice answered, "No need to worry, we are here for this scumbag, you can get dressed and go home. But do me a favor, forget you have seen this."

Now, it was her turn to smile, "See what? Oh, you think you could do me a favor?"

"Don't know if I could but try me," replied Frankie.

"You think you could kick his ass then put a bullet in him and bury him?" asked Tracy politely.

Frankie looked at her with a renewed respect, "Oh, he's in for a lot of pain and let me say this you will never have to worry about this scumbag again. I suggest you start all over cause that club you belonged to has been shut down." And with that, both men picked up Thomas and removed him from Tracy's life and into their waiting car with Jersey plates.

After hanging up with Frankie, Mario walked over to the back door of Fiore's and unlocked it. His crew would soon be bringing in Thomas from the back of the alley, blindfolded and gagged. He thought maybe being tied up and gagged would make Thomas unsure and scared. Maybe the prick would come to understand a little of what these defenseless girls he used for fucking toys felt during their captivity. Then he realized the prick was all about money and probably didn't give any thought about others' feelings.

He heard the van pull into the alley and the doors open. He could hear what sounded like muffled shouting. He then stepped back as the back door was pushed open revealing two members of his crew pulling a struggling Thomas towards the basement. The struggle and muffled yelling continued all the way down to a chair chained to the middle of the basement.

Mario walked up to Thomas who was still fighting and yelling at the men who restrained him. In one fluid motion with his right arm and fist, he swung them downward plowing into Thomas's midsection. Thomas's reaction to the violent punch was instantaneous. He fell to the floor gasping for air that was already difficult to get because of the gag. At that moment while he was down on the floor, one of Mario's men roughly pulled off his hood and gag.

Thomas looked at the men around him and for a moment decided, that they needed to be reminded whom they were dealing with so he yelled up at them, "Do you know who the fuck you're messing with. You better pick me up and untie me before I make some calls and have you all arrested," yelled Thomas.

Mario nodded to one of his men who picked Thomas up and sat him on the chair. Mario was going to say something but was interrupted by Thomas.

"That's more like it, now untie my fucking hands your fucking guinea bastards," chided Thomas looking directly at Mario.

Mario stepped to Thomas and with the speed of a seventeen-year-old pitcher swinging his right arm with an open palm struck Thomas flush across his cheek, sending him once again to the floor. However, this time Thomas didn't say a word just looked up at Mario with tears in his eyes.

"Are you really going to cry? Give me a fucking break, you pussy. What happened to that toughness? Did you piss it out cause from here I could smell it on you," laughed Mario then continued, "For a minute, I had a little respect for you standing up like that but my slap was a test to see if you would demand more from me. Guess what asshole, you just failed."

Now a scared Thomas decided that maybe money was the end game with these assholes, "You want money, I can get you a million dollars in cash just let me go and I'll take you to it."

Mario nodded his head looked at one of his men and then chuckled, "You see, Frankie, it's always the same with these rich scumbags, money. Why do they always think money would get you out of trouble? And believe me, asshole, you are in a world of trouble?"

"I don't even know who the fuck you or what I might have done to any of you," answered a despondent Thomas.

"You're here because of the young girl we consider family, Sofia who went missing a couple of days ago," answered Mario.

"I don't even know a girl, named Sofia. You obviously have the wrong man. Just let me go and no one has to know about this, I promise you," Thomas pleaded.

Mario turned serious, "Be a fucking man already. Just accept that you are a dead man. Once you accept it then you can stop your groveling."

Thomas looked back at Mario with a look of confusion. "Don't look at me like you can't believe this is happening to you. You really believe the sick shit you've been doing all these years would not come back and bite you in the ass. If you do, you one fucking dumb piece of shit and you may not know Sofia. However, you knew of young girls just like her who you raped and tortured."

"Please, Mr. let me go, I don't know what you are talking about," whimpered Thomas.

Frankie saw that look on his friend's face which he usually gave when he's had enough and decides to move the situation quickly to its end. He saw Mario frown and walk to the side of the seated Thomas towards a table containing many silver objects.

Thomas was also following Mario with his eyes toward the same table. He saw that it contained what looked like a set of knives in different shapes and sizes.

"You continue to disappoint me, Thomas with all that begging. It's really unbecoming of a man. But then again, I've come to the conclusion that you are no fucking man." And with that in another impressive swift move, Mario grabbed a silver-plated clever and swung it down towards a space just above Thomas's right knee. The speed and force of the downward clever cut through clothing, skin, and bone like a hot knife slicing a stick of butter. Thomas's leg from just above his knee fell to the floor accompanied by a torrent of blood. The cut was so quick and unexpected that it took Thomas a full minute to let a curdling scream that would have scared the shit out of anyone. But then again, Mario and his crew were not just anyone. When Thomas stopped screaming, everyone could still hear him whimpering and pleading for mercy.

"Sorry, you don't get the privilege of mercy. You did not show mercy for those poor young innocent girls or their families. It was all just fun and games to you. Well, Thomas, your fun and games have crossed over and affected our family. In our world, if someone messed with our family and we did not respond, it meant that we were weak. This family cannot afford to be seen as weak. The only way we get to hold our heads up high again is to eliminate those that have hurt our family. And you just happen to be the first prick on the list. However, the one thing we as men have, not including you, is our word. If I give someone my word then you can count on it being true."

"So here is my word to you, Thomas, I will not hurt your family because none of this was their fault. As for tonight, I will also give you my word that the pain you just experienced is only the beginning," laughed Mario as the clever came down on Thomas's left leg and knee.

At the same moment, Thomas was being cut apart systemically, Senior Special Agent, Johnson was meeting with his agents Ayala and Shula at the Popeye's located on 125th and Saint Nicholas Avenue. Chris had contacted him on his way to Dean's location and gave him the rundown on Duncan's parole officer contact. He was given instructions on what needed to be done to this turncoat and he would make sure it was carried out.

"This is how I want it to go down; you'll give me about ten minutes alone with this piece of garbage so that I could have a heart to heart with him. Once I'm done, you guys come in and read him his rights. We clear, so far," asked Johnson.

"Crystal, but are sure that this prick had a hand in Sofia's disappearance?" asked Ayala.

"Without a doubt, he's also running his parolees into different rackets for a price and if they don't play, he threatens them with parole violation," answered Johnson.

"Fuck, what a piece of shit. He's fucking worse than the cop. That means no con in his parole book had a chance to go legit," replied Agent Shula

"That's exactly what that means," replied Johnson

"I'm going to enjoy slapping the cuffs on this garbage," replied Agent Shula.

"Shit, Shula those are the first fucking sentences you've said in twenty-four hours. What the fuck crawled up your ass to make you talk," laughed her partner Ayala.

"Ha, Ha, fuck you. You know I love busting motherfuckers but sometimes we come across people who had no choice but to do the things they did just to feed their families. I know that one must do the time if they commit the crime but once they come out, they should have an opportunity to make up for their transgressions. This asshole doesn't provide that opportunity he just takes advantage, that's why I'm saying something, dickhead," Agent Shula chuckled.

Johnson smiled but then looked at his two agents and turned somber, "Now listen closely when you see him, he's going to claim police brutality but remind him that it would be beneficial for him to take his penance for the crimes he committed. Chris requested that I give him a beating. You both know I love Sofia like a niece so I have no problem making good on that request. So I'm going to put a beating on him but I will be careful not to hit him in his face, his body will take the brunt of my anger."

Special Agent Shula just shook her head, "Deserving so, where do you want him transported to?"

Johnson replied, "Definitely not any NYPD holding cell, just bring him down to 26 Federal Plaza on Broadway. Once we've cleaned up the mess, he'll be charged with aiding and abetting and any other charges you guys could put on him."

Johnson synchronized his watch with his agents and stepped into the building's lobby where the parole officer, Joseph Daniels lived. He took the elevator to the ninth floor stepped out and walked calmly to the end of the hallway to apartment 9D. Johnson knocked twice before the occupant asked who was there through the door. He elevated his credentials to the peephole and shouted his name and agency. He heard the unlocking of a deadbolt followed by the sound of two chains being released from their frames and ending with Joseph opening the door halfway.

He nodded to Johnson and asked in a snotty way, "I'm off the clock. If it ain't an emergency, you'll have to come back on Monday."

Johnson caught Joseph off guard when he lifted his right leg quickly and accurately delivered a front kick into Joseph's midsection with such force and veracity that it knocked him down and rendered him breathless. Johnson took full advantage by pouncing on top of Joseph and pummeled him continuously with his fists until he was satisfied that all his ribs were broken. He stepped away and walked out of the apartment without another word.

Epilogue

Ya ha ha-wa! Ya ha ha-wa! Ya ha ha-wa! Ya ha ha-wa! Ha ho ha ha-wa.

Ya ha ha-wa! Ya ha ha-wa! Ya ha ha-wa! Ya ha ha-wa! Ha ho ha ha-wa.

Ya ha ha-wa! Ya ha ha-wa! Ya ha ha-wa! Ya ha ha-wa! Ha ho ha ha-wa.

Dean looked over at the male dancers as they hopped side to side twirling in circles making the feathers layered throughout their garment's flair as though in flight alongside the bonfire. As the dancers continued to dance and chant in rhythm with the beating of the drums, he could feel his chest rise with pride. He once tried to explain it to a friend that was non-native that it was like that feeling one got returning home from a long journey. You realize and it becomes apparent that something had been missing while you were away. As you closed your front door, it hits you, the sense of security being in a place you created. It restores one's balance to the body and mind. Dean laughed as he remembered his friend looking at him as if he was fucking crazy. His friend had responded that the only sense of relief and security for him would have been never to return home, especially to his fucking whiny kids and nagging wife.

Dean's sister, Cha, who was seated next to him chanting and moving her upper body to the rhythm of the drums, looked over at him, "What's got you laughing and smiling. I know it's not the ceremony right."

"No, Cha, I was just thinking about a friend who couldn't understand our deep love for our culture and its traditions," responded Dean as his jacket pocket began vibrating. He reached in and retrieved his phone.

"Cha, it's a Jersey number, I got take this be back in a few."

"Don't take too long, or you'll miss the Sundance," responded Cha to Dean who was already walking away from the ceremony.

"Hey, Tonto, it's been too long," Chris, shouted in the phone before Dean could ask who was calling.

"Shit, yeah, going on two months but who's counting," laughed Dean.

Chris turned somber, "Listen about that, I'm sorry, it was rough going that first night. Who am I kidding you were there before EMS arrived. I saw you looking at her figuring she was dead. Is that why you left without saying goodbye?"

Chris couldn't see Dean nodding his head in agreement, "She was in both realms and it looked like she was trying to decide which one to go to. You asked me to find her and I did that. It was up to her to decide whether she wanted to come back. I figured out you would call me within the next few days and tell me her choice. However, after two weeks passed with no word from you, I knew she survived."

Chris cut him off, "that's right; she was in a coma for three weeks. Then she came out of it and has been in rehab since then. Were you expecting a call from me if she lived?"

"Of course, but I wanted your family to be in the process of healing before talking to you again. How is she?" answered Dean.

"Like I said that day you found her, Antonio and I thought she would not make it but your quick thinking in calling EMS when you got to the apartment was the difference," replied Chris.

Dean jumped in, "When I was leaving, they were already entering the apartment."

"Those fucking men and women are amazing. They pushed Antonio and I away and went to work immediately. She wasn't responding but she was alive. They got her to Harlem Hospital within five minutes. It was nothing short of a miracle," an impressed Chris explained.

"Does she remember anything?" asked Dean.

"Every fucking thing, fortunately, the first thing she asked for, when she came out of a coma, was to see you," replied Chris.

"I'm surprised, she lost a lot of blood when I got there," responded Dean.

"What the fuck did you expect, not many Chiefs running around Upper Manhattan, shit she probably thought she died and went to Indian heaven," grunted Chris with laughter.

"Prick and what about Elizabeth and Antonio how are they doing?" cackled Dean.

"At first devastated but that all changed when she woke up. They like me are still feeling guilty that she had to go through that ordeal but are like pigs in shit, that she's up and about," expressed a happy Chris.

"Excellent, well, if she's up for it, I'm back in Philly next Wednesday. I could come over to Jersey on Thursday morning to see all of you," offered Dean.

"I will tell her once I'm off the phone. How is the thigh is healing?" asked Chris.

"The plastic surgeon at Philly General did an amazing job on limiting the scaring. I appreciated it cause in the summer I like to wear my loincloth around the house," Dean could hear Chris almost piss his pants on that one.

Dean turned serious and explained, "I still felt unbalanced after the surgeries so I decided to come back to Arizona and the reservation where our Shaman could care for me. I was in the Longhouse recuperating under his care for over a month. Now I feel as though my spirit and mind have merged once again making me whole again," Dean explained.

"Is that where you are now? It sounds like you're surrounded by dying cats," jibed Chris.

"Asshole, yeah, with my sister," laughed Dean.

"Hey, that reminds me; you never introduced me to her. Do I have to be a fucking injun for that to happen?" cackled Chris.

"No, but a gentleman might be a start," countered Dean.

"Ouch, that was one fucking low blow. Hey, Listen, I also wanted to talk to you about something I and Antonio decided to do," replied Chris.

"OK, now you piqued my interest, talk to me," responded Dean.

"I put my papers in this week," Chris was going to finish his thought but was interrupted by Dean.

"Why, I told you there wasn't anything you could have done differently for Sofia," Dean answered.

"No, I know that but working with you and Antonio showed me that I could do more good if I concentrated on one particular case. Yes, I can do that with the bureau but the difference is with you guys I wasn't beholden to bureaucracy," replied Chris.

"But you were Chris. You still had to follow bureau rules on this case. You just had your brother and me to work the outer edges," responded Dean.

"No, there were points that I was with Antonio and did things that were not legit. Don't get me wrong, I was alright with that because it involved my niece. But there lies the issue with me, other families should be given that same consideration but can't because of the regulations we in the bureau swear to," explained Chris.

"Alright, I could understand that but how to propose to do that now?" asked Dean.

"Well, Antonio and I believe that we could do a lot of good for individuals that face the same situations like Sofia and your sister. We know that you are an established name for those seeking 'special help' who cannot approach law enforcement. If we combine that with our reputations, me in law enforcement circles and Antonio's underground connections and we could help more of those marginalized populations," pleaded Chris.

Dean interjected, "It sounds like some type of private investigator stuff and if you are thinking about asking to join me, remember, I'm not licensed in any state to conduct such investigations. However, what you just said, for people who can't afford the services of a private eye or for whatever reason cannot go to the local authority for assistance is something I can do."

"No, that's not what we are proposing, we only want to help you with cases that you accept coupled with any interesting case Antonio and I come across that fits your profile," replied Chris.

"Why would you want to do that, there is no money in what I do? It just makes me feel good," countered Dean.

"It's not about the pay for us. I have my pension and 401K plan and Antonio always has money coming from the rackets. We are grateful for what you did for us and we would like to help those families that have gone through or are going through the same as we did. Our goal is to bring the missing back to their families," replied Chris.

Dean thought about it, "Come to think about it, with your connections in law enforcement you were able to help me move things along quicker and smoother. Antonio and his people were able to do things for me that law enforcement would definitely frown upon. Add these two components with my brilliance did get Sofia back fast and more importantly alive," responded Dean.

Chris got a little nervous when he heard a loud sigh coming from the other end of the line, "You alright?"

"I can't believe I'm going to say this and I'm sure my ancestors would turn over in their graves but I agree with you. Our working together can benefit those on the fringes of society. Count me in on your fucking crazy idea," guffawed Dean.

"Nice, Antonio is going to go ape shit let us talk more next week. One more thing, do want to know the name of our new thing?" asked Chris.

"OK, I'll bite, what is the name?" asked a skeptical Dean.

"The Cowboy and Indian Detective Agency," hooted Chris.

"Real original, asshole, I'll see you next week," bellowed Dean.

CPSIA information can be obtained
at www.ICGtesting.com
Printed in the USA
LVHW080900030921
696786LV00002BA/5

9 781643 788685